AF513209

WHEN A FOREST WALKS

WHEN A FOREST WALKS

NEHA P LAL

NU VOICE
PRESS

First published by NU VOICE PRESS 2024
An imprint of Hubhawks Pvt. Ltd
www.nuvoicepress.com

Copyright © Neha P Lal 2024

The moral rights of the author have been asserted.
Database right NU VOICE PRESS (maker)

This is a work of fiction. Space and time have been rearranged to suit the convenience of the book. Except for public figures, hotels, and institution names, any resemblance to persons living or dead or the real events are purely coincidental. The opinions expressed in the book are those of the characters, and should not be confused with that of the Author.

All rights reserved. Enquiries concerning reproduction outside the scope of the above should be sent to NU VOICE PRESS at the address above.

ISBN: 978-81-970218-0-0

Typeset by Saanvi Graphics, Noida
Printed at Nutech Print Services - India
Published by Nu Voice Press

For Bhavani

Author's Note

Thank you for reading, dear reader. Outside my window, the years have passed slowly with the corruption of concrete replacing everything tree. Affluent human zoos climb the sky, blocking out the sun. My hope for us is that one day this lifestyle of human captivity in towering boxes will lose its appeal. It might require us to think out of that other legendary box inside which thoughts remain hostage.

1

A Scent of Alstonia

She ran. From the ghostly Ashoka tree and the weight of its flower bunches, through the gangling shadows between the coconut trees. She was tripping and tumbling, picking herself up as fast as she could. Her legs hurt, but to keep fear at bay, she focussed on the coconut trees. Graceful, twiggy ogres in the daytime, they were now casting kaleidoscopic silhouettes all around her. She had kicked up a trail of smashed red earth and dust as she hurtled headlong, parting the darkness, the dread in her chest so thick that she lost her breath for a second and tripped again. Then, she recoiled as the white light of day struck her in the face. She was in a garden at sunrise, and in a corner on the grassy scrub lay a dozing god, a hoary form on her side.

Alki woke. From sopping darkness to sudden slapping light, it was a dream of the day to come. Her dream time followed tormenting quantum laws. She would dream of the day to come the night before.

Late in the evening of the sixth day in January, alighting at the thatched bus stop in the village, she paused as usual to admire its split-coconut-beam architecture. She had returned for one last look before ground officially broke for her new house. She watched as an uncommon fog slid down the slope towards her. Soon she was enveloped in transparent vapour and an intense messianic scent, which led her uphill away from the simple bus station, towards a flattened mound of red earth and a house that was no longer there. Stemmy banana plants and wild curry leaf trees ringed the stark earthen mound. The peculiar scent wafted from a fragrant Alstonia tree bustling with arriving evening moths and departing bees—some big, some small, some striped, some spectacularly-hued winged gems fluorescing in the dark. She was sweating from the short uphill walk. Wiping her brow with a tissue from a little package in her handbag, she noticed the sun had disappeared below the horizon. She didn't want to stay too long after sunset. As the purple-streaked twilight waned, a strange dread and low rhythmic hum like the muted song of a blue whale crept in on the gloom. The scent of the Alstonia seemed alive because oddly she could see it. What she had mistaken for a fog of scented air started to whirl around her as if it were hot air rising on a summer's day. It glowed a pale crystal-clear light.

She lurched away from the tree overcome by the intense scent. Turning around to look at it, she was surprised by the mist. It was circling the tree. She could just about distinguish the outline of the tree trunk, but then it…the tree…started to move…towards her. In sudden fright, she inhaled audibly through her mouth. The rush of air whizzed through her vocal cords to make the rattling noise of death throes. She fell backwards. The rational part of her brain chided her for arriving so late that she was experiencing night terrors. The rapid fog was disorienting, and she was seeing things in it now. She looked up again from her position on the hard ground, adrenaline having rendered her numb to the pain of falling. The tree was just a few inches away. And its outline was no longer tree-like, it was something else…a…a…woman? Grey, ashy, her…its face formless, it…it was humming a low song… then it yowled. Panicked, her heart thumped. She got up on one knee, ready to flee.

But her flight was arrested when the yowl reverted to what sounded like whale song, once again, wailing and mournful. She stood up and despite herself, turned for one last look before she ran. There was a woman, wan and silvery, covered in what looked like bleached, broken tree bark. Her eyes were white, mouth open in an "o" shape, and there was a reverberation, a sound like crying coming from her lips. To Alki, it sounded inexplicably sad and haunting though she was now in the grip of a powerful terror, the darkness past the glowing mist making her wheeze for air. She found herself resonating with the surreal song, erupting in goosebumps, hair all over her body vertical and rigid.

She regretted the impulse she had felt to visit the land after work not estimating how late it would get. Clapping her ears to keep out the melancholy howl, she turned and ran as fast as she could, cutting blindly through the peculiar fog in the direction of the road hidden by the haze. She stumbled repeatedly, tripping on rocks, stubbing her feet, trying to keep a step ahead of the pain and whatever was left of the dimming daylight. As she hurried away from the long-gone ancestral house, the forest closed in, rustling and sighing behind her. "Wind through the trees," she said shouting aloud into the shadows, the hair on her neck prickling up in defiance of any attempt at scepticism. Still running, she fumbled for her phone in her handbag, which was strapped around her shoulder. She managed to pull it out and hit the button for the tiny phone torch, which lit up towering spectral silhouettes. Her alarm quickly turned to pattern recognition. The potential spectres were merely coconut trees. Their tall, faintly corrugated trunks were always leaning over, hunching, as if reaching out to each other in the solitude of the forest. Her thoughts were segueing, her lungs gulping for air.

The night finally got ahead of her. It engulfed her. She stopped running, having spotted the smooth ribbon of road tar through the trees. The app on her phone showed no taxis about this far out from the city. She didn't like taking taxis alone, but out late in this dark and gloom, she was desperate. She started to walk down the shoulder of the road, too afraid to glance up towards the hill, rationalising to herself that she could make it to the junction. About a minute later, she heard the approaching rumble of a little engine behind her. It was a dilapidated old autorickshaw, a model that no one drove any more, driven by an old man with kind eyes who stopped when he saw her, offering to take her to the next junction.

Inside the vehicle, she exhaled, unclenching her fist to release the compressed tissue damp with sweat from her brow. She had held on to it tightly during her interrupted hike to the junction. For a woman out alone in this part of the world, it was a gamble and ultimately a temporary reprieve to find a harmless male driver. If anything had happened to her, she knew what her family and society at large would say.

"What was she doing out alone so late?"

The first question was always about the victim, not the perpetrator. It was a cultural reflex to blame the victim, never the perpetrator.

The autorickshaw driver dropped her off at the busy junction, saying, "Daughter, you should not come to this place again at this time of night."

When she asked him why, he shrugged, "Some places here are not good after sunset. Like that hill where I found you…when boys go there to cut trees for firewood, they never come back home. Did you hear the wail?"

Alki stared at the old man, then averting her eyes, she said, "No."

"First you hear…humming…howling…then sometimes words," he said.

On another night she would have dismissed him immediately as just another conservative local, a man trying to scare women with tales of ghosts so that they didn't leave the house after sunset, effectively corralling them at home. After he drove away, she felt safe again in the company of anonymous commuters and comforting lights that shone out from the shops lining the bus stop.

<><><>

Soft-spoken and middle-aged, the architect was confident he could do a good job. He was surveying the land, which had been in his client's family for generations. Shoulder-length, dark, hippie hair swayed in the gentle breeze easing the humidity of the forest ever so slightly. He tramped down the side of the hill in his soiled work boots, instinctively calculating the difficulties of the sloped building site in his head. Almost half a kilometre above him, a uniformly flattened mound of red earth had once held up the foundations of his client's great, great grandfather's house, which had been occupied for about a hundred years from what he could tell from his client's descriptions. But the house had been abandoned many years ago. Its only occupants, before its laterite walls had gradually crumbled away bit by bit, were several generations of bats that had moved into its rafters. Examining the remains of laterite blocks still scattered around the plot, he realised the blocks had been quarried from this very hill. The quarrying had left behind a wedge of flat land in the side of the hill, with space enough to build a house and its surrounding garden. The forest had grown back over the wedge to conceal the scar in the landscape.

Looking over his shoulder up the hill at the mound where the house had once been, he was suddenly hit in the chest by a foreboding malevolence. That's when he noticed the sun setting and he felt an overwhelming desire to leave the site. He couldn't understand it. He had never experienced a sensation like this before, having never considered himself particularly brave, or particularly cowardly. He possessed average courage, which is what he would say if anyone asked. He fought off the alien sensation and forced himself to trek back up the dirt path to the mound, with the twilight now upon him and the darkness mounting. The alien presentiment returned, coupled with an unfamiliar anxiety. He did not want to use the word afraid. Not yet.

As he approached the mound, he saw the shadowy figure of a woman in the centre of the ring of trees looking down, watching him. The dark figure seemed to crouch down, menacingly feline, head between knees, the ridges of her shoulder bones prodding skyward. A second later, in the inky dusk shrouding the slope, he realised it was just a boulder and not a person trying to squat. His imagination was in sports mode. Only the thought of his brand-new car waiting for him on the road below calmed him. Maybe his client had arrived to join him for the survey without informing him, he reasoned.

Although, it was a bit late for a woman to be about in the woods alone. To check, he reached into his trouser pocket for his phone to punch in her number. He had reached the mound and its engirdling garden of bananas and trees. There was no one around. Still clutching his phone, he tapped his client's number on the bright smartphone screen. She picked up immediately, and without further ado began to ask him how the survey was going.

Confused, he said to her, "Oh, so you are not here at the site."

She said, feeling a bit tremulous, "Why do you say that?"

The architect replied, "There was a woman here, but now I don't see her."

"What did she look like?"

"Well…it's dark, I couldn't see her clearly. Long hair…that's all I could make out."

"I don't have long hair. I have shorter hair than you, sir."

"Oh yes, that's right. I didn't think of that," said the architect.

He put his phone in his pocket after their brief conversation, the darkness condensing around him. This kind of exaggerated nightfall was a common phenomenon in these woods on the outskirts of the city. Retrieving the torch dangling on a clip attached to his trousers' belt he looked around. The circling torch beam lit up the mound and the tree trunks ringing it. There it was, a roughly hewn boulder on the edge of the levelled house mound, and just behind it the Alstonia tree in full ghostly bloom. Pale, milky green, perfumed flowers hung from the branches in vast drooping bunches crowning a softly curved smooth tree trunk that evoked a botanic femininity. Perhaps this is what he had mistaken for a woman. The citrusy, smoky scent was overpowering and peculiar; almost as if someone was burning incense sticks nearby. He walked up to the tree, weary now, and leaned against the softness of it. He began to feel tranquil, the light still radiating from his torch, his eyes wandering over the strangely bare mound where nothing seemed to grow. As his muscles relaxed, he felt a band of icy cold cross the top of his chest. He looked down and a moment before he lost consciousness, he perceived a pallid hand beneath his chin enfolding him. Before his eyes closed involuntarily, he felt his heart thumping and squeezing from the most profound terror he had ever known.

2

Looking Up into the Mango

At this time of the year, householders up and down the neighbourhood would stroll out into their gardens every morning and early in the evening to look up into their trees. This behaviour would look atypical to anyone who wasn't from these parts. But Alki, and anyone else who was a mango aficionado, knew what they were up to. Mango trees in the area around her parents' house tended to start their flowering seasons. But the undertaking of coming into blossom was left to the idiosyncrasy of each tree. Some of them would decide to flower, while their neighbour, of the same variety, on the other side of the road, would not.

When this happened, there was a lot of proselytising over the walls from vegan, vegetarian, fruitarian, and lacto-vegetarian adult children of neighbours about global warming, accompanied by explanations to older, disappointed, omnivorous, tree-owning parents about why they were not going to benefit from a bountiful harvest that year. The shrunken dietarians were youthfully evangelical, a throwback to a time when their farming ancestors had nothing but grain and pulses to eat and were wasted internally, and in appearance. Their modern insistence was less self-awareness and more crusading; their mental guns locked and loaded, bullets ready to fly.

Alki was no climate change denier, but sometimes her lacto-vegan-pescatarian neighbours goaded her, by glomming onto causes, each one an organic activist tree planter on social media, their intellectual fortresses built to resist attacks. Perhaps they didn't know they were being ideological; their intention was not to question, but to posture. They had chosen lifestyle over life itself, an urban lifestyle, which was centred on the wild lives of other creatures. They believed they were non-traditional in their religious practices in contrast to their parents. Other people suffered cognitive biases, not them.

They had merely transferred the old philosophic zealotry to their food. Fanaticism once restricted to bovine aspects now encompassed the whole animal kingdom. How were they to know that dogmatism was all the same, birthed this time in the enlightenment of liberal thought? A generation ago, their parents had been truculent too but taller and less frail as diets had improved in the village with the arrival of inventions like schools, libraries, newspapers and refrigeration. But evangelical habits passed down in families. As children do, the descendants donned parental habits, and as if these were family heirlooms—honed and handed down. They caught the ideological bug from their parents and cultivated it at first to win merely their approval, but then it became about receiving validation from the world.

In her parents' front garden, under their favourite mango tree, inspecting red weaver ants marching up the trunk and efficiently preparing nest bundles from mango leaves, Alki suspected her parents' tree was about to start flowering. Not every tree would flower on cue though year after year.

Her grandmother had told her years ago that mango trees had their off years when they would not bear fruit. The old woman had not particularly favoured wild leaves, whole grains, and pulses when it was all the rage with Alki and her friends. She had insisted "animal feed" made her muscles undone, her bones and teeth crooked and swollen. She reckoned that plants put their living effort into preventing animals and humans from eating their leaves…their grains…their beans, by making the eater sick.

In her time, she told the disdaining Alki, only the poorest had eaten the doughty leaves or grainy feed given to animals, but now so much time had passed that people had all but forgotten that whole grains and leaves did not sicken animals, as these did men. Alki had subscribed to the fashionable, healthful notions of her day. Veganism had once been her thing. She had argued with her visiting grandmother, her theology needing shielding against a wizened sceptic.

The memory of it made her writhe. She did not like the remembrance of what she was once. She had had the awful gumption to ask her grandmother, "What about the animals brutally killed for food?"

Unruffled, the old woman had replied, "Why do you attach piety to the things you eat? The things you eat also eat to survive. You eat to survive in good health, just as they eat to survive in good health. Give your animals good lives, let them roam free, graze on grasses, don't keep them caged. And when their time comes, give them prayer, and be respectful."

Back then Alki had spoken with exclamation points to her grandmother.

"That's so cruel!"

Then her grandmother said something she would never forget.

"The plants you eat are also living things. They just remain where they are their whole lives. They don't run, or scream, when you cut them down to eat them."

Many years later, long after the old woman had passed from the earth, it occurred to Alki that her entire generation was predisposed towards those with nervous systems.

Rivulets of almost invisible vapour ascended the cool air above all the gardens in the neighbourhood that morning. Everyone was out with steaming cups of milk tea. Alki's parents were out too. She could hear her father debating with a neighbour, the pros and cons of weaver ants nesting in mango trees. Neither of them wanted to disturb the large red ants with their notoriously ferocious bites. The neighbour over the wall said the ants protected the tree from pests. But Alki's father said he had observed the ants farming pestilent mealybugs on another one of their mango trees last year. He tended not to look too kindly upon them. But he too was wary of unsettling the wee red monsters.

That morning Alki needed the contentment of looking up into the mango after what had happened to her two nights before. Her thigh muscles were still aching from her ungainly run down the hill, shins and toenails bruised, cut, and sore from stubbing them against rocks. Somehow, everything seemed better in their untidy garden with a cup of cardamom-flavoured milk tea in hand. Even the old porcelain cup was charming and distracting, spreading its liquid warmth into her cupped palms. The little cup painted with cheerful blue irises was a distraction with Alki wondering why these plants were so popular as crockery design, or as names of buildings, when she had never seen any irises growing in their hot, humid environs. Perhaps these absent plants evoked wistfulness from colder climes. Maybe it was more banal than that, signposts of holidays in tony temperate geographies that would later manifest on everyday objects and subsume the names of buildings.

She was rueful about the plans for her house, that anomalous night having upended cold water over everything. She had invested her savings in the venture, hired an architect against the wishes of her parents, and even he had sensed some kind of presence at the site. She didn't know what to think, how to think. How could a rational, intelligent person explain what happened that evening on the mound? Was this the beginning of previously undiagnosed, sudden-onset schizophrenia?

From the garden, she heard the landline phone jangling loudly and harshly inside the house. She watched her grey-haired, tightly wound mother, who liked to wear a permanent expression of aggrievement on her face, go back inside holding her half-finished cup of milk tea and answer the phone in muffled tones. A minute later, Alki was called in to talk to the architect's wife.

As she was handed the plastic red receiver, her mother grumbled under her breath.

"I told you not to build that house. But you wouldn't listen. This is a bad sign."

Alki took the receiver from her. The architect's wife sounded tired and strained as if she had not slept the night before.

"I am sorry to be calling you this early. But my husband did not come home last night. He told me he would come home a little later than usual after surveying your land."

Alki started a little, then quietened her nerves instantly under her mother's watchful gaze.

"He called me in the evening yesterday from the site. I asked him about the survey. But that's about it. I was expecting a call from him today."

She paused, unsure about telling the architect's wife about the woman he thought he had seen. She could not yet tell anyone about the horrifying hallucination that she had had there. When he spoke to her yesterday, she had detected an undertone of fear in his voice. It had disturbed her, especially after what she had seen, but she had tried to banish all irrational thoughts from her head. She had repeated the word hallucination to herself again and again. But now she was alarmed.

The architect's wife said, "I was planning to go to your site to check."

Alki said quickly, "Oh…I am coming too."

The woman told her she had wanted to go yesterday.

"But it was so late. I couldn't go there alone and there was no one else I could ask. I couldn't leave my daughters alone at home. My father-in-law is not at home either."

Alki sighed. The sight of any woman out after sunset was always a scandal in her town. Now here was a woman who had genuine cause to be out late because her husband was missing, but still she could not go out at night to look for him because that was just not done. It was as if women had been indoctrinated to be prey and they were supposed to be eternally vigilant, watching out for predators prowling in the dark. If women were attacked at night, it was automatically their fault and not that of "the predator" simply following his instinct. The androcentric night fell upon women like a purdah ushering them back into house confinement.

She dressed hurriedly, not bothering to iron out her wrinkled salwar kurta, forgetting her stole altogether, her mind full with the song of a wailing spirit.

Her mother's voice trailed her all the way out of the house.

"You should wait till your father agrees to take you...How can you not put on your dupatta? What will the neighbours say when they see you like that on the street? Cover up."

Alki sighed, went back in, and wound the modesty-inducing light cotton stole around her neck. The neckline of her kurta came up almost to her chin, still she was not modest if there was not a dupatta or stole over that. For a woman in her culture, modesty was the ultimate performative dance form, involving not just clothes, but a complex code of body language and facial gestures. If found lacking in these, other women, like her friends or her mother, would punish Alki passively with comments like she was too pompous or her friend Jas's favourite, that she was too judgemental. It was she, Alki, who judged other women, according to her friend, by not following the code assiduously in her own life. There were ways to cheat on the code, but that was not her skill.

Incongruously, a serene dewy morning awaited an uneasy Alki and the architect's wife at the hill. The bus had deposited her at the junction where she found the architect's thin, nervous wife waiting for her. She seemed to recognise close-cropped Alki in a crowd of long-tressed women. The woman called Alki's cell phone to confirm if she was indeed her husband's client before she walked up to her. In daylight, the land looked so different, Alki thought. She was glad to note that she experienced no sensation of dread as she looked up from the side of the road towards the flattened earthen mound. In the early morning light, through the crowns of the trees above the mound, she was also able to glimpse the colossal black rock formation that surmounted the hill above her family's plot of land. From one spot on the summit, if she stood just right, she could see a line of deep blue distant sea hugging the western horizon.

The architect's new car was still parked a little way up the road. Together his wife and his client treaded apprehensively, hurrying a little on the path to the mound. Birdcall filled the air at this early morning hour and the leaves they brushed against on their way up were tipped with cold dew. As they neared the mound, the architect's wife let out a mournful sound from her throat, making Alki jump in fright at the awful echo from her night on the hill. Both women were now able to discern the shape of a man slumped against a tree in the ring garden around the mound. On the way up, a boulder had blocked their view. The architect's wife sprinted the rest of the way with Alki following close behind.

The architect had his eyes closed, his face shrunken in deathly pallor, his back against the Alstonia tree and his legs stretched out on the weedy ground. Drops of condensation from the leaves above dotted his face. Although horrified, Alki had the presence of mind to stand back respectfully as the architect's wife bent down, tears pouring down her face. Her lips parted and the only sound that would issue from her throat was a wail.

The man against the tree opened his eyes instantly. His wife stopped mid-howl and the two women gasped audibly.

The architect's wife said, "Oh thank god, thank god."

The man looked from one to the other without saying anything.

His wife said, "What happened to you…?"

She didn't finish, realising he needed more time before he could start speaking. The women managed to get him up. Since he was able to shuffle his legs, they walked him very slowly down the hill to the road. They waited at least 15 minutes with Alki impatiently looking down at her watch and the shrunken man seated on a nearby rock. She had offered to drive them back home. But the architect's wife had appeared wary.

She said, gesturing towards her husband, "I don't think he will be very happy if I let you drive his car."

Alki did not reply. Even at this moment of great urgency, with a man looking like he needed a once-over from a doctor, no one wanted to take advantage of her ability to drive. The architect's wife had probably deemed her arrogant for even suggesting that she, a woman, could drive her husband's new car. Alki was always overstepping the bounds in her patriarchal world. Finally, an autorickshaw arrived and she extended her hand to stop the vehicle. The women bundled the shivering man into the autorickshaw with the driver staring. Then the architect's wife turned awkwardly towards her husband's client. Alki realised that from here on the wife probably did not want another woman, even though her husband was almost comatose, squeezing in with them on the ride home.

She asked simply, "Will you be able to manage?"

The wife said gratefully, "Of course, of course, I can manage him. I will call you from home. Thank you for coming with me."

Alki glanced towards the car parked a couple of metres away from them.

"Don't worry about the car, my father-in-law will pick it up tomorrow."

"Of course," said Alki and let them go.

3

The Lone Stone Bauhinia

Six feet below the smooth pate of mica-black rock that crowned the hill, in a crag on the side of the rock, grew a wild Bauhinia in mutinous flower. It clung tenaciously to its rocky understory, pinkening the very air with its striking blossoms. On her way up to the summit, Alki stopped to take in the riot of magenta billowing from orchid-like flowers also emitting a graceful wispy fragrance. Near the summit, the thick red soil and its forest had started to give way to a fruitless gravelly scrubland home to mostly dry grasses and thorny shrubs. The Bauhinia seemed to be one of only a few trees to thrive in the scrub.

It clove to the crag, thick lateral roots not allowing the rock underneath to give away during heavy monsoon drenching. Beneath the tree and its stalwart foundation, the soil had subsided leaving behind a grotto framed by thickly parted draping bands of overgrown roots. Framed by the roots, the shape of the portal was dimly familiar. Oh god! It was the face of a woman, only this was a woman with no face. No sooner had the recognition flashed into her mind than Alki chided herself quickly. Was she turning into one of those people who saw faces in toast or on Mars? There had to be snakes down there too, she thought, turning away quickly from the stunning carnival of flowers and the eerie beckoning cave entrance beneath.

The easy climb was difficult on her city legs. But soon enough she had scrambled atop the summit. From this vantage, the pinnacle was a level rocky plateau that extended around her for a fair distance probably encompassing more than one hill in the area. A million monsoons must have created this, she realised, infinitesimally eroding a peak into a tabletop. She stepped around cautiously, but not before making a mental note of her entry point so as not to get lost on the return journey.

Finally, spotting the faraway pencil line of blue sea to the west, she sat down in the sub-equatorial sunshine to ponder the happenings of the previous night and day. Beside her, there were a couple of skinks sunning themselves. The surface of the rock was gradually heating up. As the sun shone down on her back, from the rock below balmy warmth spread into her bottom and thighs, and she experienced momentary bliss. The skirmish of life always led to these fleeting quantum moments. At this time, there was an absence of when and where, a suspension of time and space.

After the departure of the architect and his wife, Alki decided to go back up to the mound instead of trying to get home. What possibly could have happened to the man, she wondered. The site appeared curiously serene that morning. Nothing seemed amiss. She returned to the spot under the Alstonia where they had found the architect. Under the tree where the architect had been lying with his legs stretched out, the dirt looked disturbed. Two metres behind the tree, there were the remains of an old mud well dating from the time of her great-grandfather. Her mother had always warned her never to try and look down there as the well wall could collapse at any moment carrying her down into the depths of the well. She had taken that counsel to heart. Even now she felt a familiar quivering of fear just gazing at the old water hole. She took out her phone and clicked pictures of the area. As she snapped away, she couldn't help but think of her mother's dismay at her proposal to build a house at the family plot. Her peeved grumbling had not ceased since that day.

Alki had drawn up prodigious plans for the land. For her brick house on the hill, she had ideas for solar panels, a vertical axis wind turbine, and perhaps even a rooftop rainwater-run micro hydroelectric plant. Up the path from the house mound, she had plans to carve out a level spot for a capacious greenhouse, which she intended to connect to the house with a brick and glass corridor. And downhill from the house, perhaps a chicken shed perched on a spaced, slatted platform so that she could collect the chicken manure that fell through. She had saved as much money as she could from her day job and now hoped to set up a small organic hillside farm.

She had learned as a child that her grandparents had decided to move back to town because of the difficulty in obtaining ever-increasing water supplies for an expanding family. Alki thought she could address this by carving out trenches along the contour lines of the hill to sink water into the landscape. She had even hired a surveyor against her parents' wishes so that he might help her with mapping out contour lines on the hill using a laser transit level.

As a woman embedded in a deeply patriarchal hierarchy, she had an innate diffidence sewn into her since childhood. Invisible boundaries plotted out a woman's life giving it a rigid grid, foundation, and edifice. This was so in every Indian family no matter their religion. A woman's life was preordained and inescapable. The Muslim woman down the road who wore a headscarf told her that her head covering was everything to her. Her own mother lived contentedly constricted within the intimate scaffolding handed down to a caste Hindu woman. Women like them were threatened when other women, like Alki, attempted to pull out the scaffolding of their lives. She represented mutant chaos that caused her mother daily trauma. Ironically, Alki lived with her own daily repressed screams. The structure that eased their lives brought her distress. Her lack of privilege within the hierarchy also meant that no one would hear her even if she did scream, or raged against her world.

When she was a child, she would watch her precocious neighbour who was the same age as her. He could talk unreservedly to the milkman, he was allowed to explore the neighbourhood, and have adventures. She would stand at the gate, gripping the bars tightly, watching his movements and imagining what he was up to when he turned a corner, and she could no longer watch him with ease. Sometimes she would call out to him, and he would tell her about his exploits, even generously bringing back a polished stone or curious snail to pass through the bars of her gate.

When she was eight, she watched him learn to cycle with the bicycle that her father had donated to his father after Alki's brother had finished learning to balance on the two-wheeler. Her father had not deemed it necessary that she also learn to cycle. At 16, she watched her neighbour learn to drive his father's car even though he wasn't of age yet. It would take Alki another 15 years to defiantly join a driving school with her father branding her arrogant for the deemed audacity.

One paternal relative had even asked, "Why do YOU need to drive?" The emphasis condescendingly on you.

When she succeeded against all odds—odds that involved the male driving instructor trying to rub her breasts on the pretext of adjusting the steering wheel and, ironically, misogyny from the female instructors—her father was upset. Scrutinising her new licence, there was disappointment in his eyes that she had not failed. Later that week, she overheard him tell relatives that he would never let her drive his car, as she was likely to dent it. This from the man who had to replace a clutch every year and at one point had simultaneously lost second, fourth, and reverse gears, stunning even the mechanic who came for the repairs.

Once, her neighbour, now all grown up, miscalculated while parking and scraped his car into the side of their gate. Alki and her father had both heard the loud grating noise and had dashed outside. The neighbour got out of his car, flicked up his broken, flaccid side mirror and examined the scratch.

Her father said to him, "Oh this isn't so bad, should be easy enough to fix."

Alki gawped, astonished. If it had been her, she would never have heard the end of it from her father, who would have used the incident to end her driving career, citing it ever after if she dared make another attempt at it.

Despite her life's impediments, she could not grumble. Others situated higher on the social ladder than she, both men and women, were allowed to complain, while it was her lot to be the designated listener. If she interjected with her own woes, they would barely acknowledge her and quickly go back to talking about themselves, one even telling her, "You complain too much." That would always shut her up.

Another modus operandi used by privileged ones against those with lower privilege was to reduce others' lives to oversimplifications, while their own problems were reckoned much more complex. In her case, for instance, they would point out that since she wore no veil, was allowed to go to school, and get a job afterwards, what did she have to complain about? They wouldn't realise till later as new ideas seeped into their little bubble world that they were not to downplay the agency of women who wore veils.

Speaking of oversimplification…her grown-up neighbour had come over one fine evening along with his family to invite them to his younger brother's wedding. To her he broached the subject of his favourite newspaper column from which he learned that sexism was an "ism" like so many other made-up "isms". And that educated Indian women had learned to repeat the tenets of this particular "ism" without question from imbibed Western concepts. She wondered later why he had thought it fit to mention such a thing to her without provocation. Was it because the neighbours were beginning to hear about her house-building plans?

<><><>

She found the surveyor's number online, easily enough. Her parents were aghast at the idea of her calling up a man to hire him for a job.

Her mother said, "He will then start to call you on your mobile phone...what will people say?"

Alki was able to solve that problem by ringing up the surveyor on the landline, thereby letting her father or mother have authority over the phone calls that came to her. Though she told herself that she was doing it this way to ease her parents' qualms, she was not ready to admit her own fears. What if the man did indeed start pestering her on her cell phone? This happened constantly. She had heard of cases of single women calling for app-based taxi services to get to work, only to have the driver call back and harass them on their cell a day or two later. Alki had always taken the bus everywhere, and she preferred the airy openness of autorickshaws from which she could jump or scream for help.

When she called up a company's repair service, for instance, the man answering, recognising the treble of a woman's voice would inevitably start up a flirtatious conversation with her. She would try to veer the conversation to professional matters, while the man would keep peppering her with personal questions. When such a man finally got around to asking her what she did for a living, she would lie and say she was a cop or a journalist, just to hear the intonation of his voice shifting from suggestive to respectful.

Fortunately, the surveyor, like the architect, turned out to be a professional, a nice man who seemed to mean her no harm. Unlike the architect, the surveyor, however, preferred to ring up the landline and leave messages with her parents if she wasn't at home.

One of his messages had intrigued her. He had found a rain-fed stream on the edge of the property. He told her it seemed to be coming from the rock formation undergirding the hill.

The surveyor said, "I don't think your land has a water problem. In fact, if you don't have enough trees to hold the soil, and if you dig those contour trenches, you could sink too much water into the landscape and cause the soil to become saturated, which could result in a landslide."

At the mound, Alki decided to find the path to the rock summit which she knew was somewhere in the forest behind the broken-down well. Perhaps she would be able to locate the source of the stream from up there. She looked down at her watch, then her phone to make sure her mother hadn't called. She would be at home waiting impatiently till her daughter returned to give her news of the wellbeing of her architect.

<><><>

Above, on the black basalt plateau, the sun had risen high, and the rock was now hot to touch. With her fingers she traced the uneven patches of white checkering banding the dark rock. On closer examination, Alki noted the rock was not really a smooth black. It was coarse and embedded with grainy white minerals. With her hands pushing down on the rock for leverage, she stood up, gingerly dusting off her kurta, scattering sunbathing skinks in the process. She stepped around, bending over the vertiginous edge, hoping to uncover a source for the stream but gave up quickly. Her want of surefootedness and haphazard search methods would yield no result.

4

The Fetid Breath of the Corpse Flower

Even at this moment of incredible danger and shock, with adrenaline pumping through her bloodstream, the stink was overpowering. Running headlong down the hill, it stopped her dead in her tracks. She had reached the earthen mound where her great-great grandfather's house had once stood. Reluctantly turning her head sideways towards the foul stench of rotten meat and the air rippling with stifling inexplicable heat, she noticed the mound was no longer barren. The skin of the bare red earth, where she realised with a shudder, not even weeds grew, was now prickling with thick, purple needle-like stalks sticking up through the soil. Almost in the centre of the mound, one of these purple stalks had unfurled into a giant elongated hourglass receptacle carrying a long pointy shoot. The spathe of the unusual flower, because this was a flower, she realised through her terror, that looked like a downside-up cape or coat stretching upwards from the back of the cup, mottled with purple and yellow. Then Alki heard the frenzied humming. Flies were crawling up and down the flower. She had never seen so many different types of flies before, some iridescent with turquoise bellies.

Bewildered, and still reeling, she turned her back to the strange floral spectacle and smell to resume her lurching run towards the road. She did not turn around again till she reached the road. Sprinting up the shoulder of the road, she looked back for a second, before the mound and its crown of rock above was blocked from view by the side of the rising hill. The two immobile men who had waylaid her were standing on the path high above the mound, almost too far away for her to see clearly between the trees. And just as the hill rose to occlude her view, an ashy-drawn figure with long flowing white hair emerged from the trunk of a tree, gazing at her briefly before leading the two men away.

As she ran, Alki passed the car left behind by the architect and his wife. She felt strangely out of body. The car, the road, and the dirt path were all passing before her as if she was watching a movie in her living room. One of the men had grabbed her breasts, and she could still feel his disgusting hand. Involuntarily, she started rubbing herself as if with a bar of soap, tears streaming down her face. Then, just as suddenly she stopped on the bank of the road. Wiping away her tears, she detached herself, looking down at her shaking hands. She determined then and there that she would get to the junction, then home, even if she had to walk the rest of the way. She was still running, frightened, the men may have come after her. Before long she began to pass houses and other people as she got closer to the junction. She stopped running, but not before looking back to make sure the men were not chasing her.

On the ride home in a city bus, she could not stop shivering from the shock. Seated beside her was a thin dark woman, hair copiously oiled and tied back in a bun. The woman who smelled of labour and sweat draped a towel around Alki's shoulders. She smiled wanly at the woman she recognised as a vegetable seller, whose woven cane basket full of the day's leafy veggies was blocking the aisle. The ticket seller came up to them adroitly straddling the basket as the vegetable seller paid her fare. Only then did it strike the dishevelled Alki that she had left her wallet and phone behind at the hill. The conductor wanted to stop the bus and disembark her when she revealed that she had no money.

The vegetable seller stepped into the commotion and paid Alki's fare telling the conductor, "Can't you see, are you blind? She's not well..."

The kindness of strangers always staggered her. She was used to the incongruity of small-town malice bestowed in a friendly manner by friends and acquaintances. A random act of gratuitous kindness from a stranger, however, was a divergence that took her breath away. Still in a state of shock, shivering and unable to thank the woman properly, Alki was moved to tears once again. She alighted from the bus at a stop not too far from her house, walked the rest of the way there and into the house, stumbling past her waiting mother, unable to speak. She just wanted a bath. By the time she exited the bathroom, smelling strongly of antiseptic soap, her skin was red and numbed from the hot water. The intense heat acted like anaesthesia sedating and comforting her. She was thankful it was a Saturday, and she didn't have to think of going in to work. It was noon when she got into bed, slid under a sheet, and dropped into weary slumber.

<><><>

She sat up in bed waking suddenly to bleached white eyes. A silvery, pale, almost transparent face was contemplating her sleeping form. The macabre image vanished in a flash but the white irises in its eyes and tips of projecting teeth between shrivelled lips remained with Alki. Her scream awakened her mother. It was one past midnight and she had slept the entire day.

Her mother came in and asked, "What's wrong?"

Alki said, "I had a bad dream…a woman with sharp bowed teeth jutting from her lips, her eyes were white."

Eyes now wide, her mother gazed at Alki in pure disbelief.

She said, "Did she have long white hair?"

Alki was surprised.

"Yes, how did you know?"

Alki's mother turned to leave the room, saying, "You brought her here to our house."

Alki laid back down and reached out with one hand to switch on her bedside light. It was already on, and she couldn't remember turning it on. A couple of minutes later her mother returned.

She bent down beside her saying, "Kalike, put this under your pillow, she won't come back."

"What is it?" asked Alki.

It was an old grey bangle made of iron.

Her mother said, "We don't know why, but she doesn't like iron."

Alki said pointing to her bedside light, "Did you switch on the light when I was sleeping?"

"No," said her mother and left the room.

Alki tried to sleep, tossing and turning restlessly. Frustrated, she got up and grabbed the laptop buried under the plans and designs for her house on her study desk. It was a little after 3 A.M. She couldn't get that peculiar reeking flower from the mound out of her mind. She had to find out what it was. She typed in 'stinking flower' into the search engine and a lot of amazing plants popped up on screen, but not the one she had seen. An hour later, after delving into interesting stories about Titan Arums and the world's largest flower, also a stinker called Rafflesia, she found her plant—a giant voodoo lily. The picture and description she found on Wikipedia matched her flower: "The inflorescence has a purplish, brown-spotted yellow spathe and a purplish brown spadix, which emit a strong odour perceived as similar to cow manure, rotting flesh, or a dirty wet dog. The odour lasts about two days attracting carrion-feeding insects such as Calliphorid flies and Silphid beetles, which can pollinate this plant." Calliphorid flies turned out to be the luridly coloured flies she had seen buzzing on and near the flower.

A tiny piece of the puzzle had fallen into place, and it consoled her after the previous day's terror. She still did not want to think about the men she had encountered on her way down from the rock plateau near the Bauhinia tree and its gloomy cave. Maybe later, she thought, and pushed back into bed perchance to sleep a little more.

Alki was up at dawn. She dressed, with the house still and soundless around her. She looked in on her sleeping parents, then tiptoed her way past their bedroom into the kitchen. After opening the window to let in the eastern light, she took down the old saucepan from its hook on the wall to boil up a cup of water. Into this she added a spoon and half of coarse coffee powder, a dollop out of her mother's stash of hand-pounded desiccated ginger, about six coriander seeds and a couple of crushed Tulsi leaves. Her hands were shaky, and she spilled some of the ingredients. The decoction was filtered and poured into a cup then sweetened with a big lump of black palm sugar.

She drank her coffee in the veranda and ate the dissolving lump of sugar from the bottom of her mug. The newspaper boy threw the day's paper in a practised arc over the garden gate as she finished. Putting aside the mug, she went to unlock the front door to go outside and fetch the paper from the entranceway. Scanning the city pages, Alki found a brief report about two young men who had left their houses yesterday to go to college and were reported missing by their parents. No one had seen them since they left their adjoining houses situated near Penumpara. The locality got its name from the honorific given to the rock plateau above the mound of her family's old, vanished house. Two passport-sized photographs of the young men accompanied the brief. Her heart skipped a beat and her breathing became heavy and short.

She had never seen them before and had no idea what they were doing on the hill at that time of the morning. They looked surprised to see her on the path below the great rock. Young, lean, scruffy, dressed in t-shirts and jeans, they were clearly not woodcutters who were known to visit these parts. One of them was clutching an empty bottle of liquor. Her muscles tightened in readiness. The expressions on their faces shifted from surprise to something a little more menacing. In the split second she intuited she had become prey, one of them lunged for her, grabbing her arm with one hand and with the other her breast. A sharp pain shot up from her breast. She went for his eyes with livid fingernails after she managed to squirm one hand free. He yelped and tried to slap her but missed and struck her hard on the shoulder as she was thrashing around trying to extricate herself. From the corner of her eyes, she saw the other man had frozen still to the spot, the glass bottle having fallen from his limp hand, horror writ large on his face. He was looking at something behind her. The youth that grabbed her, abruptly let her go, stepping away from her towards his friend. Without a moment to lose, Alki started running as fast as she could downhill, tripping and falling only once before she got to the house mound. She picked herself up and kept going.

Cosseted in the safety of her veranda, Alki examined her fingernails. For weeks she had neglected to cut her nails. They had grown untidily long and sharp. She found minute bits of skin caught in the crevices between nails and fingers. Dropping the newspaper, she rushed to the bathroom and stuck her nails deep into a softened bar of soap still wet from her morning wash. Glimpsing her strained face in the mirror, she realised her shoulder was throbbing. Beneath the left-hand sleeve of her top, in stark relief, lay a whopping blue-black bruise spreading from collarbone down to upper arm.

Like so many other women, Alki would not report the incident to the police. Her parents would accuse her of bringing them shame and notoriety, and for not having listened to them in the first place. Her relatives had warned her repeatedly to forsake the house project. It was not her place to build a house on family land.

Such things should be left to the wisdom of elders, she had been repeatedly told. They would perceive the attack as punishment from the gods for her arrogance. More importantly, how could she explain the disappearances of the two youths who attacked her? Recalling her lost phone and wallet, her heart thumped. The two items lay somewhere on the path to the rock plateau. What if a search party for the two youths came across her belongings along with their empty liquor bottle? What if their bodies were still there? She couldn't understand it, but felt certain they had died on the hill that morning.

5

The Ashy Neem

Alki's beloved Neem tree was getting a trimming. It was Sunday and her mother had been commanded by her priest to cut down a few branches from the Neem for an impromptu puja that had been organised in the morning. This particular Neem wasn't a very healthy specimen. Despite being one of the older members of their front garden, planted a yard behind the mango, it persisted in a diminutive state, its bitter feathery leaves few and far between, reaching up hungrily towards whatever light the mango would share with it. It also exhibited a curious reluctance to flower. Her mother had once ominously declared, that if the Neem would not flower and fill the house and garden with abundant fragrance, it was an indication of the presence of spirits. Digging under the tree one day, Alki found a reservoir of yellowish clay beneath the hardened red soil. She tried her best, but in vain, to dig out the clay and fill the hole with dried cow dung and compost, but after a year of modest growth, the tree went back to being stubbornly sickly. She winced at the sight of her mother and the bearded priest in ritual dhoti and over-cloth jumping up and down trying to hack into the tree's scrawny lower branches.

Alki said, "Why must you take branches from this tree? Why can't you borrow branches from the neighbour's tree?"

"Guru says it has to be from our tree." Her mother replied.

With help from her parents, the priest moved the cane furniture aside and an enclosed square brick platform was laid out in the middle of the sitting room. The cut-up Neem branches were piled into its centre. On top of the Neem twigs, the priest placed heaps of brushwood and more kindling.

Alki said to her mother, "Won't the floor be ruined?"

"I can't think about that now," replied her mother, "neither should you...after you brought her...the spirit back with you."

She stared at her mother. She had said the same thing in her bedroom last night, but Alki had forgotten about it. Then she remembered the frightening apparition.

"It was just a dream. I never should have told you."

Tersely, her mother asked, "Did you look at her face? Did you not see anything?"

Alki was bewildered.

"See what?" she asked plaintively.

Her mother looked pained and did not reply. The ceremony got underway with the scorched kindling releasing a black smoke that wafted through the house making her cough. Bits of ash and embers fluttered about the room glowing like fireflies. Alki saw her father patting his forearm as one got on his shirtsleeve leaving behind a burn hole. As molten fingers from the consecrated fire reached down towards the branches of Neem, a white smoke began to pour out of the makeshift sacred fire pit.

The priest began a chant: ".... Om Klim Kalikayai Namaha... Om Hrim Shreem Klim Adya Kalika Param Eshwari Swaha..." after which the priest dropped a spoonful of ghee into the fire.

The puja was for the goddess that Alki's mother revered above all others. The goddess her mother was sure would come to protect the house and its members if propitiated properly. With the priest's chant came billowing white smoke that engulfed the house in a smothering fog through which only a crimson flush from the fire pit was visible. Her eyes were watering, her lips had dried, and she could no longer see her father and mother though they were standing and seated right beside her. And then she glimpsed the face again, a silvery white mirage etched in a bitter-tasting smoke hanging in the air, disappearing seconds after it manifested. Convinced the vapours had hallucinogenic properties, Alki got up and staggered out the door into fresh air, her mother's scolding voice following her out.

"What are you doing? Sit back down."

After the sacramental chanting, the priest asked her mother to hand him a parcel. Inside was a set of iron bangles, which he proceeded to sanctify with more chanting. She and her parents were instructed to go nail a bangle to the wall of each room in their house, the priest following them intoning mantras. After the priest left with his fees, presents of saris, and offerings of sweets, Alki was tasked to clean up the ramshackle fire altar. She swept up the charcoal and ash, and went out into the garden to spread it out under the frail Neem. The blackened bricks were sorted away in the far corner of their garden shed. The floor of the living room had scorch marks and the ceiling above was smoke-stained. An entire Sunday morning of hard scrubbing could not get the marks out. For her mother, the ceremony had been worth the damage inside the house.

Back in the house, with the chores done, her mother was waiting.

"Did you see her again during the puja?"

Alki lied.

"No."

She didn't see any point in telling her mother the truth and cause her more disquiet.

Her mother said, "Has the architect phoned you? How is he?"

Alki equivocated.

"I am not sure how he is. He did not look well yesterday, probably some kind of viral fever with weakness. I'll give them a call now."

Alki phoned the architect from her parents' landline. His wife picked up to report that he was doing much better though he would not talk about what happened that night. Not having much else to say she then passed the phone to her husband. Alki spoke softly as she did not want her mother to overhear.

"You told me that night that you saw a woman…Do you know who she was?"

"I thought it was you. It was dark. I only saw an outline."

"But why didn't you go home after calling me?" asked Alki.

He hesitated, then said, "I am not really sure what happened after that. I am not even sure if I fell asleep or lost consciousness. My wife thinks I work too hard, and I am exhausted. Next thing I remember, I am under that tree, my wife is crying…and you are also there…it's morning."

He paused again, then whispered hurriedly, "My wife just left the room. I can tell you this much, I felt very afraid, there was something…someone there."

His tone changed again, and he spoke in a normal voice. "Don't worry, I plan to start work soon. Please give me a week to recover."

Alki said, "Of course, sir," and the phone call came to an end.

That evening after sunset in the front garden with a cup of tea in her hand, she wondered about her lost phone and wallet. She was still too afraid to go back to the hill alone to retrieve the items. She looked up then, deep in thought, and noticed a difference in her Neem tree despite the fast-approaching darkness. The fragility had abated at least to her discerning eyes. It was abruptly vivacious, its leaves seemed leafier, greener, and there were sprouts of glossy brown baby leaves on all the branches stretching towards the disappearing light almost in defiance of the aggressive mango, which liked to corner all the sunlight.

She wondered if the morning's top dressing of charcoal and ash from the fire pit could have brought about a transformation so rapidly. It was a still, quiet day with no breeze or wind to cool the skin, and yet, the Neem's branches were rustling. The effect was eerie, almost as if the tree had come alive and was trying to tell her something. She backed away, startled. She turned and ran to get a torch out of a desk drawer in the living room. Alki shone its light out the window into the garden. She was sure now that she had not imagined it. There it was in the darkness and stillness of a windless garden…the rustling Neem tree.

On the ground, at the base of the tree trunk, there was stirring. At first, she assumed grey ants were crawling up the tree. But no, these weren't ants! It was the ash and charcoal she had sprinkled under the tree that very morning. A moment before she switched off the torch, the bark of the tree trunk seemed to shift and split. An ashy figure peeled away from the bark of the tree and stood stock still in the garden facing her, its long cindery hair powdering away into dust like talc, its eyes snow-white in the torchlight. Panic-stricken, Alki slammed shut the window and latched it securely. She let out a suppressed sob and then ran to switch on all the lights, trembling. Next to the light switch in her parents' bedroom was one of the iron bangles they had nailed to the wall that morning. Leaning on the wall and resting her head beside the artefact, she felt temporarily reprieved.

"It can't get in tonight," she thought, surrendering completely to her mother's superstition and paranoia. Her rational brain knew that superstition was a type of allegory. It was her brain transliterating her anxieties into a visual, social framework. Superstitious rituals gave structure to anxieties. People who felt soothed by rituals could not possibly know how they could only be cementing their anxieties by ritualising them. She knew this, but panic had overwhelmed her anxious brain. Her mother had been right. Alki had brought something back home with her from the vanished house on the mound.

She went into her bedroom and switched on her laptop. In the search engine, she typed in the place name—Penumpara—followed by the words—local spectres and ghosts. She discovered numerous references to a female spirit called *Yekshi*, who haunted the forests in the area. There were even blog posts with folk tales and stories of women who died in terrible circumstances. They became malevolent female spirits that lured, then preyed on male travellers. The description seemed to match her apparition. She shut down the laptop and took a deep breath.

Was she perhaps falling deep into herself? Like one of those people with extensive fantasy lives. They even had a name for the problem. It was a psychological disorder called maladaptive daydreaming. People fall deep into the well of their own stories and they do not want to come back out to join the real world. But the difference between her and maladaptive daydreamers was that they knew they were fantasising. She couldn't say that anymore in her case. Some kind of line had been crossed, and she was no longer certain of reality.

Around 8 P.M., they were at dinner when Alki's father said he had to go out to the end of the lane, to their neighbour's house. There were some documents he had left at their place, and he needed them for the next day. Normally, Alki wouldn't have said anything. He often went out in the dark of the evening to buy fresh bread for their morning repast.

Frantically, she said to her father, "No, no, don't go out, Appa. It's not safe."

That was when Alki's mother perceived the alarmed and anxious weariness clinging to her daughter's face.

Alki's mother said, "She's right. You need to stop going out at night alone. It's not safe out there anymore, don't you read the papers?"

Her father decided to stay indoors that night, to Alki's relief. She slept uneasily that night. She did not wake up to any more ghosts gazing down at her, but she was nevertheless restive. As soon as dawn light was visible through her bedroom window, she unlocked the front door without disturbing her parents, and walked out into the garden, not daring to look at the Neem tree. She went straight to the garden shed to look for a spade and a sack. Only after finding these did she turn around and trudge up to her now tranquil Neem tree. The ash and charcoal looked damp and lumpy from soaking in the morning dew, but the stuff was all exactly as she had spread it on the ground the preceding day.

Was she delusional? Was she becoming irrational and histrionic like her mother? Then she examined the tree trunk. At first, everything looked normal. But looking closely, she noticed patches of grey all the way up the tree up to about her height. She pressed her index finger into one of the stains, and a bit of ash came away from the flaky tree bark stuck to the tip of her finger. Unnerved, she ran back to the garden shed, rummaged in the back, then returned to the tree with a brush. She scrubbed the trunk of the tree with the brush till the ash marks disappeared. Then she swept the hard ground around the Neem, scraping every last bit of ash and fire-pit residue from the ground to dump into the sack.

6

Pandering to the Hibiscus

Her friend's mother maintained a carefully manicured garden. Alki found a spot beside the garden's pride and joy, a prized hibiscus, and putting down her sack of ash, she drank in the freshness and order radiating from the lime green of the lawn. After the insanity of the last few days, she appreciated it today when in the past she had censured it in secret. Mostly because her friend's mother spoke derisively when she described Alki's parents' garden, which was weedy with random flowers gone to seed amongst the trees. Her parents did not believe in planning or organisation. One or both would aimlessly pick a vacant area to plant a tree or a new patch of nursery flowering plants that had caught their fancy, often uprooting another plant fallen out of favour. They never considered required amounts of sun or shade, or even the cardinal directions crucial for optimum garden setting. In contrast, her friend's mother's prized hibiscus stood statuesquely in a partially sunny location highlighted by a sea of green, finely mowed grass. It was famed for its rainbow-hued flowers and was the envy of the neighbourhood. Alki had never seen a specimen like it before. It was special, a bit too special, she thought.

Alki had laughed to herself on other visits when she had overheard her friend's family members discussing imported lawn grass breeds and each one's fertiliser requirements. This obsession with lawns amused her because she was a freedom fighter for the wild and an anti-lawn evangelist, convinced they were like big oil-guzzling sedans struggling on narrow potholed urban roads. The lawn was a status symbol that lapped up too much fertiliser and water. But the prized hibiscus beat even the lawn when it came to being fussy. As she was admiring the plant one day, its owner came down into the garden and recounted to her the history of her hibiscus. The story began dramatically with a friend smuggling in a branch of it from Florida, swaddled in newspapers inside a suitcase.

She went on to describe the first time she had clapped eyes on her favourite plant on her American friend's Facebook page as gaudy pictures attracted likes and comments from around the world. She begged her friend to bring her a cutting the next time she visited. When the cutting arrived in their small town, it took great effort on her part to save the slightly spoiling plant fragment and bring it back to life, immediately soaking it in a fungicide solution with no time to spare. The cutting was then divided into two pieces using secateurs sterilised in alcohol. One she planted with a dab of rooting hormone into good quality compost and the other was grafted onto the robust rootstock of a local variety that grew well in their hard red soil. Both the resulting plants took off to great success, and she became known as a green thumb in her neighbourhood.

The proud hibiscus owner also detailed the pains she took to grow her exotic plant. Since they were so juicy and appealing to insects, she had to spray them constantly with insecticides and they needed enormous quantities of potassium fertiliser. The plant in the main garden was a particular fusspot, dropping its flower buds at slight changes in temperature or nutrient availability. After several different nutrient cocktails were attempted, the exquisite moment one of her plants finally flowered for the first time could only be compared to the birth of a child. Ecstatic beyond measure, she distributed sweets among bemused neighbours. She spoilt her plant silly. Listening to her, it occurred to Alki that the older hibiscus-obsessed woman was possibly describing her daughter—Alki's friend Jaswanti, Jas to her friends.

Watching Jas charily set foot on the family lawn in a comical parody of Armstrong's first step on the moon, Alki remembered the first time she met Jas. Descending her home's central staircase in regal fashion dominating the world beneath: that was Jas. Unfortunately for her mother, Jas had no interest whatsoever in gardening. She hated putting her manicured hands or feet in the dirt. She once told Alki that she hated flowers, their natural fragrances, and did not understand all the fuss about gardening. She preferred second-hand perfumes in bottles laboriously plagiarised from flowers instead. Alki had a typical small-town relationship with her friend, that is to say, their relationship was not like it was depicted in the movies or on big-city television. Here, friendships were much more complicated, deeply influenced as they were by the social hierarchy in their town. Friendship was never about fairness or equality; some were always more equal than others.

Ancient, rigid, feudal structures had broken down, devolving into an egalitarian feudal oligarchy, a contradiction in terms, also commonly called the middle class. In the cities, the super elites, who had benefited the most with admittance to foreign education, had turned their backs to the system, at least overtly, and were now socialist in their ethics. But remnants of the old system were alive in small towns. As these towns morphed into middle-class, urban centres, the old system thrived anew in the burgeoning cities. The effects of feudalism would leave its indelible mark down the generations. The people who benefitted from the available resources and power structures were able to pass these paybacks down to their children's children. The descendants of the early feudal beneficiaries still lived inside their bubbles of privilege. But if they were privileged, the people below them looked at them with a generational resentment that too left a mark on society. But telling anyone who lived in one of these bubbles that they were privileged, was to invite self-justifying debate. It was like trying to tell Jas that she was cosseted and spoilt by her parents. The pampering had gifted her a supreme confidence in herself, which she used to dominate her friends and hold court. If she needed a chaperone to go somewhere as her mother didn't like her going alone, Alki would drop everything to accompany her despite her own suppressed resentment.

There was one friend Tana who used to follow Jas around everywhere, the most devoted and clingy of all her friends. This weed of a girl had spent her days imbibing all the lessons that Jas had to offer. And one day that girl drummed up the courage to be a 'Jas' in her own right. She started to dress like her and began a regime of cosmetic fertilisation that transformed her into a cultivated greenhouse specimen that could never return to the wild. Jas had been none too pleased at the transformation.

Alki had watched their fallout with anthropological curiosity, but was flustered when she had to take sides between the mirror images that repulsed each other. One hated because she was jealous, and had lost a subservient courtier, and the other hated because her friend, instead of being encouraging, was jealous that she had moved up in the world. Outwardly there was a show of tetchy sociability. It was the oldest story in the world. Though they were both hyper-thin skinned to each other's barbs, Tana had not managed to imbibe Jas's sophistication. She was Jas 2.0 without the unpredictable kind-heartedness that made Jas bearable. Tana was crudely mean, whereas Jas was understated in the way she demeaned her friends.

But the worst thing Jas ever did had to do with a boy. It was a wound that Alki would carry in her heart for a long time to come.

It all started in the month that Jas had gone to visit her ailing grandmother. Alki finally met a boy that she liked, and crucially this boy, Yug, had liked her too. Thin, pale, and very charming, he was new to their college, and he developed an instant rapport with the attractive Alki. For one blissfully quiet month devoid of drama, they talked for hours about their favourite books, playing chess in the library every chance they got. He even came home with Alki one day, had lunch with her and her scandalised mother, telling them about his plans for the future. Alki had never felt this happy. Though at first irritated and dismayed by the sight of a boy walking down the road with her daughter before the eyes of gossipy neighbours, her mother settled down and became more affable.

After he left, her mother remarked, "He's a bit too charming."

Alki was flummoxed.

"What do you mean?"

"Superficial, not really the kind of boy for you," said her mother.

It was Alki's turn to be scandalised.

"He's clever, he reads a lot, how can you say such things?"

"Yes, he's smart, and he's too eager to move up in the world."

Exasperated, Alki said, "So what? Isn't that a good thing?"

Her mother finally relented. "Yes…I suppose."

A few days later, an academic awards presentation had been arranged in college for which Alki had dressed to the nines and was feeling dapper, as she was to go up on stage. A dolled-up Jas also made a grand entrance into college that day. Alki had been on the phone with Jas in the month she had been absent from college. She had described the new boy and her platonic relationship indicating that they did have unacknowledged feelings for each other, but hadn't progressed to any admissions yet. But Jas wasn't really listening. The emotions of others barely ever made it through the dense fog of her own self-absorption.

Up on stage that evening, Alki looked down into the crowd and her body slumped, experiencing a sudden drop in self-worth. Yug and Jas were distinct in the crowd below. They had spotted each other. Each smiled invitingly at the other, and then Alki saw one approach the other and was witness to their first conversation. Their body language unsettled Alki, watching vulnerably from stage. Distracted, she flubbed her presentation.

It was still the era of landline phones in their time-warped small town, and Alki had established a ritual of waiting by the phone every evening at 7 P.M. for a call from Yug. She hadn't wanted her mother or father picking up instead of her. The day that Jas made her grand entrance, she recalled vividly, that he had called and oddly asked her a lot of questions about Jas and her family, adding that he found Jas very striking. There had been something new in his tone. After that, she waited many nights for the call that would never come again. In college, at first, she didn't notice that he was trying to avoid her as he had pending academic papers to complete.

An alarm went off in her head only days later when she found them, Jas, and Yug, seated on a step outside the college library deep in conversation. She took down the books she wanted in the library, ruefully glancing at the table with the chess set. She tried to forget herself in the relevant passages, and when she made her exit three hours later, there they were, still on the same step, with eyes only for each other.

That night Alki cried into her pillow chiding herself for having been so silly, so stupid. Jas did not even notice immediately, that yet another friend had stopped talking to her. About two months later, Jas's mother was waiting for Alki in her parents' front garden when she returned from the library. Alki swung open the small garden gate to find a familiar figure lurking politely, but disdainfully around her mother's garden-variety hibiscus. This one yielded a pretty red flower that Alki's mother used to propitiate her favourite goddess. Well at least she was polite, thought Alki, welcoming her into their humble house. Jas's mother's gracious disdain extended from the garden to Alki's house. Jas herself had often enough snickered about their lack of decor and old magazines collecting on her parents' dusty coffee table. Jas's mother did not beat about the bush.

"Do you know anything about this boy she likes?"

Alki didn't know what to say. Then she wanted to know why Alki had deserted Jas. Rendered speechless, she could only gasp in reply. Jas was apparently very depressed. She needed someone to talk to and that person was definitely not her mother. Jas's mother was upset that Alki had forsaken her duty to watch over her daughter.

After extracting a promise from Alki that she would return to her duties, Jas's mother made her own royal exit, not before she said, "You mustn't think that I am asking this of you...as you know your parents are barely involved in your college activities, and I am there for both you and Jas...am I not the one taking you for all your activities?"

Alki had to acknowledge that it was true. Other than some cursory enquiries, her own parents had barely a clue about her extra-curricular debates and science club undertakings, but Jas's mother had always been there, maintaining an open house for all her daughter's friends, volunteering her services to chaperone and ferry Jas and her friends to their venues and various activities. Alki was indeed grateful.

Observing Jas's mother leave, Alki's mother stepped into their living room and said, "I hope you are not going to go back to running errands for that girl again. I don't like the way you are always getting her tailoring...her library tokens."

Alki said anaemically, "I can't say no...when she asks...can I?"

Alki did go back to see Jas, determined to say something to her about how hurt she had felt. After two months of not speaking at all, Alki tried starting with a conversation about her emotional wounds. Wary, Jas cut her short and would have none of it. Alki finally got in a sentence.

"You can be very self-centred…"

Jas replied cursorily, "We all have our foibles."

And weakly Alki had said, "Yes we do."

Jas said, "I know you want me to apologise for things I did not do. I can't do that. You are the one playing victim, you can't blame me for that."

Alki wanted to cry, and her face was hot from suppressed tears. For years afterwards, she would think back to that moment wondering at herself for how she had remained quiet. Maybe Jas had been right all along. On that day, at that moment, she had come to her friend with her meek victim face on, hoping for sympathy from a contrite Jas, and instead, her friend had pounced. No wonder Alki hadn't even attempted to argue with Jas. Even then she had known there wouldn't be any point in such an exercise with someone for whom the purpose of logic was to justify her own actions. What happens when whole countries become Jas, lands where the accused impugned victims?

And that was that. Neither of them spoke of Yug again mostly because Jas did not want to concede that another person beside her could have drama in their lives. In Jas's narrative, there was room for only one heroine. From the sidelines, Alki watched their romance blossom into matrimony. About 10 years after Yug and Jas were married, Alki at last became aware of the strange countenance that Yug put on around her and it wasn't embarrassment. It was discomfiture. She realised she made him uneasy.

Following a global recession and a change of jobs, Jas, Yug, and their two small children came back to live in their small town. This was the time that Alki started to admire Jas for getting her way where it mattered. Her supreme egocentrism had overwhelmed even patriarchy. As Jas did not get along with her in-laws, she flouted prevailing societal norms enacting a coup of sorts. She chose to go back to her parents' house, husband and children in tow. It had taken the muscle of egotism to overcome the iniquities of patriarchy. In the struggle between two evils, one had overpowered the other, momentarily.

7

The Suffering Mehendi

Jas had just stepped out onto her mother's lawn to fetch her friend Alki, who, as she waited, had begun a distracted walkabout to check out the garden's many unusual plants. About a metre from the great hibiscus, Alki encountered a thorny little bush that got her attention instantly. She called out to Jas.

"Is this Mehendi, Jas?"

Jas shouted back, "How would I know? Ask my mother."

It was a thorny little Lawsonia bush with tiny unassuming leaves. The little leaves in her hand today were slightly crimped, hard, and stiff. When they were dried and crushed, these tough leaves yielded a soft and cooling auburn dye. She was reminded of the day before Jas's wedding.

They were all seated together in a room inside this very house getting the greenish brown Mehendi paste piped in beautiful curlicue shapes onto their hands and feet from little plastic cones. Jas's frenemy Tana was there too, beside Alki.

Gesturing to their hands, Tana turned to Alki and said, "You are like this, aren't you? You get crushed…you suffer for others."

Alki stared at her puzzled.

"What…?"

Tana said, "I know what she did to you. And you just took it. You know I stopped doing that for her."

Alki was not amused. She was laconic in reply.

"Are you really comparing me to a plant dye?"

Tana said, "Oh…I am sorry, I didn't mean it like that."

Alki said, "You stopped doing anything for her…but you sure sound like her now."

Tana smiled sheepishly, unsure what Alki meant. Was it a compliment? Was it an admonition? How was Tana to know?

In Jas's mother's garden, Alki released the small Lawsonia leaves along with her memories and ambled towards Jas.

Jas said, "What is that?"

She was pointing at the sack that Alki had left by the great hibiscus.

Alki said, "Oh." And stopped in her tracks.

The unsightly sack was incongruous in the harmonious garden, and it brought her back to her troubles. The garden's tranquillity had eased her mind just for a bit. She walked up to Jas and said softly, "I need your help."

<><><>

Alki had left the sack of ash in the garage by the garden shed under the boot of her father's car. Then she went indoors to look for the keys to her father's car. Her parents were awake by now and busy with their morning ablutions. Her father had taken to hiding his car keys from Alki. It wasn't a paternal fear for her safety, but the dent to his manly pride from the sight of her driving his car that he feared most. She looked everywhere, even under his pillows. Finally, giving up in frustration, she snatched the sack of ash on her way out through the gate. Her mother ran out in time to ask her where she was going at this early hour. She replied quickly that she had to meet Jas before work and swung the garden gate shut behind her.

Jas was still looking down at the peculiar sack waiting for an explanation from Alki.

Alki said, "Did you hear me, Jas? I need your help. I need you to come with me to the land today…right now."

Jas looked up at the change of tone and the unaccustomed assertiveness in her friend.

"What? Your land? The children are already awake, and I have to send them to school."

"Ask Yug to manage today. I wouldn't ask you if it wasn't important."

"Okay, fine. You have never taken me there before…"

Alki said quickly: "…You hate walking about in the dirt, it's not your kind of place."

Jas cringed.

"Why don't you have a little breakfast first? You are looking a little pale today. Then I'll go change and we can go. I'll drive."

Concerned for her friend, Jas gently nudged Alki in the elbow and led her into the house. The mystifying sack was left outside the front door. Inside, Jas and Alki sat down in the airy dining room and the family's morning maid and cook served them both breakfast. For years, Alki had watched the feudal chain of maids, drivers, and gardeners go in and out of Jas's house, serving as the unspoken, unwritten backdrop to their family life. Jas and her mother were also their feudal benefactors. Like the big landowning zamindars used to be in the olden days, its modern-day oblivious equivalent—the Indian middle class, had taken those duties unto themselves, taking care of the people that worked for them, the people below them also expecting and taking their patronage for granted, whether it be buying their children text-books, letting them borrow cooking gas cylinders, a steady supply of old clothes, shoes, umbrellas, advice on insurance applications when needed. Beneath the veil, this was a fine-tuned system of exploitation, in which one group exploited another, but there was some confusion about who was doing the exploitation. The elite needed the labour to be poor to take advantage of them, and the poor needed the elite to be pretentious about their compassion to take advantage of them.

Jas found nothing medieval about the goings on in her house, assertively terming it her family's acts of charity. Alki had dared to comment about it one day, prompting a burst of tetchiness from Jas who termed her elitist. Like any card-carrying member of the middle class, Jas kept up with the latest zeitgeist, which shifted on a continuum from big cars and objet d'art to organic, vegan abhorrence of all things plastic and dairy. Many affluent middle-class persons liked to flaunt previous poverty by projecting minimalism in a car purchase or insisting on retaining an old television set when they could afford the newest 60-inch smart TV. Jas's minimalism stopped with her hatchback and a dearth of artwork. These, and an ever-present paranoid parsimony, were what she used to corroborate her argument that she was not rich.

It was an irony, thought Alki, to be called elitist by the advantaged girl atop the feudal ladder. But as was her wont, Alki would back down calling herself a hypocrite for enjoying the crumbs of the feudal system at her friend's house, like on this day, breakfasting on hot idlis and green coconut chutney with a view of a bright green lawn and its stunning hibiscene ornament.

There was the morning maid, who washed the previous night's dishes and scrubbed out the kitchen and its environs, and then the cook arrived to prepare breakfast and to make sure Jas's children were fed. The mid-morning maid came at 11 A.M. to clean the house and its toilets. The cook then returned to make lunch, and start prep for dinner and the next morning's meal. The independence of Jas and her mother was completely dependent on the feminine subservience they had going.

This was one of the reasons why Jas did not like living at Yug's house with his parents. They expected her to do everything from cooking to cleaning. Love had turned to bitterness when Jas realised that she had been reduced to an indentured family servant at Yug's. They had expected her to quit her job and mind the house. She knew super women who insisted on going to work and who somehow managed to please their in-laws by also cooking all the meals at home. But the first ever bit of tangible self-awareness that came to Jas was that she was no super woman.

Alki's hot breakfast was tempered with the conflicted emotions she always felt being waited on by the family cook at Jas's house. Meanwhile, over at her house, her mother did everything, another reason why Jas's mother looked down on her mother—a woman who had stayed home only to become hostage to her house, husband, and children. At Alki's house, in the absence of a feudal system, the burden had fallen on her mother.

What kind of social progress was this that her mother's lot in life was to begrudgingly cook and serve all of them with no end in sight? Her father termed it her duty as his wife did not "work". But she did not "work" because she had to do all the "work" at home, which to her father was not "work". One day, Alki had even asked her retired father when her mother would get to retire from her duties. Her mother's simmering resentment was the imperceptible legacy Alki had unknowingly inherited. She was determined to not suffer masochistically the way her mother did. She did not want to suffer the fate of the green Mehendi leaves, to be crushed to dye and paint beautiful the hands of countless.

She decided never to marry into a family that expected her to do their housework, which only ensured that she never married. She refused to learn to cook despite her mother's scolding and cajoling. Her father had often complained to sundry visitors that the great tragedy of his life was an ungrateful daughter who refused to marry, insisted on being a burden on him, and to top all of that would not even make him a cup of tea, to which Alki would reply that she would make him one when he also made her mother one, eliciting astonished wheezes and gasps from said visitors. Of course, the visitors were firmly on his side and Alki was branded the villain.

If there ever was a universally known but unacknowledged truth, which everyone admitted to privately, it was that a man with inheritable means was never to be crossed. One of the reasons no relative would ever rebut Alki's father even if they secretly sympathised with his daughter was that this was a man who knew he could not be thwarted. Alki knew this, and one day wondered to herself if she could turn this canon on its head. She found it increasingly hard to be nice to a man to whom she and her mother were service persons, while only her distantly stationed brother got any respect as he too had become a man with heritable means. What was the worst that would happen? She would not inherit anything.

Thus, the idea of a house of her own was born. It started as an experiment in her head. Since she was not going to inherit anything, thanks to her passive-aggressive non-cooperation at home, could she not create her own means? Could her father behave like a patriarchal dictator in a house that she would build and own? How would this affect his behaviour? For one thing, her mother told her, he would never agree to go live at her house. And therefore, neither could her mother. Duty bound; she would have to stay with her husband. But Alki could not let go of what her mother called her foolhardiness. It had taken firm root in her brain.

She had secretly saved money and could now afford to build a house on land that was co-owned by members in her mother's family. It was too expensive to buy land from her savings. Her father could control all the women around him, but what about her maternal uncles? Once she got the friendly uncles to agree to give her a parcel of land; that was it. Her father was furious. One memorable evening, he had even threatened to go to court after her mother told him about Alki's house plans. He believed that since she had lived at home rent-free all these years, the money she was using to defiantly build a house technically belonged to him. For many years, he had indeed sought rent from her, which she had refused to give over to him. She had threatened more than once to move out of the house and into her own apartment, at which point he would pipe down in frustration, as the thought of public calumny would always overcome his desire for money. Alki's mother had also worked gamely behind the scenes to defuse his angry demands.

Unexpectedly, and despite her father's sputtering ire, the uncles assented to her cockamamie scheme. The parcel of land was supposed to be given to her mother, but instead they decided to give it to Alki. This was when Alki began to pay attention to the dynamics at play between her uncles and her father. She was the medium they found to act out their unspecified grudge.

At Jas's, they were done with breakfast. Yug was in the living room reading the morning paper on the settee. He hadn't looked agreeable when Jas asked him to join them at the dining table. Jas excused herself to speak with Yug. Alki made her way through the kitchen corridor towards the garage as the couple's cadences rose, then fell at the conclusion of their little argument. Alki enviously watched Jas swing open the garage door and get her diminutive hatchback ready. She got her sack from outside the front door and loaded it into the boot and the two drove off.

Looking in the rear-view mirror, Alki got a glimpse of the giant hibiscus and the serene emerald lawn sea behind it ebbing away down the lane. As Jas manoeuvred fretfully into the senseless traffic, Alki debated if she should even tell Jas about the incidents of the last few days. Would anyone believe her?

As the plans for the new house on the mound progressed, Alki had excitedly tried discussing them with Jas at their workplace. Upon Jas's return, Alki had helped to find a position for Jas at her office. At first disinterested, because Jas felt the house was just a whim on Alki's part, she too like everybody else had expressed bewilderment as the crazy idea took brick shape. How would she manage on her own on the hill? Jas had repeatedly asked, as did Alki's mother. After a while, a fixated Alki stopped listening, telling them both that she did not want to think about these things just then. Neither of them could begin to appreciate why she needed to do this for herself, by herself. Both Jas and Alki's mother had edifice to their lives while Alki had none, by choice. They seemed stingily happy where they were and Alki aspired to acquire some of that meaning, even if by other means.

It was mid-morning when they arrived at the hill. Jas wondered aloud why Alki had not called in late on her own, instead insisting Jas ring up their office to inform their boss they would be late to work that day.

As the engine shut off on the shoulder of the road, Alki said, "I left my phone and wallet on the hill on Saturday."

The architect's car was no longer where he had left it on Friday. His father must have picked it up for him as his wife had said he would.

Jas said, "What? How did you do that?"

Alki took a deep breath, then said, "There were two men on the hill day before yesterday…they tried to attack me…I ran. I think I dropped the phone on the way down somewhere."

Jas sat motionless, suddenly very upset.

"My god, this is serious. You should have gone to the police. No wonder you look so pale and scared...You should have told me at home, I would have brought Yug along."

Trying to sound composed for Jas's sake, Alki said, "I am okay. Nothing happened to me. I didn't want to make an issue out of it. You know what my parents will say…Jas you stay here, I'll go up, get my phone and wallet, and come back."

"No, no. I'll come with you," said Jas.

"What if those men come back? Better two of us than just one of you. I can call your phone and we should be able to find it when it rings."

At that instant, Alki felt a surge of love for her old friend. She opened the car door, got out and went to retrieve the sack of ash from the boot.

"What's in that sack, Alki? You dragged that from your house to my house, now here."

Alki's reply was a little frantic.

"You won't believe me even if I told you. Just…please…just bear with me."

8

The Bleached Tree

A ruby drop of blood bubbled up on the underside of her palm. A thorn had pricked into her flesh and been stained with her blood. Reaching out into the wispy leaves, she had been met with an unwelcoming spike. Startled, she recoiled, only to look up and take in the weeping shape of the tree to which she had been drawn all the way up the hill, a sack of ash in hand.

Alki had tramped upwards, Jas a little behind her, stepping with care, unused to all this "trekking", as she called it. At the collapsed old well near the mound, Alki experienced an inexplicable dread but also an impulse to wander onto a side path that led out into a patch of wilderness towards where she knew vaguely the surveyor had found the stream on the property. The uneven path was crowded with shrubs and pungent overgrown weeds scratching her, grabbing onto her clothes with hooked seeds looking to disperse themselves on the fur of hapless passer-by animals. Then all of a sudden, the jungle opened out, and it was strangely windy. She found herself standing on bare open ground, which formed a halo around a singular thorny tree bearing tiny leaves reminiscent of a mimosa. A twisting gust swept around and through the tree; and its branches swayed back and forth hypnotising Alki. She released the throat of the sack and dumped out the ash near the tree. The dust did not land on the dry mulch under the tree, but disappeared in the ascending gust into the canopy of the tree. Thereupon, Alki stretched her hand into the whirling dust and into a low-hanging branch, pricking herself in the attempt.

Swirling about in the upper branches, the ash began to slow down and settle. It started to take on a tenuous shape and her heart skipped a beat in terror. Though at first hazy and indistinct, the formless ash embodied before her frightened eyes, assuming a recognisable femininity. From an upper branch, it stood up staring down at her with the whitest eyes and there was a twiggy sprig growing out of the top of its head. Then it crouched and bent down towards her, unfolding a grey ashy arm. Alki was paralysed with fear, unable to move. A shrill bell rang out harshly behind her and the illusion, or whatever it was, disappeared instantaneously along with the wind. The tree was tranquil again. Behind her she could hear the ringtone from her lost phone, then Jas's voice calling loudly for her. Alki let out a breath, turned and ran, tumbling down the path terrified to turn back for a second look.

Back at the well, Jas said, "Where did you go? Look, I found your phone and your wallet."

Alki was still panting from her run, but she said, "You found it here? I thought I lost them on the path up there, under the big rock. There's a beautiful Bauhinia tree there..."

Noting the fear in Alki's eyes, Jas said, "No, no I found them here. C'mon, let's go home now."

Jas then paused and said, "Where's the sack?"

Alki turned around.

"Oh right…I left it back there near a tree. It's fine. I am not going back to get it. It's just some ash from a puja my mother did yesterday. She told me to dump it here somewhere…something superstitious. I didn't ask…"

Alki knew from the way Jas was peering at her that neither her words nor her demeanour was very convincing. Behind Alki there was rustling, twigs snapping. The expression on Jas's face changed to surprise followed by puzzlement, then consternation.

Jas said, pointing and sputtering, "What, what is that…?

Without turning back, Alki grabbed Jas by the elbow and screamed, "Run Jas, run."

They hurtled down the hill. Unaccustomed to running of any kind, Jas tripped and fell, soiling her white top in the red earth. Alki stopped to help her up quickly and pushed her into a run again. They sprinted till they reached the road and finally their blue hatchback. Only then did they stop to breathe.

Jas said, "Alki, what was that? It looked like a dead…bleached tree and it was moving towards us…I…I don't know what I saw, a woman was sitting in the tree, but she wasn't…and those eyes…"

Alki was looking up towards the mound. A white-haired shadowy figure had materialised from behind a tree near the mound and was gliding down the hill with its head turned sideways looking towards them. Alki almost screamed in panic.

"Jas get in the car now…drive!"

The high note of alarm in Alki's voice was unambiguous. Jas and Alki opened the car doors almost simultaneously, they got in and slammed them shut. There was a five-second hunt for car keys with Jas fumbling amongst things in her purse.

Alki said, "Hurry Jas…please…hurry."

She was sobbing, hyperventilating, hugging her knees, and rocking back and forth in the passenger's seat, looking up into the hill at the shrivelled white cadaverous thing looming towards them. Oddly, the sun had disappeared, and she hadn't noticed till then how dark it had become.

The sound of the hatchback's three-cylinder engine turning over prompted Alki to breathe again. She turned her face away from the hill and watched Jas quickly thrust the shifter into first. Jas then pressed down hard on the accelerator letting her other foot off the clutch pedal. The hatchback shot off like a jet plane. Alki was glad that there were no other cars on the hill road at that moment. There had been no time to check for blind spots, adjust mirrors, or to signal.

They drove in weary silence up to the main junction in the wooded hills into the suburbs, passing only a few cars and transport buses and then into the noise of jostling city traffic in the valley. Alki had never been so glad to see so many cars and bikes attempting to cut them off and joust with them for gaps in the road. These squabbling cars and their vengeful drivers were life itself, and where she had come from—it felt like death.

Jas brought the car back to her home's garage. She hadn't asked Alki if she wanted to be dropped at her house. They sat quietly, petrified, in the front seats of the car for a couple of minutes.

At last, Jas spoke.

"Alki, what was that thing? You haven't told me everything, have you? Is this why you've been so scared? Did two men really attack you?"

Alki stared through the windscreen blankly.

"I thought I was hallucinating…didn't think you would believe me. You or anybody else. Yes, there were two men and one of them grabbed me. Then they saw it too…that thing. I could see the look on their faces…I have never seen fear like that… I just ran…I was too scared to look back, and I don't know what happened to them."

Tears streamed down her face as she recounted the terror of that day.

Alki paused.

Then she said, "Then it came to my house."

"What?" said Jas. Alki twisted in the seat to face her friend.

"This part is really strange. My mother set up a puja on Sunday because, somehow, she knows. I think I told her the night I saw it in my room when I was sleeping. I thought I was dreaming. So, she organised a puja. The room was full of smoke from the ceremony, and I saw it in the white smoke. The priest got us to nail iron bangles to the wall of every room in the house."

She thought she was rambling by then. But peering over at Jas, Alki noticed that Jas was paying full attention for once in her life.

Alki said, "You know I don't believe in superstitions. But that evening after the puja I saw it again outside in our garden. The same thing you saw. I had taken all the ashes and charcoal from the fire and put it under a tree in the garden. And that's where I saw it in the evening, under that same tree. And you know what, it was so strange, it looked like it was made of those ashes I had dumped there."

Jas shivered a little.

"Is that what was in the sack today? You were trying to get rid of the ashes?"

Alki was in tears.

"Yes. I didn't know what else to do. I thought maybe I should take it back to where it came from."

Jas said, "Okay. Stop crying now. I want to show you something. Come with me."

Alki was surprised, but very grateful that Jas had not thrown her out saying she never wanted to see her again and whatever that thing was, that was somehow attached to her. Jas strode purposefully from the garage to the gate of her house with a puzzled Alki trailing her.

"Where are you going Jas?"

Jas merely said, "I haven't talked to her in a while. Now is as good a time as any."

She walked down the lane for a few metres then abruptly turned left into a side lane. Alki realised that she was being led to the house where their mutual friend Tana lived.

"Why are we going to Tana's?"

"Some people are so very lucky," said Jas. "Tana gets married, and then imagine her luck; her in-laws' house is just two houses away from her parents' house. It's so easy for her. And her in-laws are saints; they don't let her do anything. She's a queen there."

Alki was astounded by the overt begrudging burr of envy in Jas's voice. Could the almighty Jas be this jealous? She hardly ever spoke of Tana, and if she did, it was only to sarcastically scorn her fashion sense or remark on her laziness. What Jas termed laziness was the fact that Tana's in-laws did all the housework and doted on Tana and her children. Tana was treated like the daughter they never had, and she was even encouraged to go to work, which was the antithesis of what had happened to Jas. It had taken some mental juggling, but an embittered Jas had transliterated Tana's happy circumstances into laziness. Well, perhaps, it was a kind of laziness, Alki reluctantly conceded.

Tana did not have to struggle anymore the way Jas or even Alki did. Could the absence of struggle be termed laziness? Alki didn't comprehend that as usual; she was using conceptual jugglery of her own to side with Jas. The truth lay somewhere in the middle between Jas and Tana. If Tana was helped by a benevolent patriarchy at her in-laws', Jas had help from an exploitative feudal system at her parents' house.

Alki, Tana, and many others that revolved in an orbit around Jas were used to letting her words have power over them. They were not very good at confronting her, they would try and frequently fail to defuse those words, or at the least they should have let the wounding words deflect off of them impotently. They did not yet understand that Jas's cutting words were not about them but her own insecurities. She cut her friends down with words as she could not cut them down to an unthreatening size any other way.

When the two visitors arrived at Tana's front entrance and rang the house bell, svelte Tana, her hair perfectly coiffed, had been in the process of going to work. She was very surprised to see them both at her door looking dishevelled. Jas's white top was grey and streaked with dirt, her jeans muddy at the knees.

Without preamble, Jas said somewhat peremptorily, "Hi Tana, you are looking well, older for sure."

Not rising to the bait, and grasping the unusual nature of this unexpected visit, Tana turned to Alki and said, "Are you both alright?"

Jas spoke for Alki.

"Tana, we are fine. But how are you?"

Making an effort to be polite to Tana, Alki said awkwardly, "We are okay. We just came back from the parcel of land where I am building a house. That's why we look like this."

Tana was careful, droll in her reply.

"Oh yes, I heard about that. Everyone is talking about it."

"Ah…" said Alki.

Finally turning to Jas, Tana said dryly, "I am surprised you went along Jas. You don't do things like that."

With a short glance towards Alki, Jas said, quietly, "I will, if it's necessary."

Tana said, "So what can I do for you both today? I am getting late for office."

Alki was a little offended that Tana hadn't even offered them some tea. She was drained and could have really used a cup at that moment.

Tana said, "Why don't the two of you sit for a bit? Mamma's in the kitchen making tea for you both. She saw you and Jas from the kitchen window. Is there anything in particular you wanted?"

Mamma was Tana's jovial mother-in-law.

"No, nothing Tana," said Jas, "Alki came over for breakfast this morning. And we were talking about the old days. She wanted to look in on you. We thought we could catch you before work… say hello."

Tana said, "Oh okay, that was good of you Alki."

Jas said hastily, "You know I would come over more, it's just with the kids and Yug, I have been really busy."

Borrowing Jas's mordant tone, Tana said, "Of course. I know what that's like."

9

The Serene Shami

Occupying the northeast corner of Mamma's garden was an unpretentious specimen. For such an unglamorous thorny tree with little leaves and small, pale yellow flowers, the Shami tree was given special treatment, planted in a cement-lined podium, separated and slightly raised from the rest of the plot, festooned with sacred red threads, its straight brown trunk smudged all over with vermillion. An idol of a fierce little goddess was fixed to the base of the tree. It looked like the setting for community prayer meetings, and it was. Alki jumped a little when she recognised the weepy canopy-shape of the tree as the same tree under which she had dumped out the ash near the old collapsed well. The tree in Tana's mother-in-law's garden had long streamers of soft yellow flowers, and a glut of bees. Jas and Alki stood beneath the modest tree in eerie contemplation.

Jas turned to Alki.

"Do you recognise this tree?"

Alki said, "Why…how did you know? It was under a tree like this that I left the sack."

Jas said, "No, I didn't know that. I told you I saw something weird. You had come down the path and I gave you back your phone. You were looking at me and behind you on the path, suddenly there was this tree. It was a dead tree, or I think it was, it was white and grey, ashy all over but still it had leaves, and there was that thing sitting…crouching on a branch. I was certain

I knew the tree. You know me, I don't go around identifying trees or plants, that's more my mother's thing. But this one was different…I had seen it before. Here in this garden, and on my father's desk at home."

<><><>

Having had enough of the conversation, Tana had excused herself, leaving the two women in her mother-in-law's sitting room.

As Alki got to the end of a heaven-sent cup of tea, Jas said to the older woman, "Aunty, may we see your garden please?"

Mamma said, "Of course, my dear."

Mamma was surprised to see Jas leading Alki to her Shami tree. She put away the teacups in the kitchen, then joined the two by the Shami tree.

She told Jas, "Ohhh…you must have heard about our prayer meeting group. It's become very popular around here. People come here every Saturday and we pray to the goddess to remove obstacles from our path. We take out our prayer books, and we chant. The tree has become so famous, I've even had a couple of tree weddings here."

Alki and Jas both glanced at her perplexed.

Mamma said, "You don't know what that is? Oh, children these days…don't your parents tell you anything about your religion and great myths."

She laughed and continued cheerfully.

"Well, you see, some people are…let's say—unlucky in love."

Then Mamma whispered out loud.

"Just look at the divorces. So many couples are separating."

She resumed in a normal voice.

"Well, the priest looks at their horoscopes and checks to see if there is any possibility of death or divorce. If he finds any, then the boy is married to this tree. So, it's like his first marriage is to the spirit of the tree. Thereby his second marriage is safe from divorce. I think for girls it's a Pipal tree."

Alki wanted to laugh. But she was respectful because Mamma wore a serious expression on her face, and she was such a nice lady. She couldn't possibly be rude to her.

Jas, however, had no such qualms.

"Aunty, how can you still believe in these superstitions?"

Mamma stared a little at the offence, but not even the great Jas could dent her optimism. Tana could learn an important lesson in dealing with Jas from Mamma.

Mamma said, "My dear, if it is not doing any harm to anyone, don't call it a superstition. People's faith heals them in many ways we don't yet understand. It consoles them in uncertain times. If you take their comfort away from them, there will be chaos."

Pointing to the tree, Mamma said, "Sometimes I think, this is the only thing that holds us all together here in peace without killing each other."

Jas was silenced. Alki was still sceptical, but she kept her opinions to herself. Most of the present chaos in the world was the result of unchecked religiosity. The rules made up for life, centuries past, were no longer applicable in the modern world, but adherents and zealots alike only desired the comfort and discipline that come to automatons, the ones who had faith and never reasoned or questioned. Rituals meant to soothe would oftentimes switch on patterns of behaviour in the performer, transforming into obsessive-compulsive repetitions, adherents rocking back and forth over holy books, repetitive rituals, that if not done a certain way, made the performer of the ritual distraught till it was done right.

Worst of all was what Big Religion did to its female faithful, crushing their collective spirits till they weakened to compliant nubs, bereft of all complexity, but basic purpose. Birthing, cooking, socialising, and serving. Newspaper articles written by holy men argued against educating women lest they forget their duties, leading to the very collapse of society as they knew it. It was obvious; civilisation was founded on the bones of a fiction devised to deliberately weaken women so that they could be turned into a subservient labour force for the service of the family unit.

Powerful conditioning overrode every other part of intellect, like when women clung to their veils and dupattas, their cultural safety blankets, thwarting all efforts at scepticism. They had been groomed to be less than human, whose only job was to sympathise and care for their jailors. Alki did not dare utter these words out loud, words she knew to be contentious and, lately, anti-liberal. Evolution had made them service bots anaesthetised to their captivity, but the liberated believed that women should be allowed to have self-respect and dignity even in these situations. But Alki could not bear the cop-out of a status quo for her kind.

She began to observe the customary incongruity around her, for instance, why were most wives shorter and feebler than their husbands? A shorter wife to a tall, strong husband was no side effect of evolution, but a cultural norm. Why were a large number of Indian marriages from upper to lower castes, between dark men and fair women? Women were acquired, and even discarded if they did not bring some kind of socially quantifiable value to the new family.

Alki had a friend who had seemed perfectly reasonable at first and had no trouble scientifically detailing the flaws in other people's religions, but one day at dinner she became irrational when Alki pointed out the same flaws in her religion. Her mother's lovingly crafted dinner remained peevishly untouched, and her friend had left in a hurry that evening leaving behind a very baffled Alki. It occurred to her then that to most people their religions were their favourite nation-state or sports team. They were able to analyse the weaknesses in other teams, but were hopelessly blind to the faults of the icons in their own. Unless things changed drastically, there was nothing but trouble ahead for the world.

At least Mamma's approach to religiosity was a little more calibrated and less in your face. Alki had an aunt whose sitting room was a stark contrast to the one she had just exited. In that living room, there was a giant portrait of a guru staring down at her from an accent wall, while she would uneasily slurp down her tea. Her aunt was not a member of a cult, but existed right there on the edge of joining one. The venerated leader had been involved in unsavoury activities, but at her aunt's house, guests were polite, and her aunt would brook no denigration of the once great man. Alki had puzzled over this. These were perfectly reasonable people who all exhibited madness in just one aspect of their lives—their religions.

She wondered if religion was a channel, like Mamma's Shami tree, a medium through which people vented unconscious anomalies buried deep inside their brains. Was religion a type of prehistoric brain glitch amplified by the advent of grain eating at the dawn of agriculture? She had read several reports suggesting that humans had never really adapted properly to the consumption of grain. Was it just coincidence that modern-day religions could trace their elaborate structures back to early agricultural civilisations? Maybe, everyone living today had inherited this glitch as part of his or her human condition.

Perhaps due to the absence of a systematic religion to organise her own life, Alki's glitchy brain was manifesting spectral phantasms in the same way other people heard voices, but channelled their deviation from the norm into their religions. Religious sacraments and ceremonies were like safety valves that released the pressure of mania, or whatever it was that bedevilled folk, bestowing on their outward lives a facade of rationality. But none of her conjecturing was able to explain why other people like

Jas, her mother, or the architect were all able to see the ghost that her mind had apparently generated.

Nestled beneath the Shami tree with Jas and Tana's mother-in-law, Alki was sympathetic, and she suspected there was something there in Mamma's words. She had sat in at prayer meetings and had experienced the rhythmic, cyclic chanting of mantras, continually amazed by the capacity of the vibrating drone of invocation to put her into a therapeutic trance state. Even though there was an otherworldly essence to the phenomenon that engulfed her, she was rational enough to conclude that even these effects could be studied. If the great religions of the world had to be replaced with reason, most people like her mother and Mamma would need a little more than the cold comfort of reason to replace the release provided by religion. What that 'more' was, no one could say yet.

Then Mamma said something that caught both Jas and Alki by surprise.

"Can you imagine what would have happened to these trees in our country if they were not sacred? Let all the trees be worshipped."

Mamma lifted and joined her palms in prayer to the goddess. Alki and Jas too followed suit. When Alki's eyes shut to the world, she prayed. But hers was no regular prayer. She was able to concentrate in a way she could never do with her eyes open. There was a whole world behind her eyelids that she had never told anyone about. As she focused, she felt an inward pull in the lower centre of her forehead, a point above and between the two eyebrows. From that point, a wave of meditative intensity spread through the soft bones of her face into her neck and downwards into the rest of her body. The dark screen behind her eyelids became patchy and glowing, as if she was looking at the universe's baby picture, a portrait of the afterglow left behind from the birth of the universe, from a tiny little point. The patchy darkness started to take form, and she found herself gazing into a colossal cave. High above her was a natural, vaulted roof twinkling with minerals and she was perched at the top end of an abraded path. At the far end of the road, she was just able to distinguish the outline of a very big tree.

The recurrent image in her head would endure a mere moment. Just as Alki would make to walk down the path inside her, her eyes would open wide, shattering the vision. But this time, her eyelids lifted to a radiant face looking down at her from the upper branch of Mamma's tree. It...she was seated cross-legged; long, fecund hair, black and woven into a long braid flowing down her right shoulder. A Shami sprig sprang up from the crown of her head. It… She was smiling at Alki serenely, her right forearm raised, the soft underside of her right palm facing outwards in the universal gesture of reassurance. Her skin was the hue of dark honey. She was glowing. By the time Jas and Mamma opened their eyes to the tree, the apparition had vanished. After several harrowing days, tranquillity was finally restored to Alki. Squinting at Alki, Jas perceived a lightness in her countenance, an absence of fear. Mumbling a soft mantra, Mamma picked up a small clay pitcher placed before the goddess figurine among the yellow and saffron marigold puja flowers and poured out a libation of water into the roots of the tree.

As Mamma and Alki turned to return to the house, Jas happened to glance at the goddess figurine carved in stone, affixed to the base of the tree. She hadn't noticed before how alive it seemed, its stony cheeks a shimmering amber. The inky-painted orbs that were its eyes appeared to be inspecting her with a familiar glint. Spooked, Jas flinched and withdrew speedily to join the other two.

10

The Coconut Tree as an Indoor Plant

For something so practical, no one noticed how weird it was. The coconut tree—it lacked the universally accepted form of a tree. Shouldn't it be branching all around and outwards in ever smaller fractal tree forms of itself? In the absence of tree essence—a fundamental concept even children understood when they drew up stock, stick figure trees—it made up its own unusual form. With a little help from evolution, what came forth was the form of a palm tree, a giant herb reinventing "tree-ness", lignifying its central stem, carrying all its leaves ever higher into the sky till it was at last, after many aeons, indisputably, a tree. Ultimately, even trumping the sacred dendritic form in drier parts of the world where palms were cultivated to the exclusion of all else. As for the coconut, it was a threshold tree that liked to grow on edges, in between places not quite ocean not quite land, where salt water swirled in to embrace sand. The edge was an oddly rich place, where all things met in a melting-pot, a union, perfectly suited to the oddness of some trees. The coconut tree made itself useful, and its deviation from "tree-ness" became taken for granted: its wood had so much silica, that instead of saws cutting wood, it would cut saws. It had sand in its soul from millennia lived out on beaches, floating its seed on arriving ocean currents.

Now here it was in all its weird ordinariness, growing inside someone's house. The presence of a coconut tree in one corner signalled to Alki that this was more than just a study. It was also a shrine to the greatest tree on earth. The architect had cleverly incorporated the trunk of the coconut tree into Jas's house design. It was an anchor for a small, glass-walled atrium and a custom-built wrought-iron staircase, which squared and cornered its way around the tree trunk into a library above, situated off a short corridor. The library was distanced from the tree corner to guard the books from moisture and mould during the rainy season. To mark the start of dry weather, a frond high above the edifice would shrivel, then cast off its coconuts one by one and nut munitions would bombard the courtyard and the concrete roof of the library with loud booming thuds resonating through the study.

Jas's father was a retired archaeologist, and his study was off limits to everybody in the house including the cleaners. He had a sixth sense for the objects and books spread out over his desk. He knew if anyone had been messing about with his things. An off-limits chamber represented adventure for the children of the house. And various members of the family were in and out of his study furtively exploring his collection of curios, statuettes, rolled charts of peculiar illustrations, and walls decorated with framed seal tablets from lost Bronze Age civilisations.

Arriving at the doorstep to the study after leaving Tana's house, Alki said to Jas, "My god Jas, how come you have never let me in here before? I have been coming to your house for years…there's a coconut tree inside this room."

Jas said, "Well, none of us are allowed in here."

Pointing out the coconut tree to Alki, she said, "When they were building this house, my mother made a big fuss. The contractor wanted to cut down the tree and my father promised he would not. The architect was stumped, till he came up with the idea of using the tree to create an internal courtyard."

From the entrance to the study, Alki gawped at the magical wrought iron staircase surrounding the coconut tree in its atrium, inexplicably suspended in mid-air, a stairway with no beginning or end. It looked like a square had been twisted out of two dimensions and pulled into a twisted diamond from a deck of cards. It was an optical illusion designed to confuse those who would dare to enter the forbidden study. Jas saw Alki's eyes light up at the sight of her father's special staircase.

Jas said, "Oh, that's his..."

Alki finished the sentence: "...Penrose stairs. I know what those are...it's brilliant."

Ruffled, Jas said, "Well, you turned out to be quite the nerd, like Yug. I should have let you into this room a long time ago. You know...Yug is the only other person who knew what those stairs were."

Alki remained silent and poker-faced, attempting not to look at Jas, who observed her intently. With Jas's words came a painful image from a day long ago in the college library: Alki and Yug at a central table surrounded by a wall of books as they were trying to wrap their heads around the amazing conception of the impossible staircase. She began to understand why Yug had also been drawn into an orbit around Jas. The orbit was not centred on Jas alone, but her whole family. Alki's family was dull in comparison, obediently religious and conformist. Her house was unremarkable too; especially lacking in trees captured into its very essence. After every last one on the site had been cut down, her family house, made with dense, conservative concrete, was built to suck in the heat in boiling summer and retain it. Her family's house was as tedious as its unimaginative inhabitants. Of course, she realised with a smile, immediately letting go the fossil of her heartache, if her mother could hear her think at this very moment, she would have called her an ungrateful child. Moreover, her mother thought little of the fancy-pants family to which Jas belonged.

Jas's father enjoyed being the eternal contrarian, relishing his vantage on a super-analytical pedestal minimising people, Alki's parents among them, into simpletons. His sardonic analyses were always wordily disguised. But despite the care he took, they leaked out his contempt for a democracy that promoted conforming, mediocrity, and an admiration for the despotism of reason. As the story of populism everywhere will dictate, the simpletons take umbrage at this portrayal and strike back with a final weapon of choice, unleashing the brutality of cognitively dissonant emotions.

But in the end, Jas's father, the sophisticate was not that different from the mainstream intellectual, or the populist, both of whom he despised, all of whose rancour possessed the matching DNA of entitlement. Alki herself found it useful to dress down any intelligence she possessed when in the company of Jas and her father. He had put down Alki several times over the years at breakfast before college. She had learned to never contradict Jas in the presence of the archaeologist, because Jas's father had a blind spot in the shape of Jas. When it came to Jas, the archaeologist would involuntarily suspend his disbelief. He seemed unaware of the ultimate irony that linked him to the simpletons he had conjured up all around him.

In that moment of awe, before the illusory staircase to nowhere in the archaeologist's study, at the portal between two rooms, neither inside nor outside, Alki became unmoored and dislocated spatially. Her customary guard had dropped and risen again as soon as she intuited the hackles on Jas rising.

She stepped forward into the room and the illusion dissolved, a bottom and a top landing materialising at either end of the stairs. It was a beautiful example of wrought-iron workmanship, an otherwise average staircase cocooned in a courtyard, a coconut tree at its heart, which was neither inside nor outside. The architect must have had his work cut out with Jas's father's unusual requests, she thought.

Jas hit a few switches and the room was suffused in a muted warm glow pouring from the various spotlights embedded in the false ceiling. Alki perambulated the room and its stuffed bookshelves, examining the copper-coloured clay seals scattered around the walls of the chamber. Their unusual motifs, bull unicorns with superscripts of strange pictographic symbols, gave the study an air of mystery and theatre.

"My father is working on a paper called 'The Tree of Life'," said Jas.

Alki turned around to peer at Jas.

Jas told her, "What you were looking at, those are..."

"...Seals," said Alki.

This time Jas continued as if Alki had not interrupted her.

"Anyway, he found a few which had this tree on them...he calls it the tree of life. And in every one of...these seals...the tree is associated with a woman, a goddess."

"You think I could see the paper?" asked Alki.

Pointing to a hulking carved wooden desk at one end of the room, Jas said, "Go on, take a look. Our policy is that if he's not here, he can't mind."

A set of papers lay in the centre of the desk arranged just within reach of anyone who occupied the only modern piece of equipment in that room other than a laptop and printer. It was a heavily engineered black swivel chair.

Jas said, "No one's allowed to sit in that chair either."

Alki smiled. "But of course, you all do."

Jas beamed back at her. Alki reached out and touched the stack of papers, a shiver going through her as though she were putting her hand on sacrament. Standing respectfully beside the black insectoid chair, she began to leaf through the papers reading quickly as she skimmed along.

The archaeologist's old-fashioned and stilted writing style provided new insight into his instincts. Alki had always assumed he had built himself up by deriding any daftness he found in other people. But this was evidently someone uninterested and possibly even insecure about the rapidly smartening world around him, as he had chosen to linger with the cultural preferences and influences gleaned during his college days more than 40 years ago. Next to a cane armchair, not too far from the desk, was a well-preserved boxy record player from the 60's. A couple of Elvis albums and spy novels were wedged between scholarly archaeology journals on the shelf behind the vinyl player.

After hanging up his dusty corduroy pants and brown suede shoes at retirement, the archaeologist had been given a government anthropology institute grant to tour several countries detailing an ancient form of organised tree worship, linking myriad cultures spanning ancient Greece, Mesopotamia, the Levant region, and India. The first ten printed pages were introductory and set the premise for the whole document. These cultures had in common a tree of life. In the easternmost quadrants of these regions from Assyria to the Indus Valley, in all likelihood, a goddess was associated with this cosmically significant tree. Whilst everywhere else it had disappeared, India was perhaps the only country where reverence for the goddess in the tree continued to this day.

She turned the page and two paragraphs jumped out at her.

"Once there was a surfeit of grain and nascent trade, in these agricultural societies there arose a struggle for divine knowledge, and powerful people bidding to control it. This transcendental knowledge, at once esoteric and recondite, symbolically gathered from the fruits of particularly coveted trees in primeval epochs, really psychedelic visions, becomes so prized that many of these cultures possess a shared story of punishment meted out to those lesser mortals who attempt to steal this knowledge, which is a portal to the gods.

Despite the dangers of presentism, dear reader, imagine for a moment an ancient branding exercise. Those who effectively marketed themselves as the custodians of spiritual arcana attained priestly status and significant positions in their world's hierarchy. Exerting piety to subdue opponents and win endorsement from devotees, they can regulate the flow of commerce. At the same time, portions of this divine knowledge have been worked on by priestly logicians and spun into useful philosophy, and this is codified in scriptures. But these texts also serve to shape the edifice of society in their own image. Eventually, the embryonic tree of life is replaced with shrines and sacraria controlled by the priestly classes. Only one other group can resist the sophistry of divinely ordained power and that is a warrior class led by a regent or monarch."

After that came a series of illustrations, all of which included a central tree surrounded by several maidens and various animals. In one, that stopped Alki short as she turned over the pages, a feathery-leaved tree had a woman perched on one of its branches. Her hair lay in a plait over her shoulder. Below her on the ground were maidens and animals all bent in supplication to the one above them.

Jas said, "You've found it, haven't you? The one with the goddess in the tree, isn't that what we saw today?"

Trying not to sound too alarmed, Alki said, "Yes something like this…how old is this?"

An angry voice from the entrance to the room boomed at them startling both Jas and Alki.

"What do you think you are doing here?"

The greying archaeologist was at the door to the study with a mug in one hand, regarding Jas and Alki sharply.

The steam rising from his cup seemed to be coming from his eyes.

11

A Rose by Some Other Name

Before noon, a cup of tea in hand, the archaeologist had planted himself indolently in the portico that joined his study to the main house. Seated on the short ledge, he was wont to look out into the rose garden his wife had planted. When the house was under construction, he had wanted to house his study and library in a separate two-storey building. But his wife had disapproved of such secessionist notions, and they had compromised on this corridor. His wife, the gardener, had planted brilliant red, pink, and orange roses on either side of the corridor so that he would have something to enliven his view on his way to the study every day. He was indeed glad for the company, but not at first. He had paid little heed to the plants, and had once asked his wife disdainfully why she had left out white-blossomed varieties from her "rose exhibition".

Always the passer-by and never one to sit down and take in the sights, the roses gradually slackened the pace of his walk down the passageway. Their serrated, leafy leatheriness, and the lulling scent wafting up to him called his attention to them. Perhaps, he had been a bit too hasty to dismiss their flamboyant petalary as lurid. Since the planting of the rose bushes, hadn't he been less melancholy?

He liked to have an explanation for everything, and he didn't have one for how these prickly plants had charmed him. Some secretive depth inside him, something profoundly inherent had responded to these plants. There was no sustenance to be had from flowers, so it must be the involuntary spirituality, art, and poetry centres in his brain pinging without his knowledge. Before there was art or even poetry, perhaps flowers first stirred the primordial human brain to rhapsody. If evolution could be personified into a deity with all-seeing eyes, to those eyes the human would merely be a large, four-limbed bee that liked flowers, kept up their pollination, hybridising, and kept them going, generation upon generation.

Roses had undergone much cultivation by human hand to get to where they were today, some so voluminously petaled that insects found it hard to get inside to pollinate them, and they no longer set fruit or seed. The archaeologist was surprised when his wife told him about rose hips, the fruit of roses. It was uncommon to imagine roses, the floweriest flowering plants he knew, producing fruit and then seed. He hadn't seen any on the roses around his portico. Unbeknownst to him, his wife had been deadheading the spent flowers on the rose bushes, so these plants never got a chance to produce fruit even if they were capable of doing so. The concept of a fruiting rose seemed alien to him. An apple, distant cousin in the rose family, was a rotund, fleshed out rose hip by another name, but he didn't know that. He had been on vacation to the apple producing regions of his country, but unlike his wife, had never reckoned on the uncanny resemblance between wild roses and the flowers of an Apple tree.

Suitably be-mugged and with an elbow grasping a newspaper, he would set out on a short walk to the study to be greeted on the way by upturned green hands and fresh, flowering faces. This was how the archaeologist liked to mark the start of each new working day. He would not labour amongst them, but they were his roses now. When his wife, having finally bored of them, had wanted to convert the rose garden into a hibiscus nursery, the archaeologist had crossly vetoed the idea, surprising his wife who, till then, had assumed he had little interest in the garden or its plants. He even got into a little argument with her about the merits of thorny rose bushes over "namby-pamby" hibiscus plants. There was hope for Jas yet if her father could be brought around to the gratifications of the garden, it occurred to Jas's mother that day.

Sipping his tea on the portico ledge, from the corner of his eye, he perceived movement. A breeze had caught the heavy study door as someone had left it ajar. He jumped away from the flowers, sloshing and spilling his tea as his pace quickened with annoyance. At the end of the portico, beyond a short veranda was the hefty teak door to the study. The door was open and inside his daughter Jaswanti and her friend were at the far end of the room at his desk. It was a cameo he had walked in on many trying times before. Clutching a sheaf of papers in her hand, his daughter's friend Alki seemed to be completely engrossed in reading.

With the archaeologist's face slowly turning a hue of robust red, Jas intervened quickly. "Baba, don't get angry. I wanted Alki to look at your paper. I wanted her to see the goddess in the tree."

The redness in the archaeologist's face drained somewhat to a calmer pink curiosity.

He said, "How do you know about that? Did I talk about it to any of you, your mother? You all keep coming in here and messing about the desk. I've told you so many times not to do that, haven't I?" He paused, then said, "Why do you want Alki to look at the goddess?"

Jas and Alki exchanged glances.

Scrabbling for a coherent explanation, Alki said, "I am really sorry sir," she had always called him "sir", "well…I told Jas that I wanted to put up a feature wall in my new house. And I was telling her about the goddess in the tree motif. I remembered it from one of my old history textbooks, which I don't have anymore. Jas then told me you were working on a paper about the goddess in the tree…"

The archaeologist said, "I heard about your house. It's very brave of you to attempt a project like that."

Jas was unused to her father praising her friends. It was disconcerting. The archaeologist then turned to his daughter.

"Ask me first, before you and your friends come in here and start going through my papers."

Stepping away from the big desk, Alki said, "Sir, could you tell us more about the goddess in the tree?"

The archaeologist was at his desk picking up the illustration that Alki had reflexively dropped when he appeared at the door.

Looking up, he said to his daughter and Alki, "Do you know girls, these were all probably matriarchal cultures a very long time ago. But something changed in these societies after the invention of agriculture. The worship of goddesses continues even to this day of course, but the power the goddess represents becomes figurative and no longer filters down to the women in their worlds. The tree goddess is possibly an earth, forest, and fertility deity. She is the spirit of renewal and regeneration. Jungle trees were very important to hunter-gatherers and of course, later, to the farmers. But there is a perceptible shift in what aspects of their agrarian world they want to exalt and deify. We start seeing more seals representing the figure of the bull, buffalo, and male gods associated with these animals, and their horns. And as you know early agriculture went hand in hand with bovine animals. So, you can see how it goes for those early people. Grass plants that provide grain, and the ploughing of their fields season after season become all-consuming activities for them. Of course, the goddess of the forest is still worshipped as they need her blessing for their fields to come back year after year with the same vigour as the jungle."

Alki said, "Sir, does this goddess represent the forces of good or evil?"

There was detectable ambiguity in Alki's question. Jas and her friend were staring intently at the archaeologist waiting for an answer.

The archaeologist said, "I don't really understand that question...but I would say she represents the power of good as well as an ancient fury."

Alki and Jas were more baffled than ever.

Hence the archaeologist said, "The subject is complex. It is difficult to put it all down to good or bad. One person's good is another person's evil, you see. What haunts one person does not haunt another."

At his turn of phrase, the expression on Alki's face morphed from studied concentration to distress.

Jas nudged Alki gently, "Baba, what do you mean?"

"I mean to say," said the archaeologist, "the goddess is good, but that's how I look at it. But remember, the gods of one tribe were depicted as devils by another tribe that opposed them. For one group of people, she brings fertility and renewal. In another foundational myth, she is merely human and punished for stealing the divine fruit of knowledge. It depends on who you choose to follow or believe."

Alki said, "If she is punished...then she is weak?"

"Well, it's the 'taming of the feminine' aspect...that is just the depiction of one tribe, I think in that case, I mean a story like that is an institutionally sanctioned censuring of what they believe is a pagan matriarchy. While on the other side, the farmer-priest-king patriarchs assimilated the fierce pagan goddesses. It is another thing altogether that real, everyday women don't have equal rights. Though, it is clear to me that the popular goddess is depicted as a nurturing maternal form, which is one of the few acceptable female forms in a patriarchal world. I worry about the duality of these goddesses in our global culture. You see, either they are maternal, or else they are ferocious. It's how the male ethos sees its women, as bipolar beings, they can't begin to comprehend. If you can't understand them, idolise them."

Jas's father stopped speaking, figuring that he had gone into lecture mode. But looking over at the girls, he saw they were not bored, instead they were very absorbed. It was odd because Jas had never shown any interest before in these scholarly subjects.

To Jas, he said, "Why don't you girls come eat some lunch with your mother and me? Jaswanti, I am surprised you did not go to work today, or you Alki."

Jas said, "We took a day off, Alki wanted me to see her building site."

Alki interrupted them. "Sir, are you aware of any local myths in this area associated with earth goddesses?"

"Hmmm...," said the archaeologist. "There are, of course, the rock-cut goddess temples. I am sure you have seen and visited those cave temples. But I think you are referring to those old forest deities. Well, there is the...folklore about *Yekshis*."

Alki was immediately alert.

"Could you tell us more, sir?"

"Again, it is strange you should ask. It depends on how you look at it. In the male religious world, there is extreme disquiet about the pagan feminine. If it is not organised and controlled by them, they will call it pagan. *Yekshis* are benevolent tree spirits that people in some areas worship, much like the female spirit in the tree from the ancient seals. That type of worship is prehistoric. Here, in our area, where the hold of male religious leadership over the people is strong, villagers tell horror stories about a wild female spirit that haunts their forests. So, you see, in a world without misogyny, there would be no female demons that lured men to their deaths."

Jas said aghast, "Lure men to their deaths...oh my god..."

"Girls, these are stories. I urge you to always check the context behind these stories, as I just explained to you."

Jas looked at Alki, and then she said, "Of course, Baba."

The archaeologist continued.

"You must be suspicious because most such stories only concern preternatural female ghouls attacking men out and about in the forests. People enjoy the stories, but no one asks why it is that these angry, vengeful spirits are all female. You must try and understand the prevailing social conditions, in which women are unable to get justice in life and are granted a semblance of equal status only in the afterlife. Don't you think that is bizarre?"

Alki wanted to know, "You think there is social injustice involved?"

"Well, if you read the stories, there always is…"

Jas said, "Baba, does Amma know that you are a feminist?"

The archaeologist smiled, simultaneously taking note of the mug of cold, unfinished tea clasped in his left hand.

"I am not one. I only sound like one. The two are not the same. I am not sure if even those women are," he said, gesturing at his illustrations.

Jas said, "Baba, how can you say that? I am a feminist."

The archaeologist said, "I am not so sure."

Alki had never seen the archaeologist contradict his beloved daughter, and it felt to her like a strange milestone to stand witness to, as Jas had taken such care to never allow her such previews.

12

The Tree of No Sorrow

Usually, people can't see the forest for the trees. It was the other way around for Alki. To her, a forest was like a family. Just as people are wilfully blind to the faults of family members, she was blind to the botanical particularities of the forest. It was a Gaia-like organism to her. As to the individuals inside and their many peculiarities, she had no idea who or what they were, except for a few favoured species. But that day, by the gloomy little house in the clearing, she looked away from the stone-faced people gathered outside and into the forest surrounding the little house. The semi-darkness between the thick trees had points in it from the thorny and prickly plants growing on the ground that people called weeds, as they had no use for them. Between the patch of jungle darkness and the exposed clearing that encompassed the house, there was a twilight realm, to the southeast, occupied by a singular, familiar tree, its bright saffron flowers, a shining beacon of warmth in the gloaming. Thick round bunches of red to orange flowers sprouted like pimples from its branches as if the tree was suffering a bout of recurring florid acne.

A little girl of about eight or nine years old stood serenely in the shade of the tree, bleached, straggly hair streaming down her shoulders, and Alki was drawn to her. Neighbours and relatives were milling inside the house, and no one seemed to be watching the girl. Alki felt an impulse to steer the little girl away from the darkness of the forest and get her inside into the safety of the house. As Alki neared the tree and its bright blossoms, the girl stretched her arms around the tree trunk and hugged it. Her little arms could not get around the tree.

To Alki, she said, "This is my mother's tree."

Alki said, "Don't you want to go back inside to your mother? Why are you standing here all alone?"

The little girl said, "My mother is dead."

"Oh, I am sorry," said Alki. "Why don't you come with me? Maybe we can find your grandmother or father."

The little girl said, "My father is dead now. He was not a good man."

So, this was the child of the man who had worked at her building site, Alki thought, wracked with guilt. And now she was an orphan. The little girl let go and together they walked to the house with the child turning to look back wistfully at the flowering tree. The crowd parted and Alki perceived for the first time that there was silence, but no one was really grieving. The absence of sadness was unexpected. A plump old woman, perhaps the girl's grandmother, came out to greet them. She thanked Alki for bringing back the child. She tended to run away a lot, her grandmother said, as her father had not been nice to her.

"Her favourite place is there," her grandmother said, pointing to the forest beyond the tree.

"She's wild, this child," she added.

Secure inside the house, the little girl seemed changed. The serenity had left her countenance, and she looked smaller than her age. Alki wanted to know more about the construction worker who had died.

Trying not to offend the old woman, she said, "Did he drink… did he beat her?"

The old woman said, "No he did not drink, he was just mean. He wanted a son. And my daughter brought a girl into this world. So, he hit them both, whenever he was tired from work, or something had not gone his way. My daughter was bad at housework. She was lazy, she would neglect to prepare meals and spent her time in the forest till late in the evenings collecting herbs and plants to sell to the ayurveda doctor. My son-in-law used to curse her, saying he should have married a good woman who could do housework."

The old woman hesitated, then said, "There is an ashram on the other side of the forest. The guru there is very famous, he comes on TV. He says he owns the forest, though this has been our land for centuries. In our community, we do not own forests; it belongs to all of us. The guru told my son-in-law that my daughter is a bad woman, and she must not be allowed to go into the forest. He says only a bad woman would go out into the jungle alone. Good women have fear. My son-in-law wanted us to leave the house. You see, he got into an argument with my daughter one day, and she died. The guru made sure the police did not take him away. I think, in return, he promised our house and land to him."

The little girl who had heard every word of the conversation started to cry.

As her grandmother or no one else seemed concerned, Alki attempted to comfort her.

"Don't cry," she told the girl ineffectually. "What can I do to make you feel better?"

Twisting her little torso around and pointing to the tree, the little girl said, "I want to go back there."

"Alright," said Alki, and the little girl placed her tiny palm in Alki's, then led her out to the forest. Instead of stopping at the flowering tree, they strolled into the forest. Alki turned around once to look back at the house, but not one person had noticed that they had slipped away. The little girl was invisible to them.

Once inside the dark forest, the girl stopped to point out one of her many plant friends to Alki.

"Look at this one," she said, stopping at a little silver and purple plant spreading all over the earthen floor.

"You have to crush its leaves and apply it on your wounds," said the little girl.

"How do you know this?" Alki asked her.

"My mother taught me," said the girl. "When my father beats her or me, I have to apply this."

Glancing around, Alki said, "It is so dark here, do you not feel scared?"

The little girl said, "No, she protects me."

"Who?"

The little girl said, "She."

"You mean your mother?"

The little girl said, "No, She…You."

Alki was spooked. The darkness in the forest seemed to be caving in on her.

She said, "C'mon child, let's go back to that tree you like."

The little girl said, "Alright," and they began to walk back towards the clearing.

When they reached the tree, the little girl said, "One day, the bad man set fire to the house. And I was in here, and I didn't know. I heard my grandmother screaming and I started running towards the house. That's when I saw Her standing at this tree. She came out of the tree. She was beautiful. My mother always told me this tree was special. The tree, she, caught me when I was running, and would not let me go back to the house."

Alki said, "Your grandmother seems fine, nothing happened to her. And the house…?"

The little girl said, "You see all those people there, they helped to build the house again. The new house is not ours anymore, I don't like living there now."

Alki wanted to return to the house, as the dusk of the forest was encroaching into the clearing, and she felt a burgeoning unease. But the child insisted on staying at the tree.

The little girl said, "Please stay with me, don't leave."

Alki said, "Now let me go back and get your grandmother, please?"

The little girl sorrowfully slid her palm out of Alki's. Despite her hesitance, Alki returned to the house, leaving the child behind. The crowd was still and unspeaking beyond the small veranda. She asked a woman at the front door about the whereabouts of the child's grandmother.

Baffled, the woman said, "What child?"

Alki was irritated that all these people were indifferent to the little girl. She said, pointing to the beautiful Ashoka tree, "That one there."

But the child had disappeared.

Alki said restlessly to the woman, "I left her there a few moments ago, I hope she did not run away."

The woman was bewildered and stared at Alki with the same expression that Jas had that day near the mound when she first glimpsed the ashy tree.

The woman said to Alki, "Come with me."

Within the innards of the little house was a dark corridor that led all the way to a backyard. There were still a few people quietly chatting amongst themselves. Alki noted that they were all dressed in similar clothes, the women in crisp white saris with a brown border, matching tan blouses, and the men in brown trousers and white kurtas. These were the men who had appeared on her land to assist the construction worker before he died. The woman in white led Alki to a back room where a couple of trunks lay in a corner. Light poured in from a barred side window. She pulled up the metal clasps on one and lifted its top. Arranged inside were bits of household effects. Tall, shiny steel glasses and plates, a pair of tatty spectacles melted around the frame, a couple of white saris and faded children's frocks. The woman put her hand in amongst the things and took out a pile of photographs singed in the corners.

Handing them over to Alki, the woman said, "These were the only ones we could find in the wreck of the house after it burned down two years ago. These photographs and the things inside these trunks were the only articles to survive the fire."

Alki riffled through the pictures. She recognised the dead construction worker from her site. It was a wedding photo of him and the woman who had led her to this room. There was another wedding photo of the same man with another woman. The thin, under-nourished woman in the second photo was probably his first wife, the little girl's mother.

Alki said, "Oh I am so sorry, I didn't know you were his wife."

The woman said, "That's alright, how could you know? We helped him rebuild his life after his mother-in-law and daughter died in the fire."

After a pause, she said, "This house is now a part of the ashram."

As these last words colonised Alki's brain, she came to the final picture in the stack. An old woman stood beside a dark-haired little girl in the shade of a beautiful, flowering Ashoka tree. They were holding hands and smiling dreamily into the camera. Both were no longer of this world, but just thirty minutes before this moment Alki had inexplicably communicated with the dead. She was too stricken to mention this to the young widow. But when she looked up at the white-clad woman, from the look in her eyes, Alki knew that she knew.

The widow spoke gently.

"This house is haunted. He knew it, he had told me the day before yesterday. We all knew it though…after they died, he became afraid, he was looking over his shoulder all the time at that tree. He became obsessed with that tree. He started taking care of it. He would go around in the neighbouring areas collecting manure, drying and powdering it, then applying it to the foot of the tree. He told me he wanted to set up a little shrine next to the tree goddess. A few weeks ago, he did not come home at night. The next morning, I found him asleep under that tree. The flesh on his face had shrunk and he was white; I'll never forget how he looked. But at least he woke up that day when I called out to him. Now that he's gone, we are going to fulfil his last wish. Our guru was against it, but after this, I think he will agree."

After their conversation, Alki left the house in the clearing with weariness in her heart. No one could have possibly guessed, looking at the ordinary man who had worked for her architect, digging in the stone and mud at her building site, that he was a murderer. He had killed his wife and mother-in-law in a fit of rage and greed, and his victims would never get justice. To a vast populace inured to pain and death, psychopathy was not outlying, it was humdrum. Afflicted with sadistic narcissism, undiagnosed and disguised by the everydayness of their quotidian lives, some are even feted by the society in which they live. They show no remorse for the ones they destroy, desiring redemption only for themselves.

Before leaving for home, she turned around to gaze at the loveliness of the Ashoka tree. Alki waved goodbye, feeling a familiar prickling in her eyes from tears held back. Night was closing in rapidly around the Ashoka shrouding the little girl poised beneath the tree of no sorrow. It was important for a girl growing up in patriarchy, where mothers doted on sons, to have a loving, supporting father that would help her surmount her lowly position in the hierarchy. If she could have, Alki would have taken her home. Unseen, unwanted, the child's very substance had dissipated from this realm. Marooned in a netherworld she did not understand, the girl waved back, before vanishing into the murk.

13

How to Transplant an Ashoka Tree

The workers had downed their tools and were listening intently to the argument between the gentle architect and his stubborn client. It had to do with an Ashoka tree planted by Alki's great, great, great grandmother when the family had first moved on to the site. At least that's what she had been told. For all she knew, the first tree had died a natural death, and another had been planted in its place by another ancestor, perhaps her great-grandmother.

None the worse for wear and true to his word, a week after the incident at the mound, the architect broke ground for the foundation of Alki's dream house. She had given him permission to cut down some trees from the site, not realising that one of them would be the Ashoka that happened to mark the site of her great ancestor's now-overgrown ancient garden. When she arrived at the site one afternoon during her lunch break, she found the workers getting ready to chop down the Ashoka. Alki spluttered into an impulsive rage she did not know she possessed, astonishing her architect who had only ever seen in her an assertive, benevolent, and sometimes self-effacing disposition.

Alki insisted heatedly that the house be built around the tree. She had a good mind to ring up Jas and ask for the number of her father's architect. Alki's architect was as much a tree-lover as she was, perhaps more, but he was also mindful of his client's limited finances. The house was to be built from Alki's savings and not one penny more. She could not have illusory wrought-iron stairs or en suite trees, but it would take some convincing on his part. Finally, at his wit's end, he suggested a transplant procedure for the Ashoka, even though he was sure she could not afford the cost of it and the additional time it would require. They debated for a while and Alki was about to concede when one of the construction workers stepped forward.

Dark, wiry, and greying at the temples, shadowy-thin skin and lines of disquiet surrounded his jaded eyes. Amidst murmurs and mumbling from his co-workers, he opened his mouth to speak and Alki could not help but notice his missing front teeth, the side-effect of years of malnutrition. Alki suddenly became conscious of the feudal ladder she was perched upon. She was wont to complain of her womanly lot in life, but here was this man perched so far below her on the ladder. She often saw little children like him on the road begging for food, water, money, or selling roses and little trinkets. She, who prided herself on her empathy, had learned to turn her eyes away from them. She had "othered" them. Now here was one, defying his otherness and provoking signs of life in her entombed mercy.

He said, "Don't worry madam, I will do this for you. I will dig out this tree and dig a new hole for it wherever you want it, and I will plant it there."

The architect was bemused.

"You cannot do this alone. It will take a lot of time. Madam or I cannot afford it or the extra workers we have to pay to do this."

The worker said, "This is my *shram dhan*, I will donate my labour as part of my penance towards this sacred tree. Like madam, I cannot see it destroyed. Men from my ashram will help me. I don't want any money for this."

Alki knew not what to say at first, but after a nod from the architect, she accepted the worker's offer, although uncomfortable that she would be taking advantage of the man's poverty. She was also curious about his penance, but resisted the urge to ask questions. That would be prying, she thought. In a milieu in which the policy was pry first, reason later, she was the odd one out. The other workers sat down to watch the spectacle that ensued.

The construction worker told his audience, "We cannot disturb the goddess that lives inside this tree. We must first try and explain to her that we mean no harm."

A couple of white and brown-clad men from the ashram arrived and they performed an hour-long puja for the spirit of the tree, after which they dressed up the tree trunk with sandalwood paste and marigold garlands. Alki could not be present for all of it, as she had to get back to work.

Following the ceremony, first, he brushed the ground around the tree, removing dense layers of leaf litter and pulling out tenacious undergrowth. When the ground was finally bare after a day, he had a wooden tool with which he tapped the exposed ground around the tree. Then he began to scrape at the top layer of soil around the tree. This began to expose the surface roots of the tree. After about a century, the ground beneath the Ashoka was revealed for the first time and it was spongy and black, which surprised Alki, who had returned at lunchtime the next day. She had expected the typical rigid red soil of this area to emerge from under the tree.

As the careful excavation commenced, the worker and his friends began to come across potsherds and bits of decomposed animal bones.

The worker said to Alki, "Madam, all this is from an ancient kitchen fire. Your great-grandmother must have been dumping charcoal, manure, bone, and compost here for years", then without looking her in the eye, he murmured, "either that or there was some kind of ritual burial here..." He looked away for a second as if lost in his thoughts, then he turned to her to say, "And if you keep digging here, this soil will go down a couple of metres. If I start from this tree, I can mark out the entire area of your ancestor's old garden. Over many years, she built up all this rich black soil for her garden. Her soil is so rich, you can plant a garden here now and the plants will do very well."

Alki was disconcerted.

"How do you know all this?"

She regretted the question as soon as she finished asking it. Her amazement that a poor villager would have knowledge of this kind was classist. But the truth was that in her country, access to knowledge, to books and education, was limited to a chosen few higher castes and their children. Alki too had benefited from this ancient privilege. A fair ribbon of opportunity and entitlement wove its way through the upper echelons of society, and this band dominated culture, film, religion, literature, government, and all the big ideas of the Indian zeitgeist. The rest were confined to slums, remote forests, hills, and farmlands of the country, their ideas vastly unrecorded, their dialects reverberating incongruously in urban ears.

The worker replied peaceably.

"My wife used to be very good at finding wild medicinal plants, and she would plant them all around our house. She knew about this kind of soil. She collected coconut shells to make charcoal to bury in our garden along with manure, fish, and compost."

At these words, a pensive air settled on his face, and he turned away from her quickly to continue with the dig. Over the next few days, a deep wedge was cut into the ground around the Ashoka's umbra of roots. This was not at all easy to achieve as the roots had a mind of their own, spreading far and wide underground, forming a secret communications network away from the eyes of meddling humans. Some of them had to be trimmed and snapped from their earthen moorings. The tree and the earth around it were conjoined for all intents and purposes. The root surgery troubled Alki but the construction worker seemed sure about what he was doing. The concave trench was wide enough to fit a man. Under the root ball, the tree was propped up on stone slabs. Workers got down into the trench to wrap the root ball with gunny cloth.

The next concern, after the tree's understory had been exhumed, was how it was going to be lifted out and manoeuvred to its new spot at the bottom of the ancient garden, which had been cleared under instruction from Alki and the architect. A sheer wall of pockmarked laterite formed a natural wall marking the bottom of the ancestral garden. Ancient workers had possibly dug into this spot on the hill looking to create building blocks for the main house on the mound. Thanks to the efforts of the construction worker, Alki was able to rediscover the outline of her ancestor's old garden. And though it was not in the new plan for the house, Alki wanted to restore the garden to its old shape and form before it had overgrown and disappeared from view.

The construction worker came to the site the following morning with thick ropes and a whole set of well wheels ranging in size from big to small. The ashramites followed behind carrying a heavy board made by joining five planks. He explained his plan to rig up the tree to a system of pulleys. He only needed to lift the tree onto the board, which lay on a row of whittled timber rollers. If they were able to shift the tree and its root ball onto the board, he intended to move it on the rollers to the bottom of the garden to the new planting hole the workers had exhumed. This was day five, and Alki began to perceive a frenetic intensity in the man. His body seemed a bit more shrunken than usual. She asked him out of concern if he had been eating. He said, "Of course," and moved away. His friends from the ashram, however, told her quietly that he had taken to sleeping at her site to guard the tree and give it water when necessary. He had even gone into the forest around his house, which now belonged to the ashram, and cut down an entire thicket of long-standing bamboo, and their guru had been none too pleased. The bamboo was worth a lot of money.

Alki said, "Why would he cut down all that bamboo?"

"He's doing it all for your tree," said the ashramite, "he's going to build a frame around it so that he can pull up the tree using the pulleys onto that board he's made. Saving the tree has become his mission. He won't speak to his wife; he doesn't eat or sleep."

Watching the construction worker unload the long heavy poles of bamboo from the little truck that had driven up to the hill, Alki wished she had just let the architect cut down the tree as he had required. To her, it seemed the uprooted tree was slowly coming to life, as the life in the man trying to save it, was gradually ebbing away.

A day later, when Alki returned to the land for her usual visit at lunchtime, a two-sided bamboo teepee had been raised around her ancestor's tree. The construction worker had apparently laboured all day and night by lamplight to finish it. And by the end of it, he was gaunt. When Alki attempted to speak to him, he withdrew from her presence almost indignantly. Alki wondered whether she needed to call the authorities to have him removed from the site or would that be too cruel to the man who needed to finish his mission? She raised her concerns with the architect, and he too believed that maybe it was better to let him finish. The architect did not tell her that he believed the construction worker was manic and he might harm his client if he was removed from the site.

All the men in the ashram turned up on the day the tree was to be moved. Alki watched them, all fifty of them, stream in and wait patiently for the proceedings to commence. They seemed to be waiting for something. But no one would speak to her or the architect. After 15 minutes, a big sedan drove up to the side of the hill, and a man in flowing brown robes, sporting a long white beard and hair stepped out. The ashramites stood up to salute and hail their guru. The construction worker stepped forward and fell at his feet to receive any proffered blessings. The guru laid his hand on the prostrate man's head and the worker looked up gratefully with tears streaming down his face. A couple of ashramites had trudged up the hill with a wooden armchair for their master. The guru sat down and waved his hands. A flurry of activity then began at the site.

On the sidelines, the architect looked at Alki as if to say they were no longer in control of events. Pointing to the guru, Alki signalled to her architect that she had had enough and motioned to go and speak to the ashram head. This was her land after all. She took a step forward only to have the architect yank her back forcefully.

"No ma'am. He doesn't like women; he will not take kindly to you speaking to him."

Alki stopped herself, stymied. She would not know that her architect feared for her safety. The guru saw the little commotion and turned to look in their direction. He stared contemptuously at Alki. She stared back resisting the urge to look down or away and show submissiveness as demanded of her by this man's dominance display. Then suddenly, unexpectedly, his manner shifted. A flash of fear crossed his countenance and the guru looked away from her, fidgeting uneasily in his chair.

The construction worker had rigged up an ingenious, elaborate pulley system atop the two-sided bamboo teepee. The worker shimmied to the top and sat straddled taking hold of the heavy rope he had improvised up there. Below him, a line of pulleys led to a hook attached to a rough-and-ready rope harness fastened to the upper trunk of the tree. Alki admired the pageantry of intuitive engineering on show, but it also made her ponder the folly in all human endeavours, from the Empire State Building or the Burj Khalifa to this bamboo marvel before her.

The contriving, the inventing, it was no doubt genius, but the spine of madness riveting it in place, that was something else altogether. A little testosterone made all this difference in the world? Or was it merely gender policing? A few minutes ago, she had been pulled back into the sidelines by a religious leader's misogyny. She did not possess the free will to go into a forest and cut down a thicket of bamboo, neither could she spend all night outside, alone, joining bamboo into this marvellous teepee. Rare was the girl who would even be allowed to learn trades like woodworking. When she had tried to lift weights years ago in sports class, she remembered how the other girls in school had sneered at her, saying she would grow unsightly muscles.

At least those norms had eased somewhat today. She may have been on a higher rung on the feudal ladder, but was she truly free, like this skinny man straddling his cleverly devised teepee? When motherhood, nurturing, and hearth duties become detached from gender, the world would be a different place. Could the Empire State and Burj Khalifa buildings be replaced with something else in a gender-neutral utopia? Were these things so impossible even in her own mind that she referred to such a place as Utopia?

She was jolted from her contemplation when the old tree groaned, twigs cracked, leaves dropped, and branches shook before it suddenly levitated. Its gunny-sheathed dampened root ball was now above ground level. Another heave on the rope from atop the teepee and the tree moved forward from its former planting hole towards the board fashioned for its journey to the bottom of the old garden. After the tree came to rest on the plank, the ashramites stopped to build a scaffolding to prop up the tree before they could unharness it from the teepee and move the plank board forward on its rollers.

14

Darwin's Pea

The dark blue flowers blinked on suddenly, like the first giant stars in the gas and dust of the early universe. The Ashoka tree, strapped in for the slow ride had been inching forward, when the workers stopped to call out to their master. Alki and the architect had stepped forward curiously. The sheer laterite cliff rising at the bottom of the ancestor's garden had sprung to life. Twining all over it— as if a green, tentacled, writhing creature from a phantasmagorical tale—was a butterfly pea plant bursting with cerulean flowers. Alki watched the guru tiptoe slowly to the wall behind the dugout glaring in suspicion. He came to a stop a yard away from the floral scene. He asked one of the ashramites to bring his spectacles.

An involuntary curse escaped his throat surprising everyone in the close gathering.

He twisted round to a stunned Alki and said, "This place is an abomination."

Before Alki had the presence of mind to respond, he turned to the worried construction worker to say, "Finish this job quickly and return to the ashram. I don't want you to spend one extra minute in this place. This place will be the death of you, and me."

With these words and a glance filled with malevolence and fear thrown at Alki, he was off. The armchair was trudged off to the little truck. The big sedan drove off down the road and Alki was relieved to see the back of the master. His very presence had goaded her and vice versa. The whole time she had itched to confront him and tell him that he was trespassing on her land, but she had held her tongue out of trepidation and a lack of gumption. She, on the other hand, had been encroaching on what the master believed was the male prerogative, which governed feudal control and influence.

That first day as the work started, she had been an intruder on her own land. The workers had regarded her with suspicion, reluctant to take instruction from her in the absence of the architect. Even her relatively higher position on the feudal ladder, in comparison to the men who worked for her, did not grant her enough privilege to address them with authority. If she was polite to them, her manner was interpreted as meekness, in need of a saviour, but when she raised her voice, she was judged to be a bitch, in need of taming. It was easy to go one way or the other, and treading that fine line in between was a walk on an everlasting tightrope.

After the religious man's exit, the worker and the ashramites resumed their labour, moving the tree forward at a snail's pace, one man running ahead to slip the back roller into the gap at the front of the board as it advanced. Alki approached the newly dug planting hole in front of the garden scarp wondering what could have possibly sent the master packing so rapidly. The winking blue flowers reminded her of seashells, unconventional in their appearance, but then pea flowers were not that flowery to start with, as most people associated conventional floweriness with radially symmetrical flowers like chrysanthemums or roses.

The matrix of the flower's appearance unexpectedly resolved before her eyes and Alki was at last able to distinguish what provoked the flight of the guru. The bright blue shell-shaped flowers were mimicking female genitalia. Of course, this would outrage the priest. This was a world in which the word slut was reserved for women, with no equivalent term for men. Alki found it anomalous because the degree of sluttiness of women's clothing was often determined by the male gaze, just as the elaborate plumage on a male bird of paradise was determined by what the she-bird liked and approved. Or was it like when a woman was blamed if she was unable to produce a male offspring when all along it was the man whose chromosomes determined the sex of the child?

Her contemplation shifted back to the laterite wall, as there was something more behind the ascending carpet of the twining plant. The new leafage jacketing the laterite camouflaged a discolouration made of pale-yellow clay. Gently pushing aside the vines so as not to snap them, Alki saw immediately, without stepping back, that the buttery clay in the laterite bluff had left behind a cloudy stain resembling a woman's face. She let go of the vines and jumped back in reflexive fright. But calming herself quickly by smoothing down the front of her kurta, she looked around to check if anyone other than her had seen the apparition. Clearly, no one else had. Alki did not want to say anything that could possibly result in yet another unnecessary din.

It was almost evening by the time the tree was gently rolled up to its new planting hole. The bamboo teepee then had to be dismantled and reassembled at the end of the garden. The architect realised one more day of labour would be lost before the Ashoka could be finally established in the new pit. The construction worker refused to put down his tools and go home, contriving into the dusk to take down the teepee and drag the logs of bamboo to the bottom of the garden. The architect felt compelled to stay behind with the construction worker as he got on with the task by the light of a couple of kerosene lamps. After what happened to him three weeks ago, he was reluctant to remain on the land after sunset. The architect placed himself in the semi-circle of light falling from the lamps. A drenching darkness poured down from the mound above, leaving only a crescent of lamplight below in the ancient garden where the two of them stood. The architect sniffed at the pungent kerosene-scented vapours fouling up the air in the ancient garden.

He said to the worker, “You have been here now a few nights, have you noticed anything out of the ordinary here? Anything strange?”

The construction worker turned around to the architect. Around his toothless mouth, the skin was raw under beads of pooled sweat. The scraggy lines on his face seemed to have multiplied since the afternoon.

“I have spent the last three nights with my wife and daughter for company. Other than them, there has been no one here.”

The architect asked, “Where are they today? They didn’t want to come?”

The worker said, “Probably because you are here.”

The architect was perplexed and did not say anything more. By the time of this conversation, the architect was exhausted from all the day’s events. His client had returned to her office late in the afternoon, and he felt enough of a sense of duty to her that he had stayed at the site after sunset. He consoled himself, reasoning that at least there was one other person around, even if that person seemed extremely peculiar. After a while, the architect was so tired that he sat himself down near the new planting hole, leaning wearily against the laterite wall blanketed by the twining stems and wilting flowers of the butterfly pea plant. He did not know when his eyes closed, but soon he knew he was dreaming, because the construction worker’s wife and daughter had appeared, and they were helping him gloomily heave and erect the teepee around the new planting hole. The woman and her tearful child were grey and deathly pale, and the man scowled at them angrily through his sweat.

The architect felt a sudden stab of fear in his chest when the three of them, the man, the woman, and the child twisted sideways and stared at him. He began to gasp for breath as the three of them started to walk towards him. The architect was now mumbling in his sleep. He found he could not speak, and only ghoulish wails left his mouth.

He wanted to say to the woman and little girl, "No, it's not me, it's him.... it's not me, it's him."

He wanted to lift his hand and point to the man beside them, the construction worker, but his hands were heavy at his side, and he could not lift them. He knew they were angry, but he hadn't done anything to them. It was not him they wanted, but he couldn't speak or gesture. He was paralysed. As they got nearer, the kerosene lamps began to die down. Their movement towards him echoed the lethargic pace of the tree on its rolling board from earlier in the afternoon. He gazed at their slow-motion gait, and all he could do was lie back in paralysed fear, their shadowy visages and silhouetted bodies beginning to loom over him at the laterite wall.

Then just as suddenly, the ghostly figures halted in their tracks, about a foot away from him. Puzzlement appeared on their withered, dark faces. The architect felt a crawling sensation all over him. He looked down to find the butterfly pea plant twining over his legs, hands and chest. In the dying light of the kerosene lamps, blue flowers began to wink open all over the plant, all over him. He could barely see anymore as the stems and leaves had grown thickly over his eyes. Through the remaining gaps in his eyelids, he thought he saw a woman beside him rise from a crouching position. Eating into the night, her skin glowed a bright mango tint, and thickly plaited black hair cascaded over her right shoulder. A sprig of feathery green leaves shot straight up from the crown of her head. Her clothes were, somehow, old fashioned.

She said to the withered woman and child, "That's the one you want."

She gestured to the man beside them. With weary resentment, the shadowy woman and girl regarded the gaunt construction worker. The worker screamed at them.

"No, no, no, no, no. I have done all this for you. You cannot take me. I have a new life now."

Repeatedly, he kicked the little girl and slapped the woman, but his blows did not affect them. Long tapering hands and fingers reached out from the shadows of the woman and child to grab the man, and together they led him struggling to the new planting hole. The construction worker surrendered; fatigue and distress having dragged down his face when he twisted around, looking to the architect for help. But the architect was swathed behind a wall of perky blue pea flowers, and a gold-skinned woman was now gliding towards him. The man howled. The golden woman extended her hand and pointed to the hole. The woman, her child, and the wailing man were sucked into the ground.

At last, there was stillness, and warm light, which came not from the extinguished lamps but from the woman. Enveloped in a golden glow, she floated to the tree still waiting atop its rolling board. Without much effort, she freed the tree from its man-made buttressing and levitated it into its planting hole. When the ground around the tree was level, the golden woman struck the inside of her left foot against the bottom of the Ashoka's trunk. The tree burst into flower, burnishing the warm glow with ruddy tinges of orange. Pivoting around, beneath a halo of saffron blooms, the woman in the golden aura raised her right palm in the universal gesture of reassurance. As the exhausted architect closed his eyes and gave himself up to deep quenching slumber, the woman's aura shone brighter and brighter till there was nothing except a scorching radiance left around the trunk of the Ashoka.

The smartphone in his shirt pocket trilled out into the darkness. The architect woke with a start from the intense dream. He could not see anything except his immediate surroundings at the laterite wall from the light of his phone screen. The lamps had both gone out, and there seemed to be no one around. The worker must have gone home, he thought, leaving him behind. He answered his cell. It was his wife wondering why he hadn't come home yet. He apologised to her, telling her he must have fallen asleep while the construction worker was reassembling the teepee. He rang off, promising he was on his way home. He got up, gingerly dusting himself off. Wilted blue flowers were scattered on the ground around him. He found his car on the road below and got in, fragments from his dream coming back to him, the eerie dark faces of a woman, a faceless child, the construction worker, and a golden aurora. The architect drove home shivering in the night. He must have dreamt of them, as he remembered the worker telling him that his wife and child had spent a couple of nights with him to assist with the transplantation.

The following morning, the architect and his workers arrived at the site to find the tree standing serenely in its new spot at the bottom of the garden, the ground level around it, and no sign that the earth had ever been disturbed. It was bizarre. Logs of bamboo from the teepee, the pulleys, and ropes lay on one side. The architect wondered how the construction worker had managed to do all of this in just one night. The worker must have returned after he left for home. Alki was at work when she received an urgent call from her architect summoning her to the building site.

She arrived to a sombre scene. Work had come to a standstill and the fretful workers had all soundlessly gathered around the architect awaiting further instruction. The Ashoka tree had been successfully transplanted to the bottom of the garden. Is this why she had been called to the site?

The architect seemed upset when he gave her the news, and it hit Alki hard. The construction worker who had laboured for a whole week to transplant her Ashoka tree had died at home in his sleep the previous night. Though no one blamed her, she was instantly wracked with guilt. The remaining construction workers whispered among themselves. He had been half-dead this whole time and was finally consumed by his madness.

The architect ushered her away from the other workers.

"Something happened here last night, and I am not sure what. But he was there. I watched him tie the bamboo together. I was very tired, so I rested there," he said pointing to the laterite wall at the bottom of the garden, making Alki jump a little.

He said, "After I fell asleep, I think there were other people here. For the life of me, I cannot remember. But just look at this…"

The architect stretched out his wrists and turned his palms around.

"Can you see these blue streaks? It's on my face, even on my tongue."

Sure enough, Alki noted odd blue markings on his face and hands. But she wouldn't have seen the faint splotches if he had not pointed them out to her.

He said, "I think it's from those blue flowers at the wall where I was sitting. I was asleep. Then when I woke up, he was not there anymore. I was sure he went home. And there were all these blue flowers on the ground when I woke up."

Alki tried to sound reassuring and objective.

She said, "Those blue flowers are strongly dyed. It's called Darwin's pea in some countries. People use it to make a blue tea. It's supposed to be good for the mind. It has anti-depressant qualities. You must have got some of that colour on you when you were resting against that plant."

She wondered how the Butterfly pea had got its common name - Darwin's pea. Did it have something to do with Charles Darwin? Or were there associations between this plant, Darwin's theory of evolution, and Gregor Mendel's work on pea plants that led to the idea of genes and genetics? A man had died, and her mind was wandering. She was contrite. The architect broke into her attention-deficit train of thought.

He said, “Hmm…probably. Still, it’s strange. How could he have done all this in one night, even if he returned later?”

As he spoke, Alki’s eyes drifted to the laterite wall at the end of the garden where the Ashoka tree now stood, behind which a curling, blue-flowered Darwin’s pea plant screened a spectre in stone. Leaving the architect to compose the workers, Alki wandered over to the tree. The transplanted tree looked as if it had always been here, not one hair out of place, no trail of fallen leaves or broken twigs to show the path it had taken on its journey from the front of the garden. The Ashoka’s main trunk was discoloured in places. She went in for a closer examination. A curving pale yellow smudging traced a path from top to bottom. A second later, Alki recoiled in fear.

“No, it can’t be,” she said to herself.

Swivelling around and stepping on the fallen flowers from the night before, she took hold of the stems of the butterfly pea and pushed them aside. The wraith in the laterite she had discovered the previous day had vanished. Turning to the Ashoka with a heavy sinking sensation in the pit of her stomach, Alki took a few steps back and circumambulated the tree. The yellow stain, which she had earlier presumed to be a type of clay, had somehow transferred to the bole of the Ashoka tree; following the outline of the stain around the tree, she was more than sure she could make out the form of a woman.

15

The Jackfruit Marks the Spot

"Like the people you know, your land is hiding something under its surface," said the surveyor. As he spoke, the dappled shade under the Jackfruit tree shifted, prompting Alki to look up at the glossy Jack leaves playing in the wind. Giant pendulous fruit hanging down from the main trunk caught her attention. Distracted, Alki thought about the furtive flowers on a Jackfruit. Diminutive lime-green pendants bearing inconspicuous flowers turned into edible green monsters without any floral pageantry. Her uncle had used a magnifying glass years ago to show her that she would have to zoom right in to appreciate the tiny fruit's hidden flowers, which could be mistaken for fuzz if someone wasn't looking out for them. The Jackfruit must have partnered with really tiny insects to pollinate its fruits.

Alki looked down into the ancient garden below, now scraped clean of its protective jungly blanket. The productive Jackfruit was perched above the garden on a plateau created after the land below had been scooped out generations before. She glanced at the surveyor inquisitively. She liked him. He was a geologist, he told her, and many years before, when he was in college, he hadn't been able to make up his mind between rocks and wasps, and finally, he had chosen rocks. Alki told him she had not been able to decide either, and she had loved trees. Then in a revelatory moment, as few people were willing to listen to her story, she opened up and told the man with a sympathetic face about the unpleasantness at home and the need she felt to make sure that she had enough money to support herself. This had finally won over any love she had for trees.

"Lava tubes." The surveyor-geologist had continued with his explanation and these odd words had only just registered.

"Yes," he said, "hundreds of metres beneath your feet, this landscape is riddled with them. Let me repeat. You are in the Western Ghats. Millions of years ago, this area lay in the path of a volcanic eruption, more massive than we can possibly imagine. That eruption went on for thousands of years. After many millennia of erosion, *voila*!"

He smiled and waved his hand over the countryside borrowing the manner of a performing magician.

"You are the proud owner of lava tubes."

He was smiling at her, but Alki did not get the joke. In his blue and red checked shirt and straight blue jeans, his exterior seemed defiantly unfunny. A few days after the death of the construction worker, she had a hunch and had called in the surveyor, who turned out to be a geologist, to take a look at the laterite wall at the bottom of the ancient garden.

"Below us, behind that laterite wall is a cave. By the way, I think someone built that wall, it's not natural. That land down there, where the old garden used to be, was probably part of the cave system before someone dug it all out. Maybe they were digging here for a well, and this caused the roof of the cave to collapse. Who knows? Probably that's why they dug it out and made their garden here. You will be able to see it if you look at the contours of the garden. It has this pipe-like shape, which is distinct from up here."

Alki said, "Yes, I see what you mean about the shape. But are you sure about the…lava tubes…caves?"

The geologist said, "Not too far from here, maybe ten kilometres on the other side of this hill, are those cave temples to the local goddesses. You must have surely gone there and seen the similarities to your land. No, maybe not. I am a geologist and that is my job. I should not expect regular people to notice these things. This is a very interesting place underfoot." He tapped the ground with his foot.

Alki did not take offence at being called a "regular person".

"Of course, I know those temples, those are my mother's favourite goddess shrines."

Some distance below them, the architect and his workers were sweating over the foundation of Alki's new house. He looked up to see the two of them confabulating above him below a laden Jackfruit tree and on reflex, he decided to go interrupt them. They had a look about them, two lonely figures perched atop a broken hill. They were simpatico and shyly smiling at each other in a way that made him uncomfortable. He was a traditionalist, an Indian father to daughters. An unmarried young woman should not be talking for too long with another man, and he was paternal towards his client, having noted early on that her own father was absent from the work at the site and uninterested in helping her. He felt a little sorry for Alki, imagining one of his own daughters attempting to build a house without backing or encouragement from family. He wasn't deceived by her short hair and strict manner of dressing or speaking to the workers. He understood this was simply a disguise to help her survive in a man's world. His client was vulnerable. Men tended to pick on friendless women.

Alki heard footsteps and turned around to find the architect walking up the trail towards the Jackfruit tree. She was beginning to feel irritated with him, wary about any man's paternalistic attentions towards her. At her place of work, she had watched older men develop similar feelings, which then turned into territorial possessiveness, and then other unwanted behaviours. As to her father, Alki was relieved that he showed no interest in her project.

He would have tried to take over everything after having pushed her aside. Moreover, the workers would have ignored her completely in the presence of her father. She eyed the giant Jackfruit, recalling the time her father had churlishly argued that no woman would be able to get those fruit down, which had only goaded her into finding a long branch to show him that his opinion was perhaps befitting of prevailing cultural wisdom, but contrary to fact. He had not taken too kindly to being shown up by a young woman before his brothers-in-law.

She longed for the company of a friend on site with her, but who could she ask? Jas? Her friends were strange creatures, and any comprehension of their typical conduct would require a degree in ethology. Flying about in their youth between them were all these underlying frequencies to which she hadn't paid close enough attention. As she got older, Alki began to divine their existence—the unheeded hum from hushed grudges and apparently trivial meanness, underpinning every relationship in her life. She cursed herself for having taken so long to start getting attuned to the dog whistles in her relationships. They were, all of them, avowed feminists, but definitely not in any kind of sisterhood. Years before, Alki had been excited about learning to drive, and she had called Jas excitedly to tell her all about it. Jas, who was living abroad unhappily, was not pleased for Alki.

She had said, "Well, it's nice for you to live at home and be independent."

Only much later, after Jas had moved to India to live with her parents, and she had learned to drive the family car, did Alki start deciphering the connotations of her weirdly mean reaction. Jas was childishly combative with anyone she pegged subservient, and Alki mastering an empowering skill before she did was intimidating to her amped-up consciousness of self. But there was much more to it. She felt tied down, and envied Alki's at-home single independence, having no concept of what it was like for Alki to live at home with parents who resented her for not "adulting" in the way Jas had done by getting married and producing the two required children to show to the outside world.

Alki had unfortunately lived out her life as a foil to a friend who shunned true partnership, never letting her hog a proportionately central role in their shared lives; with Alki perpetually trying to squeeze her stories in edgeways. For a long time, she had volunteered to play a secondary role in their friendship. And until recently, whenever she tried to air her problems, they were always minimised away.

She could almost hear Jas in her head, saying, "Till now you did not have any serious problems."

As the secondary, she was presumptively meek and compliant.

As Alki's hypothesis of the secondary friend developed, she began to apply it to all the people around her. If such a person begins to empower herself in some aspect of her life, she thought, as in the case of Tana, inevitably the primary feels threatened. When Jas's mean side surfaces there is always an underlying grudge against the secondary for having contravened her rank in their pecking order. In Jas's perception, she had reinforced her power over Alki by marrying Yug. The secondary becomes trapped in the role of nurturer/chaperone, a plus one to offer support on down days or to provide company for outings to which she could not go alone.

Jas also used a technique that Alki called same-gender sexism to reinforce her dominance. She referred to the women around her by their sizes as if she were a judge at life's beauty pageant, showering praises on skinny girls, careful not to overtly disparage the not-so-skinny ones, except artfully by calling attention to a stray chubby ankle. Not even Jas would openly violate the feminist code. A fat girl in their mutual circle could provoke Jas's dormant Mr. Hyde if she lost weight and thereby changed her status. Tana, unlike no other in the group, had looked into the face of the hideous Jas and had lived to tell the tale, which she told every opportunity she got. It was not enough that Alki had to experience sexism from some men around her, but for dominant women like Jas to mete it out as well was more than tiresome. While it was easy to talk about sexist men, how could she begin to explain the absurd realism of sexist women? Jas needed to keep her friends humble, friends who were striving to earn their own entitlement.

Alki would never accept that she was perhaps the only friend for whom Jas had a soft spot. Jas wouldn't acknowledge it to herself either, but what had happened with Yug all those years ago had left behind a gnawing self-reproach that she found difficult to contend with at the best of times. Her remorse, however, was the result of hindsight and copious self-pity. A little selfishly, she wished she had rebuffed Yug. If she had let them be, it would have been Alki's lot in life and not hers to have to deal with his parents and the 'patriarchate' they had going at their house.

The house on the hill had become a beacon for all of Alki's friends, and the drone had grown louder, unmistakable. If only her plans had some semblance of docility, they would have ignored her. Authority figures were paying attention to her, even if that attention was negative, it was enough to disconcert Alki's female friends. Childhood friend Humira, neither picked up her calls, nor was she willing to even return calls. What began as nebulous antipathy had distilled into the surreal. Alki had never quite understood it until much later when her friend's inexplicit rancour had grown sizeably.

Unexpectedly Humira called her one morning, when Alki was getting ready to go to work, and she had at first ignored the call. But Humira called again insistently a few minutes later.

When Alki picked up, Humira said, "Alki, you don't pick up my calls? I had something important to tell you."

Combing her hair gingerly with the phone balanced on one shoulder, Alki paused, dumbfounded by the new technique being deployed against her. Humira had managed to accuse her of what Humira herself was known for doing. She would indicate her derision by not calling or speaking to friends not worthy of her attention, as they had not fulfilled certain benchmarks of accomplishment. Effortless scorn was reserved for perceived dunces and vainglorious malice for presumed betters. No one could be an equal.

Humira said, "I heard you're building a house, why didn't you tell me? I found out from Tana."

Alki said, "Ummm…"

"I could have given you some tips. You know…I have also had plans to build a house. It's the next step really. I have been so busy with my décor business, but you know all about that…"

Vaguely, Alki said, "No…I don't..."

Humira said, "…I have sent you enough messages about the award. But I am sure you just chose to ignore them. Even Jas rang me up to congratulate me. You were the only one that didn't call."

Alki was contrite but mostly guarded. She had indeed overlooked the messages about the local business award. To Alki, the award was trivial, but she knew it meant something to Humira, and she hadn't wanted to be cruel or petty, which Humira would have construed as jealousy. Simply ignoring it was also hurtful to Humira, Alki realised a bit late.

Alki said, "Mira, I didn't know you were an architect?"

Humira said, "Mmm…no, I am not an architect."

Humira couldn't be sure if Alki was being sarcastic.

"Really, I don't want to sound like I have an ego, but I've been in the business long enough to know what I am doing."

Then Humira got to the point.

"Don't you think it's a little arrogant to go against your poor father's wishes and try to do this on your own?"

Putting down the comb, Alki said, "Who told you my father is against it?"

"Well, Jas told me. We all think you are trying to bite off more than you can chew."

Alki was indignant and somewhat deflated, but she tried to sound acerbic when she said, "And yet, even you want to build your own house."

"Well, that's different. I have worked hard to start my business from scratch. I don't have to depend on husbands, fathers, or relatives to give me land...I am not the same person you knew in school. I am not cowed anymore by those who behave as if they were smarter or better than me. Times have changed, tables have turned."

Alki had uncritically accepted the notion that the reserved Humira like the rest of them had long been resentful of the mighty Jas, but now she wasn't so sure. She had been kept close all those years, but was she all along the real red target at the centre of Humira's mental game of darts?

Alki said, "No one starts from scratch Mira, especially not people like us."

Humira spluttered, "What do you mean? I did not have any help."

Alki said, "You already had help from being born in an educated, upper-caste family, and you have a loving, resourceful father."

Humira said, "So...what does my father have to do with anything? Next you'll say I am lucky because I was born human."

Alki said, "Lucky for you, but not so much for the earth."

A week after the prickly exchange with her friend, the architect called Alki at work. She picked up without hesitation.

He said, "Your friend is here, she is asking a lot of questions and examining the whole site. She is also taking pictures of everything."

Alki said, "That's strange. Who is it? Ohhh...it must be my friend Jaswanti. I thought she was at work today. She didn't tell me she was going there. She may have been passing that way and stopped to see how things were going."

The architect said, "No. I asked who she was, and she said her name was Humira, and she had come to help you out."

Alki suffered a sudden burst of exasperation, stomach acid rising to her throat.

The architect said, "The workers are not happy. She was giving them instructions. When I stopped her, she told me I was out of date in my research and did not understand the new ways of doing this work."

Alki said, "I am glad you stopped her."

The architect added quietly, "If I may be a little forward here, I don't think she came to help, she came out of curiosity. And I am being polite by calling it curiosity."

Alki thanked him again and disconnected the call. She sat for a while, stewing, then got up and strolled over to the human resources department to find Jas, who was not at all surprised.

She said, "I always told you she was narcissistic and big-headed."

Alki said nothing, too timid to tell Jas that she too was a different variety of the same archetype that had been pinned so effortlessly on Humira.

Alki said, "I can't understand why she would go to the bother of going there to photograph everything?"

"She's just making sure that no one else can outclass her, especially not you," said Jas.

Alki looked at Jas, askance. This was classic Jas; she would insult her even as she was making an effort to assuage her. By teatime, Humira had posted the pictures of her building site online, bewildering Alki by this nonchalant invasion of her privacy, but she was even more flustered by some of the unfavourable comments appearing below the pictures.

The one that irked her most said, "Alki doesn't like to share, thanks Mira for posting and keeping us up to date."

Alki had in the last year stopped posting pictures of work achievements or exciting purchases online because she noticed that though people prodded her on to share her life, the moment she did, they became cleverly snide as if they were unhappy to see other people doing well. They wanted to pry into her life, check her out, and then take pleasure in taking her down a peg, then be offended when that opportunity was taken away from them, hence their rancour.

Looking over her shoulder, Jas said, "Ignore those. She did that on purpose knowing what these guys would say. Alki…what's that?"

Jas was intently scrutinising a peculiar photograph of the Jackfruit tree. In the late afternoon, the angular sun had caused a whiteout behind the Jackfruit that stood on the little mesa abutting the ancient garden. The foreground lay in shadow. There seemed to be a distortion, a smudge, in the overexposed region in the background. Alki flashed back to the day she had seen the face in the white smoke in her living room during her mother's puja.

Jas said, "It looks like a woman bending to look down. What is she looking at? Is that the garden down there you were talking about?"

Fretfully, Alki said, "It's just a trick of the light, Jas."

"Look closely, Alki. It looks like…she…it's looking into the camera…"

Alki slammed down the screen of the laptop, saying, "C'mon Jas, your imagination is running wild."

The blood had drained from Alki's face, and she had gone pale.

Jas patted her friend's arm reassuringly.

"I didn't mean to…it's okay...c'mon…let's go get some coffee and drink to the wiles of Humira."

16

The Quiet White Blooms of Mango

Mango blossoms had the personality of wallflowers. First off, they were tiny, growing in big bunches away from sight, high up in the canopy. People waited with bated breath for the arrival of their resplendently tawny, sweet fruit and spared no thought for the exquisite minutia of the flowers that came before. The mango was a symbol of perfection and shape, but its flowers and streaky bees that brought it about were not as celebrated. The mango was the selfie, and its flowers—the hapless backdrop. A steaming cup of tea in hand, what Alki encountered one morning was the quiet scent of mango blossoms. The air in her parents' garden was suggestive with fragrance from trifling flowers blooming unnoticed.

She looked up and there they were, masses of them, conical inflorescences shaped like droopy snow-tipped Christmas trees, crowning leafy, brown-stemmed foundations. She hadn't examined the mango tree in weeks, what with the house project on the hill, and most recently, the upsetting manifestation in one of Humira's pictures. She had come out into the garden clutching her phone in one hand and teacup in the other, to get away from the grating breakfast chatter inside the house between her parents; her father moustachioed and clad in a starchy white shirt and dhoti after his bath, petulant that her mother had failed to bring his tea out to the dining room from the kitchen counter, her mother still in a crumpled sari from the day before, not yet having had time for her bath, reminding him that he could have gone into the kitchen and fetched it himself after his ablutions.

Having despatched hot tea down a scalded throat, Alki set her cup down in the earth. With one thumb, she clicked open the photo gallery on her phone. Humira's pictures reminded her that she too had taken photos at the site on the day she and the architect's wife had gone to fetch him from the mound where he had been found unconscious and white-faced. The pictures from that day were unremarkable and badly composed; one was of the disturbed ground beneath the Alstonia, another of the bare mound. Barely two hours after this shot, the mound had bristled with rising spikes of corpse flowers. She lowered the phone, the memory of that day making her shiver. She took a deep breath leaning into the gentle steadying scent of mango blossoms and went back to flipping through the photographs. There were three shots of the old mud-walled well. One was smudged and blurred, a result of shaky hands, followed by two clear takes.

An accustomed sinking sensation struck her in the pit of her stomach when she swiped left to return to the blurred photo of the old well. Not only had her hands shaken, but the lighting conditions in this photo replicated Humira's picture of the Jackfruit tree. The morning sun had overexposed the back of the well creating a smudging effect over the well mouth. It had been in her phone all this time, and she hadn't examined it, having been too busy, too traumatised by the events of that day. She was seeing faces in toast again, she thought, sliding down next to the cup she had placed on the ground a minute before. She told Jas that her imagination was running wild. But here it was again, that same face in the smudge she had refused to acknowledge. Pale grey eyes framed inside a white smoky face; it had been trapped in her photo gallery all this time. Curled fingers gripped the earth under the mango, the gaps in Alki's fingernails filling with grit. She faced down her fear, refusing to let it take her over again. She propped her back against the mango's unevenly ribbed trunk, momentarily looking sideways at the Neem tree a little way beyond. The Neem was unblemished, un-ashed today. Alki breathed in.

Had she made all this up in her head, and was it some kind of mass delusion, because Jas had seen it as well? Maybe she had lost her grip over reality and had even managed to drag Jas into her fictional universe. Everyone around her was constantly inventing fictions as they went about their lives, rationalising this and that, unwilling to admit to even the most fundamental of truths. Hadn't she caught herself in the act a half hour before; did she really need that fourth cream biscuit with her tea? She told herself that it couldn't hurt, as she would have only one biscuit the next day to compensate, which was really a lie. A cloud of self-delusion encompassed the really small, fourth cream biscuit and the really large, nuclear button.

Beneath the mango tree, cocooned in mute scent, Alki lapsed into reverie. All this fictionalising, did this make up the human condition? Could it be that life wasn't imitating fiction, but that all life was simply fiction, and the more human we became, the more we were unable to distinguish between life and fiction, as we're just not made to comprehend the difference? We made up everything in a bid to get a hold of the world around us: language, numbers, writing and mathematics, it was all art one way or another. We were human only because of stories. All the stories that we had ever created over our time as a species that started to talk, imagine, then write stories moulding us into conscious beings that thought about the universe and our place in it. In this dream world made real, fiction made us sapient. At a much later time in civilisation, a concept known as truth was invented as a constant to find meaning in a runaway fictional universe, to separate us from our stories, to sideswipe our deceptions for our own good. Alki needed to find the truth. She couldn't escape it anymore. She opened her eyes.

Yug, his hair sporting a couple of strands of grey, was in the front garden looking down at her. She gasped. Here was the passage of time encapsulated in someone she had not really looked at in a long time. Her breath smelled of mango blossoms.

He said, "Are you alright? You don't look so good."

She said, "What are you doing here? Where's Jas?"

"She told me to come and talk to you. Are you afraid to go to the site alone? You know…I can help you with the house. You can ask for help."

Alki was rude.

"Sure, I can ask for help. But why did she send you?"

Yug did not reply. Instead, he sat down next to her.

She turned to him and said, "Do you know what will happen if I turn up at the site with you? They will wonder what this unmarried woman is doing here with a man who is not related to her. Sure, I can be devil-may-care and not let it bother me. But my conservative architect and his workers will lose all respect for me. It took me a long time to get them to listen to me."

Yug sighed and said, "I am sorry. I didn't realise how hard things were for you."

After a pause, he continued, "Jas is up to her old tricks again. But this time she isn't trying to get me; she's trying to give me away."

Alki stared at him.

Yug said, "I don't think she ever told you about what's wrong between her and Humira. Do you know why she doesn't like Humira? A few years ago, I said I found her beautiful."

Surprised, Alki said, "Yug, no…you led on Mira?"

Yug was offended.

"I didn't lead anyone on. Okay, I may have flirted…a little bit. And you know Humira…her giant ego. That was enough for her. She always looks a bit triumphant around me. Jas can't stand that."

He continued, "Do you know Humira calls me every fortnight? She calls to talk about business strategies and to ask about Jas's situation with my family..." he rolled his eyes, then said, "and Jas fumes every time she calls me. She says it's sexist that Humira will call me to talk about business and not her. You know, in front of Jas, I can't even call her Mira..."

He laughed.

"Alki...you haven't called me once in all these years."

"Why do I need to call you?" asked Alki. "I see you all the time with Jas. And well, Jas keeps me up to date."

Yug asked, "Aren't you interested in my side of things?"

Alki replied, "You already have Mira calling you for your side of things, you don't need me for that. My god! You are just like Jas."

"Alki...I know you are angry...whenever you speak to me, that anger...I can feel it. Do you know how rude you are to me?"

"Can you blame me?"

"No...I guess not...Jas doesn't say it, but she thinks you and I were perfect for each other. Maybe she's right."

Alki finally stirred, squirming away from him.

The moment was awkward, but with some finality, she said, "Did you ever consider that maybe she's not right...you better get back to her. I need to get to work, and so do you."

Yug stood up, rubbing the dirt off the seat of his pants, and moved towards the front gate.

He stopped then turned around to say, "I meant what I said. I want to help. I will drag Jas to the site with me, if that will help, alright?"

Alki smiled at last.

"Thanks, Yug."

After his exit, Alki got up and looked around. No one had witnessed their exchange, no need for neighbours to gossip. She went back into the house to have breakfast with her sullen parents.

At the table, she remained distracted, thinking about Jas. Sending Yug over had evidently been some kind of self-seeking manoeuvre. No one made up more convoluted stories in their heads as well as Jas did. Even though she had some relief living at her parents' house, only Alki knew how asphyxiated Jas felt with Yug and his family, having to compete with his mother for his affections. Jas had decided that she needed to get away from Yug and for that he would have to leave her. Since he would not do that consciously, she would have to furtively manipulate him. Had she somehow convinced him that Alki was pining for him? Oh my god, thought Alki, if she was ready to go to that extent, the world in Jas's head was crying out for help.

At work that day, Alki found Jas at lunchtime.

"Jas, why did you send Yug to talk to me today? He caught me by surprise."

"I thought you could use the pep talk. He came home and told me from now on, the two of us should go to your site as often as we can to help you."

Alki laughed out loud. The expression on Jas's face said she hadn't wanted that outcome.

"Then maybe you shouldn't have sent him over."

Jas was sheepish, but she was also smiling.

"You know I don't like to muck about. But I guess I can for a little bit."

Alki brought out her phone and showed Jas the shaky picture of the old mud well. It was not just in Alki's fancy anymore, because the picture of the old mud well also seemed to frighten Jas, who kept wordlessly looking at the picture and then back again at Alki.

"I am not imagining it, right Jas? You can see it too?"

Jas waited, then said, "It's that thing…the white woman… Alki…what is going on there?"

"I think it has something to do with what the surveyor told me the other day. He said the whole site is riddled with lava tubes."

Alki smiled when she thought about the geologist.

Jas was mystified.

Alki said, "Underground, there are all these caves connected to each other. You remember your father mentioned those goddess temples?

"Yeah…?"

"There's one on the other side of the hill. You know the Bael temple. I think these caves go all the way to that temple."

17

The Spectre in the Banana Clump

Her hair started to clump around beads of sweat, eyes darting around rapidly under their lids. She was asleep, she was sure of that. But she was back again at the thicket of banana plants on the land where Alki was attempting to build her house, following a group of workers up a dirt track into the hill. The path led to a banana clump growing on a carpet of ash. She watched them leave offerings of fruit, flowers, and burning incense; one of them tied a saffron-coloured sash around the tallest plant. The men then kneeled and closed their eyes to pray. She stepped forward, wary, eyes focussed but shifty. There was something there, hiding, waiting. She took another step into the dread and the outlandish features of the banana clump took over her sight. The plants seemed proudly un-tree, with no woody bark on thickened squelchy stems and, therefore, no timber to be had from inside them, and those gargantuan leaf straps towering over her like alien receiving antennae turning to track her movements.

The men had their eyes stubbornly closed and they could not see what she saw emerge, birth itself in trails of incense smoke, peeling off from the tough greasy skin of the tallest banana stalk, leaving behind long threads still attached umbilically to the thick green main stem. A sparkling grey-green wraith with long hair and eyes to match raised its hand and pointed a bony finger at her accusingly, instantly drenching her in an unknown remorse.

She was so afraid, suffused with a genus of anxious terror that only came to her in the earliest part of the morning, when it was twilight outside. She looked around for reassurance, but the men had stopped praying and were staring at her. One of them got up, a man she recognised, and he grabbed her from behind and wretchedly she allowed him. With both hands, he held fast, around her middle and just beneath her neck, and she wracked her brain for excuses, for any gambit, to make him let her go. The thing was watching, and it was infuriated now. It began to hover, burgeon in size, umbilical threads ripping. She noticed that its feet were turned back, and she could only see its heels. A screech rent the forest, scattering the offerings brought by the men, their faces spattering with stinking gobs of blood and a shower of sparks. The familiar man, blood-stained and scorched, let her go, he cowered and shrank from the thing. The bananas had all bent down around the angry floating spirit, their elongated leaves, now rugs of chlorophyll.

Even in bed, Humira was tall. She awoke, dripping with sweat, covers having been kicked off by long legs. It was the same early morning dream again, and she could still feel his hands, dripping around her, tightening, choking her. She coughed into the air viscous with evaporating perspiration. It had been the same dream for ten years. A man attacks her, and she is helpless, but this time there was the sparkling wraith that was both distressed and furious. Humira's waking life had suppressed the incident with the cousin who grabbed her, but her sleeping brain had kept the terror of it going all these years.

In her waking life, there were weddings to attend that she refused to attend. She couldn't tell her parents that he would be there, the reputable man, charming everyone into believing he could have never done what now lived on in her sleeping life. She could not even talk graciously to his mother, her aunt, a woman who suspected, but resisted the knowledge of what was wrong with him.

The day after; all those years ago, she had tried to tell his sister something about what happened. He happened to be present, and he said to the girl, "Whose side are you on?"

Humira had to let it go. No one would take her seriously, especially when the reputation of a good, handsome man was at stake.

How many times had she let things go? In traffic for the umpteenth time, when the driver behind her deduced the presence of a woman behind the wheel. The roar of sudden acceleration was also the sound of a ballooned-ego-pricking followed by dangerous overtaking. The automobile was a proxy for the ego behind the wheel and just by observing vehicular manoeuvres around her, she became skilled at detecting the flavour of the temperaments cocooned inside their cars, like the darty ones who always felt free to troll the good-tempered cars. At work, she had to talk louder than all the men to be heard and respected, so that they could then call her a mad shrew. What about when she and Alki had cut their hair so short all those years ago, Jas had derisively called it their 'boy cut'; Jas was almost a man, in the way she did not hide it when she couldn't bear anyone besting her in anything, which included haircuts, body weight, or work exploits. That's how she knew that the hairstyle suited both her and Alki, as Jas had hated it. And it hadn't been just Jas.

What visited her vividly after the 'boy cut' was the palpable loathing of a woman assistant in a shop that sold light fixtures for her business. That girl had been dressed traditionally in a salwar suit, forehead *bindi*, and dangling metal earrings, and Humira, with her elegant new boy cut and freeing blue jeans had been a call to arms. Though Humira was polite to the patriarchally-indoctrinated girl, she represented all that was wrong with the modern woman, shrill and demanding, independent and slutty, un-checked by either by head scarf or dupatta.

More than the men, it were the women who could not abide by her prosperous spinsterhood, her independence—an object of abstract desire, just out of reach, the one thing the patriarchally-privileged girl could not have, transferred from father's to husband's house. Although Humira had failed to take that final step and continued to live in her parents' home; it troubled her more than she would admit that Alki of all people had taken that first step. The women she knew were always subtly making things hard for her with their unceasing subliminal antagonism, and their insistence that she play by their rules of manipulative subterfuge instead. And by far the worst of them were the women who stood by the reputable man—possibly a son, a brother, or a husband; women who would not believe her because they begrudged her, her independence, her freedom from the patriarchy they defended.

But one thing she would not let go of, and it was also something women could not tolerate about her, was her repudiation of the virtue of humility. Humira flaunted her arrogance. She enjoyed being a business owner and talking down to people, undercutting them, especially women, and making them feel insecure and threatened. Someone like Alki, with her show of meekness offended her theory of everything.

Intuitively, Humira knew why she was expected to be the personification of humility and timidness, *a la*, Alki. It was just that much easier to control her if she was pliable. After the incident with her cousin, Humira began to understand how the world operated. He had taken advantage of her modesty, literally. Women were trained to be submissive, and if they were dutiful and sacrificial, good things would come to them in the end, like inheritances, devoted progeny, and suitable husbands. But she reckoned the opposite was true. The more submissive they became, the easier they were to govern, with crumbs of destiny being thrown at them to distract them. Women could plot away from the sidelines like they did on her mother's serialised TV shows, but they were perpetually ancillary to the principal story. It was altogether egregious that she was not allowed to star in her own life, and she took pains to flout that subconscious rule every opportunity she got.

She swung her long legs out of bed that morning and hurried into the bathroom. It was her younger sister's wedding day, and this one Humira could not avoid, as she had done all others. Her mother had thrown down the gauntlet that she don a sari and she had capitulated in the face of her mother's vehemence, a woman just as forceful as she. She hadn't worn one in years; in fact, she had her hair long on that horrible day and she could not forget the slick polyester of the yellow sari on the day of the incident with her cousin, try as she might. She had felt so guileless and demure. Since then, she had not liked long hair, saris, or the resulting exposed midriff. If someone grabbed her again, she would ensure there was fabric between her skin and their creeping fingers. On that day, the yellow sari had tied her up and tripped her. She remembered the tremulous running, hair streaming into her eyes, taking focus away from the stony ground, the containing, circling fabric congesting her legs, and it catching under her slipper, and she falling hard on her face, with him behind her chuckling at her childish fear.

At the entrance of the wedding hall, when Humira and her relatives arrived early that morning, they were greeted by two banana plants propped up at the portal. As her aunts and uncles streamed in, Humira stopped, overwhelmed by a sudden foreboding. The bananas were harbingers, signalling something. She was about to enter a netherworld where there would be no separation between her sleeping life and waking life. One of her aunts turned around and called to her. Snapping out of it, Humira walked through into the big hall packed with a disarray of plastic and metal chairs.

Up front, a four-sided wedding platform had four lush banana plants set up at its corners. As they entered, five priests were finishing up a consecrating ceremony at the foot of the platform, leaving behind offerings of fruit, marigolds, and burning incense. Hypnotised by the scene, Humira walked up to them, and they stopped to glare at the uppityness of a trousered woman, impudently stepping in their midst. Humira gawked wondrously at the strange recreation of a scene from her dream world, before the angry male scowls made her look away at last. She turned towards the dressing room milling with female relatives and friends of the bride, all assisting the bride with her embroidered sari and make up. Her younger sister handed Humira a package.

She said, "Didi, this is for you…Mamma and I chose this for you, I hope you like it?"

Humira was not thrilled, as she knew the package contained a sari. She had not even wanted to visit the shops with them and choose one on her own, so they had bought one for her. Her sister's friends offered to help her, but she said no, telling them that her friends were on their way. Tana, Jas, and Alki arrived within 15 minutes and went straight to the dressing room. The friends tore open the brown-paper package and Jas cooed a bit at the folded sari inside. Humira did not even want to look at it, she just wanted it over with. They took it out, unfolded it, and as they started to wind it around her, Humira began to feel breathless.

She said softly, almost inaudibly to them, "I can't move, it's too tight."

Alki who was crouched down pulling at the pleats in the sari at floor level heard her and looked up at her friend. She had never seen her this uncomfortable.

"What's wrong Mira?"

"No, I am fine, just a bit tight…constricting," she replied, noting the kindness in Alki's face and grateful for it.

Jas said, "You feel this way because you never wear saris. Look at me and Tana, we can run and jump in these if we want."

Humira took a good long look at the bejewelled twosome.

"I will hold you to that. I will arrange for long jump and high jump at the track at our college tomorrow, and you both better turn up in those," she said, wagging her finger at their elaborate ensembles.

Alki laughed out loud, she couldn't help but enjoy the crestfallen expressions emanating from both Jas and Tana. Humira was caustic, therefore alive and well. Jas and Tana did her hair after finishing with the sari, dotting her head with small diamante clips.

At one point, Humira said, "Enough," peeling away from them.

"I need some air…a glass of water."

The four left the hubbub of the dressing room. At the entrance to the hall, there was a clamour with relatives gathering around to receive new arrivals stepping out from a brown SUV. Humira's mother was at the head of the congregation. The reputable man had arrived with his mother and sister. Alki and Jas simultaneously observed a shift in stance, almost a shrinking of Humira's posture. She was flinching. But after a fleeting instant, Humira metamorphosed, pulling herself up in height, her face stony and angry, the faux diamonds on her cropped head catching the light to match the stormy grey green in her eyes. She walked forward into the gathering, with her friends close behind.

She came up next to her mother and whispered fiercely into her ear, "I want him gone. I told you not to invite him, I don't want him here."

Stunned, Humira's mother said, "This is not the time. I told you before…Go away…please for god's sake."

The reputable man had walked up to the gathering just in time to witness the frantic whispering between mother and daughter.

He said, "What's this, Mira?"

Humira turned her full fury on him.

"Don't ever call me that again. I want you to leave now."

The reputable man said, "You are stuck in the past, Mira."

Then he skulked back, humiliated, livid. An abrupt quiet descended on the group, which only emphasised the whine of Humira's mother pleading.

She said, "Please don't do this here…please, I beg you."

Humira's father appeared.

He said, "Mira, listen to your mother…please. Don't spoil your sister's day."

Her father's words withered Humira. Then, dark eyes flashing in a face framed in rosy, amber hues, Alki stepped into the breach, and so did Jas and Tana. The three stood next to each other, a wall of women, their saris iridescent, closing the gaps between them, so that not one of them could ever fall through again, overlooked and disregarded.

Alki said to the reputable man, "If you have any self-respect, you will leave now."

This seemed to dumbfound the man, Humira, her mother, and even her father. A stamp of stupefaction appeared on the reputable man's sister's face. She had no idea what was happening. Alki's cloak of empathy extended for a moment towards the girl who was collateral damage trapped in her brother's deceits. That girl would be an easy target for Humira's thwarted wrath. There was a pause, a torpid few seconds in which everyone was silent, immobile, and no one knew what to do, moments in which Humira un-shrivelled, gathered herself to her full height once again and joined her friends. Together, they glowered.

From the interior of the hall behind them, a loud crashing noise broke the spell. All of them wheeled around reflexively. One of the banana plants, propped up in the corner of the wedding platform, had toppled aslant into the offerings left behind by the priests, scattering fruit, flowers, and lit incense sticks into the spectators. No one was injured; only the wedding guests up front were a bit shaken. By the time Humira and her friends turned back around from the commotion, the reputable man, his mother, and sister had disappeared. They had left. Humira's mother teared up, mortified and anguished by her daughter's outburst in this public forum. Her father tried to comfort her to no avail.

To Humira, she said sobbing, "How could you do that to a mother with a son? I am just a mother with daughters."

Humira said, "Someone should have taken on a mother with a son years ago…"

Around them, relatives hissed and mumbled indignantly.

Her father said, "You are heartless Mira, please stop now..."

Humira stepped aside, hurt, and so did her friends. They found some seats away from the throng at the back of the hall. Relatives strolled past them whispering at a safe distance, treating the four as if they were untouchable. During the ceremony, however, her sister called out for her, and so the four friends made their way to the wedding platform.

Humira heard her mother muttering urgently to her sister, "Get your cousin to do that, there's no need for her."

And her sister said, "No…no…I want Mira."

As she neared the platform, her mother seemed increasingly pained and aggrieved and Humira could not look her in the eye. The groom entwined the black wedding thread and pendant around the bride's neck, and it was left to the bride's sister to tie the knot securely in the nape of her neck.

Humira bent down, knotted the *mangalsutra* and her sister whispered in her ear.

"Didi, you did not spoil anything. Don't listen to them."

Humira's eyes brimmed, and she kissed her sister's cheek quickly before letting go.

Back at the distant chairs, Humira said, "Do you know how many times in my life I have been told that I was making a scene? My mother gets this weary expression on her face…she starts rubbing her brow as if she's got a headache coming on. I think I like to make a scene just to see that expression. My whole life she has wanted me to be quiet and not call attention to myself or her…I couldn't do it..."

Alki said, "Mira, you are better than me. I ran from "scenes". I hated being stared at when I had to confront anyone. I hated feeling embarrassed because others would look at me thinking what's wrong with her, why is she making a scene?"

Tana said, "You probably feel that way because in every shopping mall almost every day some woman or the other will be making a scene because she was frisked or wanted to cut in line. You…should…feel embarrassed. We don't feel it enough."

Jas said quietly, "That's different. You are talking about silly entitled women. I don't think that's what Alki meant."

But Tana said, "See, that's the problem. Because of them, no one knows the difference anymore."

There was a pause, and then Jas said, "I don't think I can sit through another wedding lunch. Let's go to my house for lunch."

Alki and Tana were both relieved.

Jas said, "Mira, you coming?"

Surrendering, Humira said, "Yes…thanks Jas."

Jas said to Tana, "Call her sister later and tell her Mira's with us."

On this strange day, Jas would call Humira Mira, and as Tana's guard was down, she would take orders from Jas.

18

In the Shadow of the Bael

At the admittance to the Penumpara goddess caves was a gnarled illustration of an old Bael tree. The famously trifoliate tree had become such an object of veneration that a temple had been constructed around it to consecrate the tree. This temple then became famed for the elixir made from fruit collected from this tree and other Bael trees growing around the caves. A temple priest offered this elixir as prasad in dollops on cupped palms of supplicant devotees circling the sacred structure. It was also sold in small lapis blue apothecary jars at an authorised shack at the bottom of the hill, as gifts for relatives who were unable to make the little trek up the steps to the rock-cut caves. The blue jars had made their way to far shores, into the temple rooms of migrant devotees where they shared mantel space with bottled Ganges water and other sacred trinkets.

The elixir was cooked in batches whenever the ripe fruit came into season in an ancient cavern kitchen behind the shack. The potion was made from a secret recipe handed down in the family of the chief priest. A passage from the kitchen led into a misty cave deep inside the hill where jars of the stuff were sent to be preserved. Scientists investigating the caves and given permission to examine jars dating back more than a hundred years stumbled upon a previously undiscovered troglodyte microbial species living inside the cave that had lent its qualities to the elixir.

From distant places, pilgrims disembarked at the nearby bus stop hoping to pay obeisance to their god, and then imbibe the blessed elixir, renowned for its rejuvenating properties, legend turned datum, to which pious wayfarers gladly gave attestation. Long before the microbiologists, botanists had examined the Bael trees on the hill and declared, that though these were indeed Bael trees just like all the others that grew in various temples and countless gardens, the ones that flourished on the hill around the goddess caves had apparently sprouted from wild seeds, and each one was therefore different, unique, unlike saplings got from nurseries, which were mostly grafts of preferred popular varieties.

The mystery of the temple's elixir was far from Yug's mind when he got down at the bus stop with his mother-in-law, his wife, and friend Alki in the heat of high noon. His father-in-law had promised to see to the children that day after they returned from school, as his mother-in-law had been keen to accompany them to the Bael temple. Alki was not so keen on the famous Bael temple as she was about the abandoned cave temples behind it, which were maintained by the government as a tourist attraction. Yug watched with a sense of detachment as Jas tried to beg off from the trip saying this was more a Yug and Alki thing, and besides she had to see to their children. Curiously Alki had persisted, sponging arrows from his wife's quiver, suggesting calling Humira to accompany them, as she was downcast after her sister's wedding. Finally, someone was getting their way with Jas, and Yug was surprised that it was Alki.

Humira had insinuated herself into Jas's family in the few weeks after her sister's wedding with only Jas to seethe in silence at the intrusion into her most intimate space, her family home, into which she had let in only a couple of her closest friends, including Yug, now her husband, and Alki, both of whom had always maintained a respectable distance, choosing not to meddle in her dominion over her parents. Ostensibly Humira, who had years before detected a tautness between Jas and her mother, was coming over to learn gardening and landscaping from Jas's mother as part of a new business tangent.

Jas's family had presumptively taken her in after Humira had become more or less an orphan in her own home, persona non grata. Even Humira's father had turned away from her. Unlike other men, emotionally he knew where his bread was buttered. Most wives were desperate for their husbands to choose them over their mothers-in-law and even their own daughters, and her father had figured that out for himself for the sake of his peace of mind, although he would continue to work at his daughter's office, acting as the peaceable intermediary between her and her many angry dealers. Bereft, Humira was grateful for this one paternal concession.

Humira's influence began to reshape the mother that Jas knew. She began validating her mother in ways Jas had never done. Her mother, for her turn, becoming simultaneously silly and more Machiavellian than usual, using Humira's regard as a tool to have power over her own daughter, power she had not enjoyed before. What Jas begrudged most was unsolicited advice from her friend about how best to deal with her mother, with Humira declaring to her one day that her mother talked more to her than she did to Jas.

Humira and Alki envied friends like Tana and Jas for the extended network of friends and family surrounding them in imperceptible webs of love and affection. They were never ever really, truly lonely, though they bemoaned their friends' betrayals and complained about sophistries in their mutual circles. But there was always someone to turn to for solace on these occasions. Humira had unravelled her web and so had Alki, for people like them there was no consolation to be had from any quarter. But here was Jas getting a taste of something that previously only Humira or Alki had suffered. Both had at least one parent who did not love them, while Jas was loved by both of hers. They could not get away with anything the way Jas routinely did. But with Humira inserting herself into Jas's intricately woven web of familial comfort, Jas suddenly experienced the displacement of looking in from the outside, with not even her father taking her side when it came to Humira, who was definitely no Alki, the outsider; Humira was far more insidious. She was an in-betweener.

According to the world in Jas's head, there were three kinds of people in this world. Insiders, who were self-run folk, surrounding themselves with love and useful networks that helped them through life; the outsiders, who for reasons unbeknownst to them, lived by eschewing the conservatism and conformity of such networks, even though they wanted to be loved just as much as the insiders. Either they lived completely off grid, or they ended up unable to get any work done. Then there were the sneaky aspirational in-betweeners, they were neither inside nor outside, and they wanted what both the insiders and the outsiders owned by default, and were full of resentment till they got at their unnamed object of desire, which changed with time and shifting goals. Ultimately, they coveted the same things—they wanted love, they wanted validation, and they wanted their peers to salute their worth—but used different tactics to get there.

The most important aspect of the three kinds of people, which Jas had not yet understood, was that all of them claimed to be the other kind, even though their real status was mostly obvious to others. Each one's perception of what he or she was, differed from what they really were. And there was no quiz to take to find out either. The insider was always defensive, contending they were an outsider; the falsely modest outsider would say they were in between. The in-betweener was always spiteful. Even after they got inside, from the vantage of having attained "insidedom", they tended to look grudgingly at its inhabitants, as if they were still on the outside looking in. Because boundaries were never exquisite, they were really all in between, intersecting to some 'nth degree.

From Humira's new vantage in the sanctum sanctorum of Jas's house, the days were sunnier than usual as long as the divine Jas wasn't glowering around. She loved being loved, softening and flourishing in the company of a less paranoid, more sanguine foster family. She didn't feel like a hostage anymore, except when she went home at night to be confronted by the discomfiting fact that her mother was trying to flip the narrative in her absence, prudently playing victim to prying relatives. At Jas's house, Humira could let down her hair, figuratively, which she had never done in her own home in the presence of her own mother, who had a chronic repugnance for her and vice-versa, an ailment that sometimes took root between mothers and daughters. An astrologer had told Humira's mother a few days after she was born that the child would bring her no good. Her mother had told the tale for years, so much so that even Humira knew that she was the cursed one. No one told her mother that an astrologer's prophecies could be self-fulfilling. To have a cursed child, there was really no need for divination, all she had to do was to go about treating the child in such a manner as to bring about the prophesied transformation.

Humira did not tell anyone that her mother was trying to replace her with a changeling of sorts. A cousin of theirs had come to stay and her mother more or less adopted her, snubbing Humira and showering all her underlined affection on the new arrival. That cousin became a constant companion to Humira's mother, accompanying her to weddings and other family events. As Humira's status in her house became untenable, her mother stopped calling her to the table when lunch and tea were served. When relatives visited and asked for her, her mother would pretend that Humira was at the office, even when she was at home.

She tried to stay in the office longer, deciding not to come home for meals or she would sneak off to Jas's house for a quick tea-time snack. One night, her mother even reprimanded her about spending so much time at Jas's and that she should come to her own house for tea, as people were starting to ask about her prolonged absences. Through it all, her father, the good man, stood by, unwilling to say more than one excoriating word or two to his wife.

When Jas got down from the bus at the stop near the Bael temple, she didn't note the crowds or the pervading smell of ripe fruit at the junction from all the fruit shops. Humira's intrusion was on her mind, more than she wanted to admit. She had tried to complain to Alki about it, but Alki remained adamantly reluctant to denounce Humira, no matter how much she led her to say the words, which only made Jas promise to herself that the next time Alki complained about someone to her she would not take her side. Everything always came down to sides. The world was sectioned off into sides and to Jas, "whose side are you on?" was the only question ever. Alki was trying to complicate a very simple question.

The party of four did the temple run with other pilgrims, accepting their dollops of the indefinably citrusy Bael elixir before Alki made them all tread the trail to the abandoned caves, which took them through a thicket of spiny wild Bael trees. As they neared the cliff-side cave entrance, sunshine and bird song fell away to be replaced by a sullen cold damp, created by the soaring hunk of basalt before them blocking out the sun. They entered with trepidation. Alki found it beautiful, as only she would a wild place, and looking over at Jas and her strained expressions she knew what most other people would think of a place like this. There were discarded flowers and lines of ash from burnt-out incense sticks under raw stone reliefs of fierce earth goddesses. There was still worship going on even though the focus had shifted to the Bael temple years ago.

They switched on their phone torches and walked amongst the stone rubble. Jas's mother, put off by the dark musty damp, announced she wouldn't go any further and would wait for them at the entrance. As Yug and Alki regarded the reliefs, which had been painted once, Jas sighted an orange glow at the end of the path. She started to proceed down the uneven track tentatively, trying not to trip herself up. The path descended, the glow at the end getting brighter as she approached. She came upon a natural cave amphitheatre that even had a step row carved into the rock just before a glowing wall. Mesmerized, Jas sat down on the step and gazed up at the luminous wall.

As her eyes adjusted to the shimmering darkness, shadow words began to appear on the wall only to disappear an instant later. Jas blinked her eyes at the vanishing words. "A plot…A plot…A plot…A plot…"

The words seemed to shift shape and become humanoid. A woman's form manifested on the wall, and Jas started to hear a whisper, which got louder, and raspier, then she heard a woman's angry voice speak in a slow shout.

"You grew up in a miasma of invisible resentments, mostly yours and those of others that you could sense. Then you learned to channel and hone these into intricately crafted stories, which said just enough, but never a lot so as to give your sly game away, which was to take potshots at the people you still resent and have always resented. It is the same people you talk of over and over again, the people who did not take you seriously when you were low. You are careful not to praise or criticise too much the people you admire, the ones who you assume have used their cunning to survive just like you. And you will never forget those who saw through you and labelled the thing they saw in you… you will always be their high enemy and tell them that labelling… judging…that's the word you like to use, is a low art. You can't stand labels because the cunning work by skirting categories always avoiding, being pinpointed, knowing the difficulty in describing instinct. But…words…your words, each one is a label, they have meaning, they will give away your true intentions, your contradictions…"

The voice trailed off.

The shadow grew, its two-dimensional hair springing up in the flatland of the wall, its voice guttural, accusing, "…if a label lands on you, when someone has found you out, you will try to shake it off, you will rage against it, your quick anger will unhinge your cunning. All your intricately crafted high equivocation will return to its origins in spite..."

The strange speech riveted Jas. It seemed to soak into her very being, echoing deep into her, it was awful and bizarre, even though she had no idea what any of it truly meant. Never had she felt this uncomfortable, never before had she felt found out.

Then another voice behind her, a kind one, called out her name making her jump in fright, although seated.

It was Alki.

"Jas…where are you?"

The enchantment over, Jas said, "Here…I am here."

Slowly she got up. The cave was dank and dark now, with no words on walls, no glow, and no voice. Jas switched on her phone torch. Alki found Jas standing, shivering at the end of a descending path. Jas squinted and waved her phone at Alki.

She almost fell against Alki hugging her close, then in her ear, she whispered, "A plot."

She paused, then said, "I am sorry."

Alki was bewildered. Her friend must have been lost and frightened. But Jas's mind was turning over rapidly. Her burst of remorse was quickly overcome by abrupt quiet rage. Alki's madness was contagious, it had spread to her. She needed the rage to overpower the snarling voice and its brood of words. It was so much easier to blame Alki than the Bael trees and their famous potion.

19

A Hum of Sunflowers

He sat down among them, the sunflowers and the buzzing bees, in a warm yellow meadow feeling lit from the inside. The steady hum of insects coming and going from their plentiful nectaries enclosed him completely. Yug had been examining the cave walls a little unglued by the glaring eyes of the goddesses following him around, wondering about the expertise of the people who had carved those angry, fish-shaped eyes here a hundred or more years ago. Even more bizarre, the angry eyes were familiar. He hadn't noticed the path he was on, which seemed to bring him to a cave entrance, another one. The dark cranny opened out into an open field of wildflowers dominated by sunflowers, bounded on all sides by walls of basalt.

The lost humming meadow immediately stopped the whirring in his head, a welcome pause in the ever-present disquiet over wife or children or mother. The strange yellow came with a hypnotic frequency that made him more self-aware than usual. With their winking dark-brown centres, these one-eyed yellow aliens standing up on one green leg each heralded the existence of a new conscious realm that he hadn't paid attention to afore. Gazing into the earnest ochre of the sunflowers, he wondered if he had been depressed before this moment.

Yug had always been charismatic and brilliant, and most ordinary, when he was self-absorbed. He had succeeded in his start-up business where others had failed because of his calculated everydayness. Except for a few, not everyone saw through his quietude, it had been enough for him to pass among most people basking in the glow of the boy-next-door archetype. The products of his narcissism were the interesting ideas he came up with, that he sold to his company for enough money to keep his wife happy, only that she wasn't. She seemed to be depressed too. But he had chosen her over Alki.

And how could he ever tell Alki that she hadn't been interesting enough for him? He disliked how she wallowed and disappeared into nothingness; she was a wallflower, although, he could never break her heart by telling her that. Jas, on the other hand, was beautiful, self-absorbed and devastating to his happiness, his stability. He could be mean to her, and she was mean right back, and in all these years together, he had never known her to shrink in defeat. Sure, he was at this pass today because he had chosen her, the person who was eternally animated. She wanted to live so much she would hurt the people around her. Jas spent so much time ministering to herself that she had no time to minister to others. Jas was of the opinion that everyone should be ministering to themselves, she had learned that from her father.

Yug was a lot like Jas, he had to concede that to Alki. Like Jas, he had crafted his self-absorption into a fine art, so that hardly anyone called it out anymore; except Jas was touchy when someone did, and he wasn't. In his case, the person who called it out was usually Jas, especially when she liked to say he suffered from male entitlement. He had worked hard his whole life to get to where he was today, even personally, having had to compromise both with his wife and his mother. For his wife's happiness, he had agreed to go live with her at her parents' house. He was always apologising for everything to his mother, so how was he entitled? How had he taken away their space or agency? He had heard that last word a lot recently and wasn't even sure what it meant. Instead by compromising, he had given away his own space and 'agency'.

But while admitting this last thought to himself, he knew he had to be careful, as there was no sympathy in today's world for a man complaining that he had lost his entitlement and power to label a manipulative pushy woman, like Jas, or that one woman shark at work he knew, an ignorant imbecile, which he was often tempted to do, but didn't. Now a male imbecile to Yug was a very funny, piteous creature who no one would defend and was expendable.

He was one step ahead of both his wife and father-in-law because they could not really be sure anymore if he was mocking them. He had learned from the best, his father-in-law. He had been sly enough to learn. His father-in-law had never bothered with ordinariness, and had no need for it, which was one of Yug's most important defences. Yug had worked on it, paring it down to an unseen badge of honour, using it to spot other people's weaknesses, even his father-in-law's, a pompous self-regard that rendered him blind on occasion. Yug mastered the art of prodding him quietly without getting him riled up. If he had been an entitled male as his wife insisted he was, he would have made a spectacle of his contempt like his father-in-law.

Another useful defence he learned from him was that fine-tuned satire was a cover for biases. He could pass off his prejudices, hypocrisies, and contempt for others very easily in the cultivated ambiguity of satire and most smart people would be forced to swallow it, even though they took offence, because the satirist had the advantage of the emperor in his new invisible clothes. His audience of smart people, who always admired any evidence of satire, would idolise it. They had to continue to appear smart in the face of satire directed against them, disarmed by the very thing that they had fawned over, they would have to grin and bear it, and say they understood it. Or God forbid, they might be called humourless!

In many ways, the legacy of satire from his father-in-law had saved Yug. Unlike Alki, he had transformed in the tutelage of Jas's family. He was no longer diffident or self-defeatist, instead he had developed a talent for multi-speak, a defensive tactic he used while speaking with competitors and naysayers, never articulating a single idea, but multiple conceptions designed to disarm and confuse, which helped him cope with the malicious, disabling disdain of others. Ultimately, he would realise it was not just directed at him alone. The clever ones disparaged anyone around them that puzzled or threatened them. Their disdain was their insecurity that he had come from behind and had somehow outstripped them.

Yug would surpass his smart father-in-law, who was a blustery man at the best of times, indignant that others did not immediately acknowledge his importance. Yug had the same predilections, only he was mindful to go about them furtively from behind the cover of the boy next door. He had not progressed, however, to the extent of other men he knew, walking among them unobtrusively, successful boys-next-door, who hid their conniving and casual malevolence in melodrama and a desperate need to be liked.

He could live without what he knew to be a toxic variety of aggrandising self-regard. Such men were always careful about how they appeared to others. They would turn the women in their orbit into objects of fixation, or nurturers and coping mechanisms, something he had never done to Jas, perhaps his mother, but not his wife. Jas had taken a leaf out of their book for sure, as one part of her misogyny consisted of her trying to turn meeker friends, like Alki or Tana, into providers of comfort, a home-grown support staff. Tana had womaned up long ago to the duplicity and quit in loud protest. Alki, on the other hand, had submitted to his wife's dissembling, which said a lot more about Alki than his wife.

Around him, the bees seemed to be buzzing shriller. Their winged acrobatics were somehow, if it were possible, synchronised;

the movements were not random as they were moments before. They swarmed into the open sky above the field streaked with orange and purple clouds, flying hither and thither, pitching and yawing in a mesmerising display, like a murmuration of starlings. They formed a dark cloud above his head, as they moved en masse toward the cave entrance to hover and buzz in formation. The sky above him dimmed, greying the yellow of the sunflowers. He blinked his eyes again, then one more time, because there was a dark shadow of a woman at the entrance from which he had emerged. The darkness was not from shade, but from a shroud made of a heaving multitude of bees, her skin was crawling with them. Yug stood up straight, alert, afraid.

The intense drone of the bees resolved into a voice, a woman's voice, and it spoke to him.

It said,

"Why have you divided the word into light and dark?

Because there is a day and then night?

Why did you think light was everything and night its opposite?

Did you not see how the light of day only lets you see the earth around you,

the green of trees, the yellow of flowers, and it wipes out everything else?

Did you not see more at night?

You can see other worlds in the heavens,

You can even see in the moon a ghost of sunlight

from the other side of the world.

Why did you divide your life into good light and bad dark,

only to sleep it away?

Why did you make me frail, and take away the power of the night

to see more than you?

You made me dark and gave yourself, the sightless light,

all the essence of my world."

The last words dissolved into the drone. It, the woman, was now closer to him standing in the field of sunflowers. She was so close, his heart was thumping hard, and he almost stopped breathing. From inside the heaving mass of bees, he could suddenly see beautiful dark eyes glinting at him angrily. All he had to say was one word for the swarm of bees to dissipate, for his world to return to what he knew it to be.

"Alki."

A cloud of woman-shaped bees roared into the sky, levitating, lifting the angry, staring eyes with them. The insects suddenly scattered in all directions leaving behind a hovering woman to fall into the field below. He ran up to the fallen woman, bent down on one knee and gently lifted her head and torso, cradling her, the blacks of her eyes had rolled over into her head leaving behind only white. He was more than worried, he was terrified for her, having no idea what he had just witnessed.

Again, he said, "Alki?"

She blinked, turned her head and stared up at him with those familiar brown eyes he had loved. There was no more anger, only weariness.

She said, "I came looking for you and I couldn't find you…Jas wanted you, she got lost. There was this light at the end of a tunnel and then it went dark."

Yug said, "It's okay…you're okay now."

Alki said, "I don't understand, what happened? Where are we?"

He let go of her when she tried to sit up and sidle away from him. She looked around at the sunflowers.

Yug said, "I found this place. I think it's a wild meadow inside the hill."

After a pause, he said, "You must have been sleep-walking."

"What? How can that be? asked Alki.

"I was very much awake."

Yug did not tell her about the bees or the strange voice that had spoken to him or what it had said to him. He must have been sleep-walking too, he thought unconvinced. The two of them sat silently together among the sunflowers, and just for a moment after a sideways glance, Alki wondered about what could have been, but quickly marshalled all such ideas out of her head.

For Yug, the vision of Alki and the bees was a revelation. He had been wrong about her. The woman beside him was perhaps a wallflower, but it was because he had chosen to see her that way. It was a perception that he had created and participated in, as he had been unable or perhaps unwilling to see in her anything besides what he wanted to see. As soon as he thought all this, he knew his insight had come too late.

Perhaps he had been struck by madness in the meadow. Was there a dormant malfunction built into his brain that something on this basalt hill had triggered? He had heard stories of such things happening all the time. Didn't people see ghosts? Weren't his friends seeing ghosts?

Malfunction was probably built into the brain and served a very important biological function during pre-religion, such as a primitive form of precognition and soothsaying. Some people would go to sleep at night and their brains would stitch together known images and objects, and they would wake the next day to find a strange connection from their dreams the previous night to happenings of the present day or the next. But whatever primitive perceptive function these glitches served; they could easily go awry. If a child lived in a family of glitchy people, exposed long enough, the child would imitate those glitches, Yug believed. In the absence of religion, children could be saved from imitation through a decent public education system that could expose the forming faulty brain to texts and fiction that the brain could feed upon to reason with itself. Reasoning could overpower fundamental error by acting as a type of useful mindfulness.

Yug savoured the possibility that the same glitch responsible for the birth of religion could also be causing some forms of psychiatric anomalies. Could it be that we just coded our glitches and turned them into things like prophecy, religion, and astrology?

He was deep in thought, but then he gazed at Alki and said, "Come, let's go back. Maybe I should tell you what I saw, though you might think I am crazy."

Yug told Alki about her, the bees, and the strange speaking drone of the insects.

Alki said, "I don't think you are imagining anything. There's something about these caves and the land where my house is coming up, which is not far from here. I was told that the caves in this hill might go all the way to where I am building the house. This place is somehow connected...to me."

She paused.

"Yug…I am being haunted by something…a woman I think."

She had her head in her hands.

"I am tired, but I need to know why this is happening."

Yug said, "I was sceptical before. I tried not to believe any of it, but I do now. I don't know how you did it, but those bees came to you, they knew you, if that is even possible. And I believe I am a rational man."

20

Skinny Jasmine Petals

Early in the evening, Alki's mother was alone in the garden under a gargantuan jasmine vine, which had lost itself in the crown of one of their Jamun trees. She sniffed the air to take in the last of the previous evening's divine scent that still lingered. This plant had small, white, non-descript flowers with skinny petals, but they emitted a stout, intoxicating scent in copious amounts, seemingly in violation of bloom size. Unbeknownst to observers, the plant reached massive proportions, misplacing its entirety over a wall into a neighbour's garden and the canopy of a tree next door, climbing into the vast skies towards sunlight, broadcasting its existence only through its moth-enticing scent that would make late evening walkers look around enquiringly in awe.

The vine had sprouted many suckers and several of them were yielding flowers at a height convenient to reach for flower gathering. She would have liked to pick them later in the evening when they opened, but this part of the garden was too dark and weedy for late evening flower raids. She had a knack for picking buds, which were about to open, so she concentrated her efforts on those nascent blooms. The goddess she worshipped was black, rich, and red.

The only way society and culture had found to domesticate her was either by maternalising her or what Alki's mother did instead, which was to imprison her wild attributes in a little framed picture set up on a makeshift altar table in a corner of her kitchen, propitiating her in the evening with the lighting of an oil lamp, and offerings of red hibiscus and the perfume of wild jasmine. Alki had stared at this picture on her way in and out of the shabby kitchen in her childhood and adulthood. The goddess was stepping on a man, had her tongue hanging out and wore a necklace of skulls. Eventually, she was struck by the tremendous paradox between what was depicted in the picture and the world that existed just outside its immediate frame. Her mother appeared to be worshipping a deity that was nothing like her. The goddess violated all the rules of feminine conduct set out for "females" of their realm. And yet this was a popular goddess. The goddess must be providing something that her mother desperately needed because her mother's worship had continued fervently and unabated for almost 35 years. Maybe long before that, possibly a month into her newly married life to a man who pocketed her salary and would not buy her clothes to wear or adequate food to eat. When her first child came into the world she would gladly stop working. What was the point of having a job that only remunerated her husband and she could no longer buy herself a new sari to replace the faded old one?

Under the jasmine, there was tranquillity and obliviousness, and the wild goddess too helped with her melancholia. She could forget her clownishly cruel husband, wilful daughter and cherished son now ensconced in a foreign land, who had announced to her one vacation that his young wife believed his mother complained too much about his father. That had muzzled her, what else did she have to talk about with the people closest to her, other than her anguish? There was no one left to confront her husband, her son would not, and while her daughter did, both husband and son regarded female dissent as insolence.

Surreptitiously, from a depth of which she was not yet aware, she tended to agree with her daughter, as much as she could. But she had to be careful, for her own survival she had to side with the "males". They had everything and she nothing, she lived off their scraps of money and the food that she cooked and was offered to her, at least that is how it felt to her most days. After a time of siding with the men in her household, she began to sound and behave like them, even though she was at the very bottom rung of the boy's club. Alki sometimes was exasperated by her mother's flaccid hostility towards her, as if she were a newly grown stegosaur displaying its plates to keep up with the other males.

But Alki's mother believed her daughter was foolish to build her own house and she had even begged her mother to join her there, but how could she take such a step? Anyway, since her husband had refused to move to the hill, she could not go either. How could two women, one of them old, possibly survive by themselves on a forested hill without male guardianship? They would need protection from male prowlers, ready to rape and take down a woman. Fear of rape was what kept women trapped as nurturers. As men valued and even worshipped feminine nurture, they would protect those types of women, others they would attack or chastise, whenever possible. If something did happen, it would be their fault for daring to venture out into the male realm. This fear and her husband's demanding malice had birthed her agoraphobia. She was sharp in every other way except for this one undiagnosed malady.

When guests came around, she would blend into the surroundings and let her husband do all the talking. No one noticed how she would quietly drop out of conversations, that she had stopped attending weddings, and if she went out to visit relatives it was only when her husband took her out in his car. During the journey, she would keep her eyes closed or she would have taken some of her husband's cough syrup, falling shrewdly asleep and keeping her eyes averted from the outside world. She hadn't taken a walk outside in the world beyond her walled garden in 20 years. Either Alki or her husband fetched things from the shops.

Sometimes she would even get a sympathetic passing relative to collect her tailoring. No one need measure her, as she would always send ahead the measurements the tailors needed. The measurements were never quite true as she refused to go for fittings. As a result, her sari blouses were ill-fitting and made her look common, which provoked the disdain of cultivated women like Jas's mother. If Alki left, who could she ask to fetch her intimate necessaries like the old-fashioned stiff brassieres she liked…her husband? Certainly not. And she was not looking forward to being left alone with her husband with no Alki to act as a buffer in between them. Maybe she was experiencing feelings of abandonment, she had read about that in the newspaper. She had been so ingenious about the workarounds that not even Alki suspected that she had a problem.

If only she had stepped out, she could have observed her husband at work in the neighbourhood during his daily walks, pleasantly chatting up the neighbours, turning them against his wife and daughter, describing the first as a woman who would not support him in his time of need and the other as a disrespectful shrew. If he had one agenda, it was to gain sympathy, he was obsessed with obtaining it, hoarding it. A sadist at home, outside he cut a carefully crafted figure of wretchedness seeking and thriving on the pity of others. It would kill him to lose it one day. His wife and daughter must never, never tell on him. He even cultivated other women, sometimes even in front of his wife, maybe always in front of his wife. His wife was not blind to the message he was sending that she could be easily replaced if she did not measure up to his demands. He often loudly admired Jas's mother for her sophisticated good looks and urbane elegance. When Alki had secretly cried into her pillow for weeks after Yug had thrown her away for Jas, her mother had partaken in her child's pain knowing all too well but unable to tell her that men who sought to commodify the worth of the women they were with were not good enough for her child. It had happened to her but the same should never happen to her daughter.

But as much as she sought to build her daughter up, thanks to implicit cultural norms she also sought to tear her down. Alki's mother assumed that a house of her daughter's own was not only a waste of her hard-earned money, it was also a logistic impossibility. How could her feeble child possibly command an all-male team of workers? Alki's mother knew her gender was weak, men had been handling her affairs for her all these years, and after her husband, it would be her son. Unbeknownst to Alki, her menial role in her mother's life was to be her caregiver. What she did not know was that Alki had found her own workarounds around this presumed weakness. Her daughter's persona at the worksite differed from the one she presented at home. At first, the workers had treated her like a damsel in distress giving her instructions, instead of taking her notes. Even when she told them she wanted it one way, they ignored her. Frustratingly, she could not shout at them or assume a militaristic guise, because a woman shouting at them would prick them, and they would actively rebel or try and take her down. A man giving them commands could get away with a lot more.

Instead, she learned ego-defying patience and became unrelenting about having her way every time. She overheard the workers calling her stubborn one afternoon, a term they would not call a man in her place. Although irked at first, soon enough she was okay with the tag, because stubborn seemed to get her work done. If all she could get from them was a begrudging deference, she would run with it. She could have assumed the dragon-lady facade of female Indian chief ministers to be then left with only those who wanted to mollify her. She needed all hands on deck to give her ideas for her house.

Alki's mother believed she had a child who refused to listen to sound advice and she feared for her safety. She would try again and again to cloak Alki in her own agoraphobia to keep her out of harm's way, but to no avail. She would insist on rejecting the safety net of humility engineered for their gender. Nothing good could come out of a woman's derring-do. She had watched a documentary on television one evening with Alki about the evolutionary ancestors of mammals and what happened to them when the meteor struck 65 million years ago that killed off the dinosaurs. She was engrossed by the information that mammalian ancestors had been scurrying rodents living underground, coming out at night to feed. They were so good at hiding themselves that the exploding meteor could not get to them and when all the dinosaurs were dead, the miniature mammals had the world to themselves. She too had to wait it out. She had heard the legend of her maternal ancestor, a woman with a cruel husband who had waited till death to start living.

Her husband was fiercely opposed to what Alki was doing. It was a dent to his manhood that his daughter would dare build a house of her own. The man had not let her drive his car for the same reason. Alki could have bought her own car, but she never did, and her mother had assumed she had wisely conceded defeat to her father. But then she had upstaged him by starting this house project. Now, all he could do was ineffectually complain endlessly that he had lost face.

She was willing to commiserate with her husband, but she held back sensing that he wanted their daughter to fail at the task she had taken up. That's where she drew a line. The male ego had brought war, monotheism, atheism, militaristic polytheism, populism, and here in her house it had overcome a father's paternal instincts. He resented his daughter having her own money and would rather she failed and have tragedy befall them if something happened to her. He behaved as if he was jealous of her, which was odd and beyond rationalisation. She did not like that her own husband was wishing their daughter harm. She could do nothing about it but watch helplessly and lose herself in the goddess. Alki was now in Her hands.

Lost in thought beneath the jasmine, she hadn't noticed the creeping twilight or the darkness setting in. She began to pay attention only when the jasmine started to release imperceptible clouds of fragrance. She had never been out this late and the scent was overpowering. She turned away from the plant tucking the flowers into the end of her sari drape, and looked toward the house only to stop abruptly torpefied. Most of her flowers fell to the ground. Ahead, two snakes lay coiled and facing the empty space between them, they were separated by about four feet. Then from the reptilian circles they had formed, their scaly rippling bodies rose in unison. She had never seen snakes up this close before. She was bathed in an oily snaky odour her mother had warned her about when she was a child. Living in the city for 66 years, she had been witness to the urban extinction of serpent-kind and the rise of their mutual enemies—the rodents. Suburb dwellers had beaten all the snakes to death, having forgotten the old knowledge that snakes were also the best rat catchers. Living on concrete, humans had left behind most of their ties to the earth, but not forgotten was an ancient dread that made them want to kill anything that moved furtively near them.

Alki's mother was paralysed to the spot, afraid to make the slightest movement. As the two reptiles twisted their bodies, their heads were pointing into the house. She turned her head too and gazed at her house. The window to the living room was open and the lights were on inside. Her husband must have sullenly switched them on in her absence. Past the settee and an old, stained coffee table, there was a wall on which a hall mirror gave the illusion of space, or so her Alki had insisted. Her daughter had hung it there a couple of years ago in an attempt to brighten up the room. She was now able to see into the mirror and its reflection. The two snakes shone back in the mirror image and in the space between them stood a woman in white. Her hair was long, ashy, powdering away, and so were her eyes. The white woman was speaking, but there were no words, at least she could not hear anything. Terrified, she turned her face away from the house, and back towards the two snakes. In the space between them, a golden aura manifested, which contained a familiar woman. She had the darkest hair, her skin was the colour of amber, and from the crown of her head, from atop her thick hair a sprig of leaves shot up into the sky. The woman turned to look at her and smiled. She raised her hand in the universal spiritual gesture of reassurance.

The golden woman opened her mouth and said one word, "Shiuli."

Alki's mother was suddenly gusted by a strong wind, and it almost swept her off her feet. She was astounded…by the sound of her own name…Shiuli. No one had called her that in years. Her husband always referred to her by a colloquial term used in his family to call women. Most Indian cultures had insolent words to refer to younger people and women, ironically, these 'calling' words were deployed casually and it conveyed the sense that such family members were of low status. In their house, the term carried with it all that her husband felt towards her. It was used to put his family's women in their place when they were uppity. He had tried to call Alki by that word once. Her daughter had straightened like a cobra and spat back at him with such venom that he had never called her that again. He tried to teach all the little boys he came into contact with that word. He needn't have bothered, as little boys were very good at imitation.

Her own children called her "amma", and she was "aunt" to her nephews and nieces. The only people who knew her name had died years ago. She wasn't even sure if even her son knew her name anymore. Her husband's name in contrast was everywhere, on all their ownership documents, on the mail that came to their house, and displayed on the marble frontage of their house, he had even shoved it into hers and his children's names. Tears started to stream down Shiuli's face. She sat down in her fallen flowers to be soothed by the scent of jasmine. The woman and her snakes vanished leaving behind a balmy gold aura. Then her husband's voice rang out in the darkness, dispersing the warmth and sending a chill into her bones. From the living room window, his head appeared. He called for her irately, and of course he would not use her name. He was cross, not because she was missing, but it was late, and his dinner had not been arrayed on the dining table. Shiuli got up, looked up for one final whiff of jasmine then walked back into captivity.

21

A Breath of Marigold

She blamed it on the square of fluffy orange blooms. A patch of marigolds, plump saffron jewels studding a mat of thick green, had brought out in her a happy benevolence. Others would have called it her muliebrity, her feminine warmth. Humira hated that word—muliebrity. Why did a fancy word that described the softness of womanhood sound suspiciously like it had something to do with distance-trudging animals of burden? Although it had nothing to do with mules, she had often thought of womanhood that way, as a baby-producing condition that carried the menial burden of Indian joint families across long interludes in time and space. This particular condition seemed to unite the major warring religions and races. Even the hunter-gatherers on lost islands that ran out to throw spears at the unsolicited modernity of helicopters and proselytisers were all men. Where were the Amazons? Once womanhood had done its work, it was pastured out, retired to the position of a dominatrix mother-in-law lashing an unseen whip on unsuspecting, unrelated younger mule women. Manhood, on the other hand, had synonyms like virile and courage to describe it. Even the words in the language reduced her, despised her. But here were the sunny marigolds defying her self-loathing, rewiring her brain just by her looking at them. She was thankful for this interval of orange.

Mothers-in-law were on her mind as Jas's in-laws were on one of their routine visits, having arrived to spend time with son and grandchildren. Jas's mother kept busy with her garden work, and unmindful of her daughter's burden had called in reinforcements in the form of Humira to intersperse her garden spaces with square-foot patches of marigold plants. Her neighbour, the mother-in-law of her daughter's friend Tana, had extolled the gentle spiciness emanating from these plants as very good pest control. Jas had offered to help in the garden that day and though this pleased her mother, the older woman was sceptical and had asked her to watch and learn as she and Humira got the patch ready for the marigolds.

Very happy to be called in, Humira arrived ready to overlook the delicious annoyance on Jas's face. But then despite herself, she started to feel sorry for her friend. Jas's mother-in-law was rude and commanding. Mira watched as the family endured her politely without any of them trying to confront her. The woman was very possessive of her son and doted on her grandchildren, but Jas was another matter altogether. She was a fanatical vegetarian, and Jas's mother kept a second refrigerator in their kitchen to store Yug's mother's food separately, as she would refuse to eat at their house if an egg or a chicken leg had been placed near her food. As this was a non-vegetarian household, she always sniffed at all the food distrustfully. She complained about meaty odours lingering in their house.

Jas had been stage-managing the production of egg sandwiches for her children that morning when her mother-in-law strolled into the wafting aroma of cooking eggs. Humira was in the garden with Jas's mother, and she heard a loud scream issuing from the kitchen. She dropped her tool and proceeded towards the sound in time to see various people, including Yug, scattering in different directions hurrying to remove the offending egged pans, spoons and bowls from the room. Jas was fixed to the spot, chagrin writ large on her face.

Hot pan in hand, Yug was saying, "I am sorry Amma, I forgot. I should have told Jas not to make eggs today. I am sure she didn't mean to..."

Jas said nothing. From her determined countenance, Humira knew Jas had indeed meant to.

Yug's mother said, "No...you always take her side. She did it on purpose."

There was an awkward pause during which no one said anything. Countertops were washed and cleaned in hunched silence by the morning maid and air fresheners were sprayed. Jas removed herself from the kitchen after glancing sullenly at Yug.

Yug's mother noted the appearance of Humira and said sharply to her, "Why are you here?"

Arching her spine and without missing a beat, Mira said, "I heard you scream."

Yug's mother said, "I was not screaming."

Jas, who turned around for a moment to witness this terse interchange did not know how to feel. Jas's mother-in-law kept a watchful, irritated eye on Humira from the windows of the house as the young intruder worked gainfully to plant the marigolds. Jas too was out there looking less molten than usual when her mother-in-law was around.

At one point, when Yug joined her at the window, she said to her son, referring to the stranger in their midst, "Why are they letting this outsider interfere in our affairs?"

Yug said, "Amma...Mira is a very old friend."

She gazed at her son and was struck by the way he referred to Jas's friend Humira as Mira.

Outside, the sun warmed their backs and though Jas was hot and did not like the slimy sensation of mud on her hands, neither did she want to go back inside to the woman whose eyes were boring into her scorched back. Humira was sitting down in the grass undaintily, separating the plants from their plastic receptacles.

She said, looking up at her stooping friend, "For heaven's sake Jas, just sit down. You can change your pants if they get dirty."

Yielding, Jas said, "Okay."

She sat down.

Humira said, "I don't think she likes me."

Jas asked, "Who?"

"Yug's mother."

"Oh, welcome to the club," replied Jas.

Humira said, "I knew she was difficult, but I didn't how much."

Jas smiled.

"People think I am the difficult one, and arrogant to boot, especially now that we live here."

Humira said honestly, "You are difficult…but I am surprised you are not standing up to her more."

"I can't," said Jas. "My mother won't stand for it. And Yug won't either, not after I made him come here to live with my parents. We couldn't afford to get our own house."

"I had to get away…" said Jas, then stopped quickly.

"Sure", said Humira, "I can understand."

She didn't really.

Jas said, "I don't think anyone knows the full extent of it… nobody really wants to know. If I start talking about it, they move on to other topics to shut me up. Do you know she would not let us close our bedroom door at night? I don't think my mother wants to hear such things."

Humira wanted to ask why someone would do that, but she didn't. Perhaps she too didn't want to probe too deep. Poor Jas! My god, she had never thought a day would arrive when she would think the words "poor Jas". She had been abandoned by friends and family to deal with her tribulations as best she could.

As privileged as she was, Jas too could suffer the slings and arrows of gender's fortunes.

Jas said, "I started to worry about my children. They are little sponges…Akku and Dozy…and in the one year that we stayed at Yug's, the kids started to imitate her many superstitions. They were getting fastidious about what they ate, especially about fish and chicken. You don't know with kids, they have these inner lives that no one knows about. They may be one thing outside with their friends, but what they absorb in their homes makes them what they are, their politics, their secret ideologies, school doesn't touch them as much as home does. Even now I have to watch out for them and mind what she's telling them. No one else will. Yug won't, and my mother is too afraid to tell them not to listen to their grandmother."

Jas smiled.

"Of course, my father has no such qualms. He didn't even want to buy that damned second fridge. He said to keep all the meat and veg together. At least that way we would be subjected to fewer visits from her. But my mother insisted…and that was that…"

Humira then said something that would restore Jas's rancour towards her.

"You know your mother doesn't feel like she has a place to say anything or be forceful in the same way you or your father are."

Jas went quiet with anger. Alki would have never said that; she would not have presumed to get in between her and her parents. If Humira could hear her thoughts just then, she would have said that Alki did not interfere because Jas had always treated Alki like a lesser being. Jas liked to make underlings out of all her friends if she could. Neither of them would have given Alki the privilege to think for herself. If Alki had been there that day, she would have been unobtrusive with her opinions. Alki considered Jas's mother's silence only slightly odd. Could the woman perhaps even be grateful to Yug's mother, the only one capable of effecting a take-down of her super touchy, supercilious daughter, who with her father had set up a power structure that kept out both her and Yug?

Jas said tetchily, "I should go back inside wash my hands… change my pants."

She got up and marched away without making any more eye contact with Humira. After washing up and changing, Jas felt an impulse to ring up her friend.

On the phone, she said, "Alki, it's Saturday, what are you doing?"

"I am at the building site," said Alki.

Jas said, "Didn't you say you were not going to go there anymore without us?"

"The architect called. I had a few decisions to make. The brickwork is all done now. The floor tiles are in. It's about the wiring. Anyway, I did call you and Yug. Neither of you picked up. Then I remembered it's Saturday, I thought you might have visitors."

"Oh, I am sorry, my mother-in-law's here. You know how it is. When you are done there, why don't you come over? Humira's here too."

The sun had set, and Yug's mother was taking the air outside on the veranda surrounded by patches of blooming marigolds. It had been worth all the effort of the morning. There was something about all that persistently cheery orange. No wonder people liked them at temples and weddings. Inside, the house still smelled of eggs and her husband was no longer in the mood to listen to her plaints about it. Jas had got her wish, and the old woman was out of the way now. It upset her because she did not get to spend enough time with her grandchildren. The children had a conspicuous preference for their maternal grandparents now. She needed to do something about that quickly. She had insisted and Yug was bringing them over to spend two days of every week at their house. And she made it a point to visit them on Saturday. That was a start anyway, till she got Yug and the kids to move back altogether. Jas could stay with her parents and her servants if that's what she wanted. She and Yug would take care of the children. She would do anything for them.

Jas had walked out one morning two years ago. She had not let her take the children then. Jas and Yug had been at each other's throats for weeks. Two days after Jas left, Yug announced he was leaving with the children to go stay with his wife as the kids were missing their mother. It had been the most traumatic day of her life.

She had asked him angrily, "How can you do that? She left us, abandoned us and the kids. And now you are just going to take them away from me. Just like that."

Yug was suddenly very angry. To this day she could recall how he had jumped up from the dining table, the chair falling to the floor clattering loudly. Akku and Dozy were big-eyed listening to them talk from the other side of the room.

He said, "You cannot talk about her this way in front of her children."

She had replied, "These are my grandchildren and your children. Why are they only hers all of a sudden? The children are becoming rude and pretentious like her and her father. They will only eat fancy food and won't eat the food I make. Sometimes I see they want to, but one look from her and they turn away. Why haven't you noticed any of this?"

Yug knew his mother was right. It was awkward for him. He had indeed noted the burgeoning of affectation in his children, but he loved them and his wife, and more than anything else he valued his peace of mind. He simply chose to go along with whatever Jas wanted for them.

In the veranda, a timeworn unforgotten anger bubbled up inside the old woman once again. The wrath had coiled up deep within her and she had worked away at it, scratching it down to a sore aching nub. And with it came the stench of rotting eggs and meat. Yug's mother lurched back and clutched her nose, pivoting her body towards the front gate. Though it was dark now, the marigolds planted on both sides of the gate cast their orange glow on the gateway, as if it were a portal to another world, and there was a woman there, at least she thought it was a woman. She… it…was old and abnormally white, even its face…her eyes…the chalky white was in her long hair. In contrast to all that awful white, was a garland of the most profoundly orange marigold flowers around her neck.

Yug's mother was overcome by the sour stench of what she could only describe from memory as raw chicken livers, and she collapsed to the floor. For a millisecond before her eyes closed, a sad ashen face gazed down at her. Its dry flaking lips had parted and inside were bowed and buckled, tipped teeth. Its breath was pungent, redolent with marigolds. The bell rang inside the house and Jas opened the door to find Alki standing at the door, pale and alarmed.

She said unsteadily, "I am sorry Jas, your mother-in-law fainted."

Pushing Alki aside, Jas and Yug ran outside followed by her parents and Yug's father. The older woman was coming to now. She sat up surrounded by the whole family. Yug was anxious and concerned.

Slowly, melodramatically she said, "Where are the children?"

Then she stopped suddenly, dumbfounded by fear. She had remembered the white woman, her white eyes…

Alki, still standing at the entrance flanked by Humira, said, "I think this is my fault. I startled her. I came in about ten minutes ago, and I was admiring the garden. The new flowers were so lovely…those marigolds…I didn't see her standing there in the veranda. And then she saw me..."

22

The Dent under the Curry Leaf Tree

Hometown was a dimple in the earth beneath the curry leaf tree, and Alki knew it intimately, the springtails in the leaf litter outside her circle of bare earth, the many ant species that migrated through, carrying their defenceless translucent white babies clutched in mandibles, even the occasional golden rat snake that sent her scurrying, leaving her book behind. Her mother had sat her down there many years ago to be a scarecrow or scare-fly to be exact. Bug-eyed, unibrowed green caterpillars of Common Mormons, brown-red slow-moving butterflies, could strip down a curry leaf tree when a householder's back was turned. Her job had been to shoo away the graceful sail-winged Mormons and stop them from landing on the tree to lay eggs.

That other hometown, which sprawled outside her gate, its many-laned conversations and cultures, was no woman's land to her, never having been allowed out of the house as a child except with an escort of either father, brother, or trusted neighbour. The derriere-warmed ground beneath the curry leaf tree outside her mother's kitchen was the spot where she experienced the reverence that other people called home. There was even an indentation there where nothing grew because she had sat there for hours, for years in the afternoon after school before the mosquitos came at twilight, reading or daydreaming, her life turned inside out. As outside was a place denied. And inside—the house was her father's domain.

This is where she had lived her life, inside herself, the world beyond, a mirage till she happened upon the idea of building her own house. This internal life was mostly unknown to friends, but some friends like Yug would find a way there only to leave. Others who didn't have enough of one were envious. People had evolved to live their lives on the outside, from very early in childhood to imitate the outsideness or the inclinations of others. Among a tight-knit group of family or friends, the internal life was tranquilised by the happy sameness of companionship. The sameness, when enforced was incongruent with interiority. Friends traded traditions, rituals, customs, and body sizes, which were all trends, valuable social currencies, memes and markers of lives lived on the outside in the company of other people.

But Alki soon realised that a rich internal life was even more valuable going by how less magnanimous, intelligent people, deficient in their own interiority, reacted when they intuited signs of it in acquaintances and new friends. Intelligent people prided themselves on their internal lives and they would look out onto the world at other people grading their internalities on a scale. The trouble with that was they would inevitably come across more internalised friends, which would either make them warily malevolent, or the smarter ones among them would make mental lists of their friends' habits and persuasions to take back home to cultivate their own core gardens.

Alki learned to keep her leaky interiority in check when it caused her friends to be mean to her in many ways. While in school she had looked at herself in the mirror and found the image therein to be pretty, dark-eyed, and amber-skinned, not fat or thin, but soon enough the words she would use to describe herself would take a negative turn under the tutelary eye of her friend Jas. Then she lost Yug. And even that had been an internal wound. No one would know to what extent the loss would hit her and undermine her being; they would have called her silly if they had known. It would take her many years to regain a normative mirror image, to realise that the dysphoria, if any was not in her but in the minds of her friends, that they would feel compelled to lash out at her for even the merest suggestion of discernment.

The internal life of literature had saved her. Under the curry leaf tree and its flying Mormons, she absorbed stories. In the imaginary lives that authors created for her, she recognised the forebodings and grudges of her own friends. Fiction turned out to be an extraordinary treasure trove, which contained the secrets of unexamined internal lives. Make-believe was a bridge to the undisclosed, undiscovered country that so many people harboured inside them. It was a weird business, Alki thought, to begin to comprehend the outside world, she had to turn within. Somewhere in that well of stories deep inside was born her house.

She was in her mother's kitchen one hot evening, noting the grease and soot that had collected in clumps on her mother's counters, imagining Jas's mother's reaction to them. She had walked past the goddess corner clutching a steaming cup of ginger tea. Night had set in beyond the dusty steel mesh at the kitchen window. This was her favourite spot in the whole house. This was where she placed herself every routine morning with her fleur-de-lis patterned cup brimming with milky tea when the house was quiet, straining her eyes through the dusty mesh to contemplate the curry leaf tree. At dusk that day, her tree was in bloom. Its secretive sweet floral scent was wafting into her on a breeze, distracting her. She hadn't realised the power had gone out until she heard her parents' voices calling out.

Her mother and father were yelling for candles. The power cut set upon them in the darkness, like a cat among pigeons scattering her parents in a hunt for non-electrical sources of light, stowed away on the grimy tops of cupboards. Alki got one down and timorously walked to the en-suite bathroom in her room, carefully palm-cradling the flame from the puffing breeze ahead of her. She set it down on the basin countertop and flipped up the tap handle to release a fall of water to splash over her sweaty face. She gazed into the mirror, a dampened visage staring back at her. Behind her, murmuring shadows came to life playing about in the dark matter, the candle flame lit up her face in unnerving sepia tones.

It took merely a fraction of a second for the nerve cells in her brain to send electrical impulses across synaptic gaps, for recognition to sink her like a weight strapped to her body under water. She had seen the face again, the face that had haunted her for months now, the white face that had stared down at her sleeping form, the outline in the laterite wall, the face in the ashy tree, the face of the golden woman seated in the tree; the angry eyes in the goddess caves, here they were in the mirror staring back at her, it was her own face, her own eyes.

Alki stumbled out of the bathroom gasping, possessed by the purest fear. She shrieked, calling for her mother.

"Ammaaa."

Her mother was in the kitchen when she heard her daughter's scream. She came rushing into her room with another candle, wax dripping painfully on the older woman's palms and on the floor. Alki was seated on her bed bent over, head in her hands.

She looked up at her mother and said, "You knew, didn't you?"

"What are you talking about Kalike?"

"Amma...why does she look like me?"

Alki's mother teetered and took a step sideways to steady herself.

"I am sorry...I didn't want to scare you."

After a pause, her mother started to speak softly.

"It is a very strong family resemblance that passes down in the matriarchal line. It skips a couple of generations sometimes. I have only ever heard stories about it. The person born with the resemblance is…marked…haunted."

Alki's mother paused, sadness and worry etching her face in the darkness of the room. She sat down beside her daughter.

"My grandmother told me when you were very little that you looked like her. She told me to be prepared. One day…she would make contact with you. All these years, you were okay. I tried to stop thinking about it. I was very disturbed…angry with my grandmother for telling me. I told myself they were just stories and superstitions. I prayed to the goddess every day to protect you."

Alki experienced a surge of anxiety she had only ever felt before in a private dream time that sprouted around her slumbering head at 4 am. She had always thought of it as a strange slice of temporal space generated by her sleeping brain, a realm with no inhibitions or any sensation of up and down, she could be on Earth or on the other side of the universe, inside the skin of her doppelganger, whose life had proceeded in another direction, a dream time in which one day she felt the fear of approaching death and on the next, she tasted unrealised victory.

She said, "I don't understand…I don't understand any of this…"

Her mother was quiet, unsure of what to say.

"...This is why I was against you going up there, to the land, and disturbing things. She had lived there, and she had disappeared there."

Confused, Alki said, "Who?"

Her mother said, "This is just the legend. I am not even sure if it was my great-grandmother or someone much before that, but the story…it keeps passing down. After what my grandmother told me, I never wanted to tell it to you. I thought I could stop the haunting by banning the story, by not telling it anymore."

"She was very unhappy in her life. Now, you must imagine a time long before yours, when there were no opportunities for women. When they were children, they did housework, helped bring up their little brothers and sisters, and cooked for their older brothers. Then in their teens, they were married off. I think she might even have gone to school for a short while, I am not sure if there was a school... you see, the story changes as each person tells it...but one that ended quickly as they needed her labour at home. I don't know if she got enough to eat, it was mostly watery rice and lentils, no meat, no milk. Her teeth grew deformed, and she was very short. She was sure no one would marry her. But one man did. This man was interested in assimilating into the higher station of her family. He would do her the favour of marrying her. She was grateful for a while, but then he became very unkind. If she had been a servant before, she became indentured in her wedded life. Her family knew, but no one would say anything, as they all had their own reasons to keep quiet. Then one day she disappeared."

Her mother looked troubled when Alki asked, "What do you mean, disappeared?"

Her mother said, "No one really knows what happened. Some believe she jumped into the mud well. Others say she just walked into the forest on the hill, never to be found again. They say she was attacked and killed, her body left to be eaten by small animals, and her bones, sucked into the fallen leaves into the earth below. Villagers said she became the forest. That's why they say she didn't just disappear. People in the area kept sighting her. She appeared on forest trails on moonless nights. Some men were found dead in the jungle with no marks on them, their faces seized up, frozen into masks of terror. Her husband was so panicked by the goings on after his wife's disappearance, he took off one morning for another village with his young son never to return, leaving his daughter behind, a girl that looked just like her. After the vanishing, another girl was born in the family that looked exactly like her, and the people in the village said she was a goddess, and they worshipped her. It happened again and again. Every time a girl was born that looked like her, that child would start seeing her, and it would drive them mad, generation after generation. Finally, the family decided to move away from the hill to save their girls. In a nation of prized sons, ultimately something had moved one family to think about its daughters."

Alki's mother laughed out loud.

Alki stared at her mother. There in her face were things she had never before chosen to observe, wildness and grace.

The older woman's countenance softened, then she turned to look at her daughter to say, "And now you want to go back there."

Alki was quiet.

Then she said with resolution, "I do want to go back there."

"Why?" asked Alki's mother, Shiuli.

The daughter said, "I don't think she wants to hurt me Amma. I am terrified every time I see her…but when I think about it… her…there is sorrow in her face…it feels more like she is watching over me, maybe all of us, you, me, even my friends. I have to find a way to get over my fear…I can't help myself, I am still very afraid. I need to understand what she is, why she is here."

Her mother said, "She is a ghost of course."

Alki replied, "Maybe…but that's the name we have given her… goddess…ghost…but what is she really? If we call her a ghost, no one will believe us. There has to be an explanation."

23

The Persistence of Wood Sorrel

Humira could not understand it. She was always angry. Even the mundane task of pulling out the clover-clone wood sorrel, which owned minute yellow blossoms, a persistent garden weed in Jas's mother's garden, proved infuriating. It hadn't been as simple as Jas's mother had made it out. Humira had been warned about their tiny seed pods, which when ripe were rigged to burst open at the slightest touch scattering little black seeds everywhere. She had carelessly seeded the garden that day with a whole bunch of new wood sorrel. As for the tiny spreading plants, they were difficult to pull out, as they shot roots down into hard clayey soil, and once those clasping roots were in the ground they could not be budged. They had to be dug out with effort. In frustration, she ended up shearing away the tops of many of them knowing that they would sprout again bigger and more stubborn from the shaved root tops.

Pottering about her friend's garden, she mused on life, a thing she did not do at work or at home. As she pulled and strained her yoga-honed body, she had the time to dwell on the essence of her indefatigable anger. Her frustrations were not confined to tackling obstinate weeds. She was angry at home, at work, and yoga sessions. What was it about her life that she had not been able to identify? What was it that home and work had in common? She was always having to confront low-level hostility. Was that it? She had become so inured that she had not deigned to pay attention to it. Infrasound hostility was the background noise of her life. When she opened her mouth to speak to someone, their hackles rose immediately, they became subtly truculent with her. What was it about her? Hunching over the persistent wood sorrel in the garden that day, it came to her. It was how her friends went about their lives—in their mannerisms and gestures, in everything they did and said.

All her female friends observed the boundaries of gender as if they wore an invisible veil all the time. Friends like Alki lowered their heads more, made less eye contact, appeared more submissive when required, they made an effort to be sensitive to the ego of the men they were with. She had spoken to Alki's architect a few weeks before, and her friend had later insinuated to her that the man had not taken too kindly to her intervention. Some women like Jas were flirtatious, as they knew how to employ their sexuality in the absence of other kinds of power, others like Tana were artfully obsequious, unassertive and passive; at least she once was. And still others employed religious piety to get their way.

Humira, on the other hand, spoke assertively and articulately, never flubbing her words, a characteristic that annoyed her listeners. Her speaking boom conveyed both self-assurance and grievance. Her defence was that she constantly found herself the lone woman in groups of men, who would insist on talking down to her, infantilising her, "damseling" her. An aggressive, enunciated speaking voice made the more obnoxious among them take notice of her ideas, the men who would have dismissed her directly without notice if she had been a softer, humbler woman. She often heard the words "dumb" and "bimbo" muttered sotto voce in her presence, her punishment for diverting attention away from them.

Somehow, Humira had resisted gender indoctrination and policing when she was growing up. She could never sit still or decorously enough to please her mother, who was constantly frustrated that the girl could not keep her legs together while sitting down, befitting the social graces of a good little girl. When she was thrown a pink party that required her to don a traditional girly outfit on her seventh birthday, she had cried and then thrown a tantrum to upset her mother, who in all these years was never quite able to figure her out. She loathed the elaborate jewellery, favoured by Jas, and most cosmetics. But through it all, she cut a striking figure in her office and among her friends. Even this was resented by some women.

Jas told her sarcastically one day that she was too loud, liked to play 'the man' and treat women badly. That had made her pause for once. Was she unkind to other women? Or was Jas only saying that because Humira was perhaps the only one who made an effort to stand up to her? Did Jas not realise that she had to be loud because no one would hear her otherwise, that everything she did, felt exaggerated to women like Jas or Alki. After all, she was not resigned by nature, like them.

Unlike them, she possessed agency. What was that? She had been hearing that word a lot, that women did not have it. Instinctively, she grasped what it meant. Bizarrely, she had never felt a lack of it in her whole life. She had learned very early on that to have agency or whatever that meant, she could not be humble or docile. She had to exude authority, which also meant thwarting her parents at every step, which she achieved successfully, though at a cost. They found her very difficult to love. Sure, she had never adhered to any feminine grace, she walked with confidence never slouching, and she got things done, never taking no for an answer.

She had been neither deferential, nor rude, and had never been defeated by the processes at work in a man's world, waiting around in corridors with the rest of them, greasing the wheels if she had to, getting requisite permissions for her projects, learning all the tricks, and she had not resorted to feminine wiles. Did all this make her a man? Perhaps it did in the eyes of other women.

She was what they used to call a tomboy, except she had hung on to her tomboyishness as a functioning adult, twisting the accepted norms for her gender. The one time she had allowed herself to be an alluring woman all those years ago to please her mother, she had been preyed upon. She had broken that day.

When a person is shattered by an outside entity, there are many ways to react. Some shuffled through life clumsily, dragging the broken pieces behind them, never quite able to self-repair; still others raged incoherently against the broken pieces and at anyone that got in the path of those shattered bits; then there were people like Humira who stitched themselves back together and made sure that no one would ever view her as prey, ever again. Only prey were forced to be manipulative, and passive-aggressive, only prey would evolve to find workarounds to get the job of living done, only prey would be obedient, only prey would lose their voice, as they did not have agency, or whatever it was they meant by that, damn it to hell! They would have to find other means to strike her down.

She was a pioneer, someone who could go where no one else would, and thrive despite the best efforts of those intent on uprooting her. Even Alki recognised that, albeit reluctantly and enviously. Humira intimidated her. Alki swallowed her spite and tried to study her, and learn from her, especially now that her house project was afoot and she needed the guidance of someone better than her, not Jas…not Yug, but Humira, the conqueror.

A shadow fell on her hunched form and the weeds beneath her. Humira turned around, shading her eyes from the sun. For a split second, she was startled. Her imagination had run wild, probably as a result of the blinding sunlight and sweat in her eyelashes. She thought she saw again the green sparkling wraith from her dreams. But no, it was just Alki, who seemed to have also caught the fleeting expression on her face.

Alki said, "Mira, you alright? Did I startle you?"

Humira said, "You seem to be doing a lot of that these days. What are you doing here?"

Then she smiled and asked, "Have you come to help me with this thankless task?"

She waved her hands over the ground at some small plants that to Alki, appeared to be Irish clover, but not quite.

Alki said seriously, "Why don't you take a break? I need to ask you something."

Humira glanced up at Alki's tone, then put down her tool and straightened her back.

"Okay."

Together they strolled to Jas's mother's garden shed that housed a pretty, fluted washbasin, alongside bags of soil, compost, and a wall decorated with colourful packets of this year's seeds awaiting planting. The wall facing it sported all manner of dedicated garden tools.

Alki regarded the room and said, "Wow Mira, you have become a horticulturist."

Not one to be humble but because it was Alki, Humira said, "C'mon, stop teasing, you know none of this is mine…well, okay, maybe, I am a gardener now."

Alki retrieved her smartphone from her handbag and started to scroll through pictures as Humira dried her hands on a clean towel that Jas's mother had thoughtfully provided for her.

"Mira, do you remember this one? You posted this online? Did you notice anything unusual about it?"

Humira took the phone from her friend and examined the photo inquisitively. It was one of hers. She remembered the day she had taken the picture. Alki prompted her again.

"Mira, what do you see?"

"Impatient much…hold your horses Alki."

Alki waited, stymied, letting her friend take her time.

Then abruptly Humira let out a breath and said, "Ohh…"

Alki jumped.

"You saw something, didn't you?"

"My god Alki…that's…that's…a face. What is that? Why hasn't anyone seen that before? For god's sake, it's been online all this time."

Alki took back her phone and silently scrolled back through her pictures. She stopped at one, then gave the phone back to Humira.

"Look at this one. I think you saw the mud well near the house site. I took this one about a month or so before you took that other picture."

Humira eyed the picture and gulped. Dazed, she could only mutter, "What is this?"

Alki said quietly, "You wouldn't believe me if I told you."

Humira's grey-green eyes shone with light.

"Try me."

They pulled down two packed stools from the tool wall, unfolded them and sat down. Then Alki started to tell her about the haunting.

A few minutes in, an upset Humira interrupted her with, "Alki…no…they attacked you? No…I can't bear it."

Humira got up and hugged her still-seated old friend, which shocked Alki, having never been at the other end of a sincere embrace from her friend before this moment.

"I am fine Mira, nothing worse happened to me. It's weird, I think she took care of me."

Humira took a step back from her and sat down again.

She said puzzled, "She took care of you…?"

Alki finished her story and then without pausing she said, "I want you to tell me if you saw anything that day at the site when you visited."

Humira said, "This is all…too much."

"I am sorry to have laid all this on you," said Alki sadly, "...I... need help."

Humira looked over at her friend in distress, and then she said, "No, wait, let me think about it. I walked past that mud well in the picture. I didn't see anything. I kept walking and I came to a fork in the path. I took the middle path that went slightly uphill, not the one to that beautiful magenta tree and the rock you mentioned.... Oh! yes, I came to this clump of banana plants."

Humira paused, her eyes opened wide.

"You know, I felt something there."

Leaning forward, Alki asked, "What...?"

"Something...was watching me approach. It was inside that clump. I didn't take another step forward. I was overcome by this strange feeling...I don't know how to describe it...maybe... intense dread. I didn't like feeling that way. I turned around thinking maybe someone was following me. But no, there was nothing, no one there. I did not wait around, I went back down to the site."

Alki said, "Why didn't you tell me this before?"

"I didn't think there was anything to tell...what, you wanted me to tell everyone, that your land spooked me and sent me packing? It did not feel benevolent to me, Alki."

Alki was desperate.

"But that's our fear talking Mira. You may not want to say that you are spooked, but I am terrified...my god it looks like me. After I heard my mother's story yesterday, and after all this...I feel different. You know, that's what I was trying to tell my mother."

They were quiet for a bit.

Then Humira said, "Maybe you are right. Do you remember my sister's wedding day? That happened, maybe a few weeks after my site visit, I don't remember exactly now. The dates are blurring. For days before the wedding, I kept having this recurring dream about those damned banana plants on your land. It was weird. And this woman, I am not sure what it was, it was sparkling and green and it had long hair, shining eyes, it emerged from those plants, and it's like you said, it was angry…but not at me, it was angry for me. Then after the wedding, she went away. I never had that dream again."

Humira spoke with some assertion. "You know what you have to do, right?"

"What?"

"You have to get into that hollow below the rock, the one under the pink tree. There's a cave down there, I am sure of it, and there's something there that you need to…confront."

Alki asked quietly, "Why do you say that, Mira? Now you are scaring me."

Humira said, "I feel it in my bones, there's something there. Those caves at the Bael temple…if you all experienced hallucinations there and if those tunnels run all the way to your land…I feel sure there is something down there. And, aren't you the one who said you want to find out what that thing is? Don't worry. We'll come with you. You are not alone."

24

Tomato Red

It was the turn of the tomato plants to go feral all over the garden in the front and back yards. The home-made compost had been chock-full of juicy, slimy tomato seeds, which had survived the heat of the compost pile, and had run the gamut of fat, squirming soldier fly larvae and earthworms to emerge intact. The plants were hairy and off-putting. On being touched, they exuded an odorous watery ooze that vanished like hand sanitiser when Tana looked down at her wet, then magically dry palms. She had been tasked with transferring many of the bigger, stronger ones to the veggie patch. In the patch, where they were safe from weeding, they were staked and allowed to grow monstrous till they spat out tiny, ugly yellow flowers that attracted giant midnight-blue carpenter bees and yellow-bellied bumblebees.

Months later, after pollination, they yielded their ruby red fruits, which is when the plants and their hippy hirsute droopiness were at long last appreciated. No wonder this South American plant had found its way around the world. It had all been for the colour of the fruit, which had in historical times scared people at first. How could such a smelly, offbeat plant produce something so beautiful? The Europeans had been suspicious, even about its taste at first, till they weren't, and the umami flavours of the tomato became ubiquitous in their world. The ruby fruit that helped everyone forget its ugly plant parent had gone on to describe a shade of red.

In Mamma's garden, it was early morning, Tana was awaiting that exact moment at dawn for that intersection between cold night and the warmth of the rising sun. She enjoyed the exorcism performed by the sun expelling the cold from her body. The start of a new day made her feel like she could hit reset on life every 24 hours. The iridescent saffron disk of a new sun, vertical on the horizon, was a fresh poetic start, not anything like that technical point in the orbit of a yellow star when a glob of dirt, gravity-glued, turned and faced its star in space.

As she watched the sun rise over a distant hill, she had her back to the gate. But she turned, startled as soon as she heard it grating. Who could it be this early in the morning? The milkman and newspaper boy came much later.

The gate had opened in a wedge and her irritating neighbour popped his head in to ask, "Why don't you come out for a second, I have something to show you?"

Tana was instantly wary, but she had already been very rude to him on previous occasions and told herself that she would go out and make it as brief as possible. As the gate closed behind her, her back to the blinding sunrise, she failed to notice the sudden, furious rustling of Mamma's favourite tree, the Shami.

<><><>

She got out of bed at 4 am and made time for herself before going to work, before her mother-in-law Mamma and the children awoke to begin their bustle. She got ready without peeking into the mirror, an old habit from childhood that was difficult to root out. She had once detested her mirror image. She was still afraid of that old ugly creature still living beneath her now beautiful exterior. She was beauty and the beast all in one person. Her mystery workout that Jas was always so curious about was the work she did in her mother-in-law's garden at the crack of dawn.

On this day she needed to transfer the unbridled tomato plants to the veggie patch before Mamma could come out into the garden, take inventory, and notice that Tana was behind on her garden jobs. Although she knew Mamma wouldn't mind, she would just mutter "tch tch"… and let her get on with it. Tana was not much of a gardener, but Mamma hadn't paid heed to that and had expected Tana to help her around the garden, rather than in the kitchen. Tana liked that choice and adhered as best as possible to Mamma's garden schedule. Mamma was more than a mother-in-law to her, she was a mother that loved her as if she were her own child.

In the pre-dawn murk, she noticed one early fruit had started to rouge up and Tana was glad that she was not in charge of its culinary journey. She had trouble telling women that she did not cook. She did not enjoy it, nor did she take part in the activities of the kitchen. Not long after she got married, she began to notice that if she expressed this dislike out loud to women, then most of them and even men took exception to this aversion. Some women's entire lives were wrapped up in the culture of cooking. And their families exhibited a patriarchal pride in their culinary calibre. At Tana's in-laws' house, days were spent discussing and devising recipes for the humblest vegetables. She took little interest in it like some men took no interest in sports. It had got to a point where she was afraid to tell people of her dislike lest she offended someone. But Mamma knew and shielded her.

Her mother-in-law would tell overly inquiring relatives, "Do you know what her salary is? Why are you not asking that? She earns very well."

Some men were especially obnoxious about it, like the annoying neighbour, who liked to barge in on them in the evenings every couple of days. Visitors were usually accommodated in their airy veranda in a cane-henge of chairs and a glass coffee table placed at the centre of the circle.

When it was time for tea, the neighbour would pointedly turn to her and say, "Why don't you fetch us some tea and fry up some snacks?"

She would rise, irritated and unsure, then Mamma would motion her to sit down. And would step into the kitchen on her behalf to conjure up the tea and perfect snacks that magically appeared on the glossy tables of domestic goddesses around the world. One evening after Mamma had left for the kitchen, the neighbour commented to Tana's husband that he shouldn't be allowing his old mother to do all the kitchen work after a snide peep at Tana. And she had remained silent but exasperated.

Finally, a day came when she couldn't bear it anymore, and she told him, "I'll get the tea today, tomorrow you get it."

She regretted her rejoinder the moment it escaped her mouth and laughed awkwardly as if to indicate that it was a joke. She had mortified everyone in the room, including her husband, the neighbour's sullen wife, his noiseless mother, Mamma maybe not so much. She hadn't been able to help herself. It was like Jas had arrived before her in male avatar and was giving her orders again. After a brief interval, the neighbour piped up.

He said, "I have seen this unhealthy change in many of my friends' houses. You know...where the husbands cook because the women don't want to...and they don't hide it either, like before, they are quite open about it...This is what the world is coming to...next they will say they don't want to look after their children. I heard one woman say she needs space."

At this point, observing that his wife and mother were reddening and unwilling to respond, Tana's husband hopped up from his cane chair and ushered the neighbours out, saying he had some important documents to examine for work and it would take the whole evening.

This particular neighbour also liked to pounce on women who expressed themselves. During general discussions, if Tana spoke up, he would immediately, as if it were an unwritten rule, contradict her. Tana's husband observed this one evening and countered the man, catching out the presumptive misogynist, who acted as if he was deaf to Tana, just as he was starting to expound on how he had helped out some very poor women back in his village. Before this, glancing at his wife and mother, Tana had tried to explain to him but to no avail, the counter-intuitive fact that women wouldn't need any help if they were allowed to help themselves. Her husband's steady response had silenced the young man, not anything Tana had said, though they had said more or less the same thing.

Her husband had taken her aside later that night to tell her she needn't be so meek, that she should express herself with more gumption. Tana thought to herself that she had learned diffidence in the company of her friend Jas. Now she was in the middle of undoing the brainwashing of childhood.

Sometimes the undoing project went too far. She didn't know anymore where to draw the line. She found herself being so mean to Jas, that even Alki and Humira were compelled to defend their friend. When Tana was rude, on cue Jas became a concert conductor, enacting the role of the aggrieved party, gesturing appropriately to her other friends, triggering their protective instincts for maximum effect, thereby wangling advantage out of Tana's malice. She sighed, she could never win, even once, with Jas. Ever since her ugly duckling transformation back in college, her friends had been a little distant with her, even Alki and Humira, which she had not anticipated. Jas, she had expected, but not the other two. The three had all complained about Jas for so long that she was full of consternation when they did not automatically take her side. She knew they were both over at Jas's a lot, and neither of them would ever take the time to pop over when she was just metres away in an adjoining lane.

Alki had informed her on the phone that Humira was over there learning to garden. Tana then hinted indignantly and vigorously to both Alki and Humira that her mother-in-law was the more nuanced gardener. Unlike Jas's mother, Mamma did not use either fertilisers or pesticides. Mamma had turned to permaculture years ago when it had not yet been fashionable. At that time, the neighbours, including Jas's mother, had labelled Mamma's garden messy and disorganised. Mamma had even offered to teach them her natural techniques in her usual cheerful way, feeling a little bad, but ultimately choosing to overlook their condescension.

Years later Jas's mother would adopt the organic method after several surreptitious expeditions, disguised as casual visits to Mamma's natural garden. Having no ideas of her own, she would shadow Mamma on trips to garden centres to pick up tips from her and have her point out new things. When her own garden's natural makeover was finally complete, she was more than keen to not give Mamma the credit for the transformation, wary of being labelled a copycat. She took offence if someone innocently compared her garden to Mamma's.

Tana had even been eager to get Yug together with her husband, but Jas had not taken to the idea. Tana hoped that Yug and her husband would get along as they had both gone to the same school, and worked in software, and she assumed they had a lot to bond over. But whenever Jas came over for one of her rare visits, she made it a point to never bring Yug, as if to let Tana know that she must banish the thought of the four of them being best friends and dinner buddies. She knew that Jas and Yug did go out on dinner dates with their work friends. Tana would never know that Jas had tried, even if ineffectually after many unrelenting calls from her friend, to get Yug to go out with Tana and her husband, but Yug had been patronising and had rejected such a get-together.

Yug had known Tana in college and had not liked her much. He deemed her to be a caricature of Jas, and that was just too much. Yug only went out for networking dinners that helped him in his career.

But Tana had not imagined it. Ultimately, Jas was relieved that Yug showed no inclinations so that she didn't have to manipulate him into saying no. Tana's eagerness had not just irritated Jas, it had agitated her. It was all just an upward mobility project with Tana, which had nothing to do with friendship. Tana had always treated Jas as if she had been a step to a better station in life, copying her tastes, and clothes, modelling her behaviour, and now hoping to get their husbands together, secretly resenting Jas the whole time, maybe even hoping to pull her down a peg, when the time was appropriate.

And Tana was clever about it. She would imitate Jas, then she would visit at a later date and emphasise to Jas, "You know I figured this out on my own…" and repeat to Jas whatever it was she had learned from her friend, but in such a way as if to show that Jas was not the primary source of that information.

Jas found Tana's little manoeuvres comical at times. Tana was trying to pre-empt Jas labelling her a copycat, but much to her chagrin that label did fall upon her. Jas did not like those of her friends, somebody like Alki, who put up an obsequious pretence of equality with a friend like Tana. Alki was always dissembling, adjusting her speech to suit others, dumbing herself down in the company of those she knew to be mediocre. Jas believed it to be a comedy of manners, the stupidity of the smart feigning ignorance to mollify the average person, just like the cleverness of the dunce masquerading as an intellectual. As for Tana, it was not Alki that she desired equality with, but Jas, who would never permit her friends to be on an equal footing with her.

Tana had stuck to Jas in school, coming home with her, insisting on doing homework there till late hours, almost as if she had not liked going home. Tana's own modest tiled-roof house was not all that bad, according to Jas, not as musty as Alki's house anyway. Her school principal father, and hospital nurse mother were very nice, if very disciplined, ambitious people, who had tried to teach Tana that education was her means to a better life, but their daughter had outstripped them in her aspirations. She aimed for the refinement of Jas, the blue-blooded demeanour of her parents and even their grandly designed house.

Unlike Alki, Tana had stuck to Jas so closely that she had actually made it into her archaeologist father's secret study, to be taken in by the grandeur of it all. She could remember the defining details of the study even today. It had felt to her like the set of an adventure film. She had made all the right admiring noises, and at that time, unsuspecting, Jas had taken Tana under her wing. It was Jas who taught Tana to use makeup judiciously; it was Jas who had insisted on sharing her exercise regimen with overweight Tana.

But Jas started to get disconcerted when Tana actually lost weight and changed the way she dressed. Those transformational days were the happiest of Tana's life, except for the drone of a persistent antagonism from Jas. One memorable night, Jas had deigned to step out into the lane to visit Tana at her house at dinner time, she had come by, she said, to make sure that Tana was not starving herself to a smaller body size. A week later, she returned, bringing her obviously disinclined father with her, who said barely a word to Tana's own cowed father. The great man had aloofly looked around at the interiors of the small house, its strict, unfashionable furniture, and the doilies on cushioned chairs with unconcealed contempt. Jas had brought out the big guns to put Tana in her place, who had been chastened and humiliated on cue. But Tana would not stay browbeaten for long, her path to refinement was inexorable. By the time Tana got married, her metamorphosis was complete, and Jas was glad that she had the excuse of being abroad with Yug to beg off from attendance at her wedding.

From day one, Tana had loved her husband's mother, whom she called Mamma. She was the antithesis of Jas's father. If Jas's father was a Bentley, Tana's mother-in-law was a rocking Baja Beetle. A year after Tana's wedding, the great ones—Jas along with her mother and father—had called at Mamma's. Jas's father had the habit of being insufferably taciturn in company, occasionally muttering titbits of a serious nature that he knew no one else would understand. At one point, his wife was forced to admonish him.

To which he said, "I suppose you would say the same to Wittgenstein."

There was mystified silence in the room, and then Mamma's clear voice rang out. "Language puzzles…? Okay then, don't words suffer from relativity? Take the words that describe us women. To you, they mean one thing. But to us, they help explain where all the women went. Why…all the great philosophers were men! Women? They were 'virginal', 'hysterical', 'maternal', 'fair', giving birth to philosophers, keeping their houses and making them meals. Two thousand years ago, a Greek man pointed out that women should also be allowed a life of the mind. After that, nothing."

Along with everyone else, Jas's father gaped dumbstruck at Mamma. Tana was on eggshells, but then he went on to smile beatifically at Mamma, surprising everyone, especially Jas, who had never before observed such a countenance on her father. If Jas was none too pleased, Tana was nothing but. The day marked the birth of a platonic adoration that became a thorn in Jas's side, with her wishing that she had never met Tana.

The two older people talked in the lane whenever they passed each other on their morning walks, the archaeologist trying to persuade Mamma to join him either on his walk or come indoors for a cup of tea with his wife. Very old school about being seen in his company, she would always decline both offers. When Jas got wind of their intimate lane conversations, she began to join them as often as could and had even tried to persuade her mother to accompany her father but to no avail.

She told her mother dryly, "You seem okay with him being 'friends' with Tana's mother-in-law."

She hadn't known what other word to use.

Her mother replied gloomily, "He needs someone to talk to."

To which, Jas asked with derision, "And that someone is Tana's superstitious tree-worshipping mother-in-law?"

Her mother had said, "Don't be so much like your father. People surprise you only because you choose to underestimate them."

One evening, the archaeologist arrived in state at one of Mamma's prayer meetings. Tana and her husband watched astonished as her mother-in-law accompanied the dignitary through the throng to a focal point before her favourite tree. Tana remembered how they stood there conversing warmly, unaware, perhaps unmindful of the buzz they were creating in the prayer group. Tana had tried to distract the gossipers from staring at the two by the tree, by distributing snacks and tea from a huge vat they had prepared earlier for all the attendees. She recalled how she had listened in on snippets of the conversation by the tree.

Mamma had even 'introduced' her favourite tree to the archaeologist: "…this is a tree of life, and its worship goes back thousands of years…" After having handed out clay cups of sweet cardamom tea from a laden tray, Tana had made her way back to the two as the sun was setting in a divine orange and purple haze framed between hills. The archaeologist and her mother-in-law were both gazing up into the tree.

She heard Mamma whispering to the archaeologist, "Can you see her now?"

He had appeared wistful, then he said, "Yes."

Tana had mechanically looked up. There was nothing there except an inexplicable golden glow from the setting sun reflecting off the white walls into the tree.

25

The Migrating Hibiscus

Jas rested her back against the garden-variety hibiscus in Alki's parents' garden having some idea about the adventurous history of her backrest. The experts, said her father one day when he was trying to rationalise her mother's hibiscus obsession, were sure of one thing: that the hibiscus had travelled the South Pacific on the catamarans of migrating Polynesians. But no one had been able to solve the botanical mystery of its origins. Upon her mother's insistence, her father had dug a little more and concluded that the plant surely had a volcanic past, sprouting and evolving on a mercurial, neurotic landscape that had formed itself out of incipient lava. The old bush was flowering that day, plain, red blossoms her own mother would have pooh-poohed, but were beloved to Alki's mother, who had found her loitering in the house and put her to work collecting red shoe flowers. Her own mother would fuss over her prized rainbow-flowered hibiscus every week, applying fertilisers, and spraying smelly pesticides. This one, on the other hand, didn't seem that nagged, but was thriving nevertheless in its own scraggy, understated fashion.

Alki's mother had asked Jas to go out and fetch the flowers for evening worship. She didn't mind complying. She liked Alki's mother, a petite, insecure woman who looked like she needed taking care of, but was unfortunately married to a man who took care of only himself. Alki's father reminded her of Yug sometimes, also someone who did not want to take care of his wife. Jas had driven down to pick up Alki and take her to her construction site, but she was still finishing her bath. Jas gazed anxiously around at the wildness of the garden, as her mother had warned her there could be snakes skulking in the undergrowth of an unkempt garden. After that warning, she had made sure to never be alone in her friend's garden until this day.

Looking around at the towering, weedy borders, Jas suddenly felt a freeing. Her hair came loose from a binding ponytail. The breeze had caught it, playing with it as if the strands were wind chimes. Patches of unusually azure sky were visible between tree crowns, floaty, wispy clouds filtering beatific motes of sunlight down to her. She had never experienced this in her mother's garden. Her skin should have crawled from the lines of ants marching past her or the wasps making their air raids, but she was okay, more than okay. In that moment, her neediness ceased. She let go. Nothing would be perfect in this garden, not even if her mother came and dug away all day, every day for a year. This garden simply had no ideal form.

Jas could not tell how long the perfect ones had possessed her. Gods, goddesses, superheroes, and ideologies—the people she worshipped had seeped into her and she had not known that they were there, that their claptrap had taken possession of her. She had not resisted when they tried to mould her in their image. This had always been the problem with worship, but who knew that the problem was not with her, but with the gods and goddesses. A god, or a person with expectations of worship, was a creature of the society that created her. They were tropes: male gods were masculine and paternalistic, goddesses endlessly maternal, or beautiful and infantilised, requiring protection and care. How long had she carried their ideal forms around in her head crafting herself tortuously into something always out of reach?

Is this what was missing between Yug and her? The worship… they started having problems after he stopped treating her like the goddess she was. She had become a screen deity, light-skinned, her body trained and toned to sharp edges, having sculpted away her cheeks to leave behind fashionably high bone structure. She didn't like looking at her childhood pictures because she no longer recognised herself in them. And she didn't want to be a showcase for a before-after metamorphosis like Tana. In her mind, she was always this, and there could be no before pictures, taking posed selfies day after day to reinforce the after picture on social media so that no one could have any doubts, especially her.

She wished to destroy her family's yellowing photo albums when her mother wasn't looking. She hated how her mother clung to them, and fished them out for their guests. Her mother had loved her flawed little girl, but Jas had transcended her old self. Goddesses did that, they were supra-mortal. Being a god was addictive, and she could not get enough of the high. The high was succour from agonising self-diffidence, which caused her to hit out like a nervous, skittish animal at friends and the people she loved. No other friend was allowed to be unhappy, they dared not compete with her pain. No other friend could be loved, as the melodrama of a kitschy, classical romance was reserved only for goddesses. But gods were human creations, hence not really omniscient, they could not be everywhere at once. And Jas, desperate to be worshipped, had failed to see that her mortals were tiring.

She believed that Yug had stopped worshipping not just her but even his mother. He was fed up with their vulnerability, their compulsive need to be revered. But unlike her, his mother had not come to terms with it. Or maybe she had, lately the old bat had been nice to her rival Jas, and this new nice had descended on Jas entirely unexplained and without warning.

On the breeze came a thought.

"What have I done? What have I done?"

A tear flowed down her face. It had been so clear to her that he had loved Alki. And she had coveted that adoration, at the time not realising that what the two of them had wasn't adoration, or worship, the thing that she wanted. Then, just as quickly, as the torment had washed over her, she forgave herself. Perhaps her presence had been a test, and he had failed that test. Alki should be with someone who would not give her up so easily for a goddess. Worshipping the ideal was like being led astray by shiny advertising, it would always lead to disappointment. She knew of husbands who adored their wives, someone like Humira's father, for instance. But Yug was not like that. There were wives for whom the adoration of their husbands was not enough of a high. Then Jas thought to herself, what was the ideal anyway? Who decided what was an ideal form? Why were they all so furiously chasing these forms, one shinier than the next? Aesthetics were protean, they changed rapidly from decade to decade, and even she was tiring of keeping up with them. Jas closed her eyes. It was restful, leaning against the old hibiscus, its gnarly branches curling around her in a warm embrace.

Alki finished her bath. She heard her mother's voice calling loudly. She dressed quickly and jogged past the goddess corner into the kitchen.

"What is it Amma?"

Her mother said, "Do you know how long Jas has been waiting for you?"

"Oh no…I forgot…"

Her mother said, "I sent her out to the old hibiscus to fetch my flowers. Go and get her, both of you can have lunch before you leave."

Alki moved swiftly into the living room, but before she could step out into the garden, she glimpsed something from the open window that made her start in absolute fright. Under a sunny, blue sky with cotton-ball clouds, was Jas leaning against the hibiscus, facing the house, facing Alki. But it wasn't really Jas, Alki could not be sure anymore. Jas's torso and legs were twisted in the form of a tree trunk, and she was pinned to the thickened hibiscus bole, her forelimbs splayed out, as if she were a god, crucified. Her hair had come loose and the skin on her face was grey and flaking like bark. Jas was staring at her insensate. The branches of the old hibiscus were closing around her. She was being absorbed into the hibiscus. Alki bawled into the garden.

"No, no, no…. you can't have her….no…no…NO."

She tore out of the house and grabbed the curving branches of the hibiscus, prizing them apart.

Adrenaline had kicked in, and she roared, "Let her go, leave her alone…"

The knobbly branches cut into her palms, hands, and elbows, but nothing would deter her. She grabbed Jas's peeling limp hands; her friend's head having fallen back into the tree.

Alki heaved her friend forward with both hands. Jas would not budge. Alki relinquished her friend's hands to grasp hold of Jas's upper arms just beneath the shoulders.

She yanked as hard as she could manage, then she said fiercely, "You will have to take me too…I am not letting go of her."

By then Alki too had been snatched inwards by the branches of the hibiscus and squeezed against what was left of Jas's body. Alki was being suffocated, while Jas had stopped breathing. Suddenly, the branches sprang back propelling them forward, releasing them both. Alki and Jas tumbled to the grass below. Alki gasped, then got up, frantic. She was on her knees desperate to see to her old friend. She checked anxiously to see if Jas was breathing. She was.

Shaking her friend, she said, "Jas…Jas…wake up."

The flaking effect faded, and her skin flushed with colour. Jas came to and opened her eyes.

She said looking up at Alki, "Ohh… I think I fell asleep. I had the strangest dream…I was turning into a tree."

Alki looked down at her hands, wondering if she too had been dreaming, sharing Jas's dream, or whether this was another one of her hallucinations. But there were scratches on her palms, and small cuts on her elbows. This was no dream.

Jas said, "Alki, what happened? Look at you... you look frazzled?"

Calming herself down, Alki said, smiling feebly, "Me? Jas, go inside and find a mirror. You don't look like yourself anymore. This is the first time I have seen you without make-up in years. The last time you looked like this was back when we passed out of seventh standard."

Jas smiled, then she shrugged and sat up to examine her grimy palms.

She said, "This is so strange, I have never fallen asleep before like this outside. Oh my god! Why do I feel so tired?"

She sat back again gazing skyward lost in thought. Alki stood up wondering whether to tell Jas about what happened. All this time Alki had her back to the house. She turned around, suddenly conscious that her mother might have heard her scream. The sun was shining on the living room windowpanes. It was perhaps an artifice of the light, but she thought she saw someone reflected on the glass pane, and it wasn't her mother. Neither was it really a face. It was simply the outline of a woman's face. There were no eyes or mouth. Alki recognised the faceless face. It was the grotto entrance she had walked past on her way up to the great rock on the hill above the mound. How could she forget that day? Or the beautiful mauve-magenta flowers of the Bauhinia that marked that spot. Alki turned away from the house and regarded Jas, still seated beneath the hibiscus about a yard from the Neem tree.

She said, "Jas, could you move?"

"Why?"

"I want to check something."

Jas got up wearily to position herself beside Alki, who bent to inspect the thick root base of her mother's old hibiscus. Why had she never seen it before this day? At the foot of the hibiscus was a miniature grotto. At the most, it could have made a nice home for a mongoose, for even their archenemies, snakes. The roots had spread out from the base of the plant, thickening, and hardening over time, leaving behind a hollow that resembled a woman's face when viewed from an angle close to the ground. Undaunted this time, she reached a hand into the hole.

Jas slapped at her arm, saying, "Alki stop, there could be something inside."

"Jas, you were here all this time, nothing bit you."

Alki extended her arm into the hole and felt around for a bit. When she took out her hand, it was covered in a whitish grey powdery substance.

Jas said, "What is that?"

"I think it's ash. All this time, I thought I brought her back with me from the hill the day I was attacked. But she was visiting us all this time maybe for years and we just weren't aware of her."

"I don't understand. You are talking about that thing again… aren't you?"

"Yes…she tried to take you today. That dream you had, it wasn't a dream Jas."

26

Dry Grasses from a Muzzled Past

Tana was itchy all over, lying, left side of face pinned to the ground, blinking her eyes rapidly at thin blades of poking weed grass, the tiny white flowers on curving spurges and purple-coned thistles, thinking about how Mamma used to tell her about the many native grass species, and how they should not get rid of them as native butterflies needed them for their survival. Her children had loved butterflies, the only time they left the television room and abandoned their iPad screens was to come out to the wild verge that housed wildflower insectaries, and makeshift wild bee houses that Mamma had especially devised from bundles of hollow twigs and straw. Mamma loved to tease the children and tell them how she loved those gaudy creatures more than she loved even them. They had pleaded with her—the kids, and she had relented, telling them she would change her allegiance only if they promised to take care of her butterfly garden. They had promised.

She remembered how bored she was as Mamma had droned on. Lying there on the ground with energetic black ants crawling up her ankles, her face being intently examined from a safe distance by a common house lizard frozen to its spot, she suppressed her squirming instinct, and wished she had bothered to memorise the names of the grasses. She hadn't dared admit, even to Mamma, that all that talk of native plant species had bored her, because she could not come across as ignorant. She was very thin-skinned about other people judging her as stupid, as she now looked a certain way. If anyone talked about matters she had no interest in, she would vehemently claim interest in them. She listened to her co-workers attentively, especially the smartest among them and made mental notes of the things they said, so she could repeat them later as if these were her ideas. After some time had passed, they would become her ideas.

Inadvertently, Tana had stumbled into the secret of individuality, that no one person was truly unique or original, though they were capable of occasional insight. A person was simply an assemblage of fictions, interesting traits derived from all the influences in their lives, then adapted into a neat human package. Although blind to her own inspirations, frequently she was startled to find the people around her, echoing family members or even friends. Like her friend Jas, who imitated her archaeologist father's gestures, or Alki who subconsciously emulated the meekness of her mother, or even her husband, who not only sounded like his father, but also borrowed his catchphrases.

Where her own private thoughts ended and the thoughts of others began, she did not know anymore, her mind was a collection of useful notions she had gathered from all around, like a crow bringing shiny baubles back to line its nest. She had an intense interest in appearances, both outward and internal. To some extent, she had detested not just Jas, but also Alki and Humira, as one represented what she aspired to be on the outside, and the other two were what she wanted to be on the inside. From time to time, their words betrayed what they thought of her, that she, Tana, was dim-witted. She was not.

Then, she was sad, thinking about how she was going to miss the subliminal quarrels with her friends and her family so much. She lay sideways on the grass filled with regrets. She should have offered to help Alki, who was struggling with her house and did not have the kind of support that she enjoyed at home. Instead, she had been envious of Alki's new-found individuality. Deep inside lived a part of her that did not want Alki to overcome her difficulties and prove herself to the world. Why she should even feel that for someone who had less than her? She lay there on the dry itchy grasses, amazed at herself, trying to understand human nature and her own self-delusions. She felt a tinge of shame, and for the first time, intuited Alki's desolation. Neither Jas nor Humira wanted to admit how alone Alki was, her mother a shut-in that no one saw anymore, and her father a stealthy sadist. Her friends knew and were silent.

The corners of her mouth were now beginning to hurt from the gag, her legs and hands had been tied and twisted behind her back. Why was it that she had never noticed the big empty plot, almost an acre in size, facing her gate on the other side of the lane? She had passed by so many times, and sometimes cautiously paused there to note the numerous butterflies visiting the plot due to all the wild grasses growing there, exactly as Mamma had said. As a woman, she had been too guarded about exploring the world beyond her front gate. Her explorations were restricted to television shows about her area, and visits to said places in the safe company of her family.

A couple of yards away, in a corner near an unplastered brick wall, he was digging very slowly, solicitously, cutting out flat pancakes of hard red soil, and it looked like he was taking care not to disturb or destroy the wild plants growing there. It seemed to Tana, from what little she could observe, he was going to put all the plants back after he finished with the spade work. Did he want the site to look undisturbed? Probably. She could scarcely see from her vantage on the ground as the grass in the plot was knee-high. At first, she had had no idea what he was doing, but then it came to her. He was digging her a shallow grave. She was not scared, only surprised that he thought he could get away with it. Only a man could have such confidence. Maybe he had relatives in the police department or government who could slow down the investigation, which would surely follow. As the adrenaline kicked in, she was sure her husband and Mamma were not going to take her disappearance or death lying down.

Why did men do such things? How could she have provoked him? She had sensed the man's envy, but she had thought nothing of it, because everyone she knew was petty and jealous all the time, except her precious Mamma, of course. Whether it was her friend Jas or Alki or her neighbours, no one could stand it that she had pulled herself up by the bootstraps. This neighbour insisted on coming to visit them every week. To her, it seemed he came simply to compare and stoke his own envy. He looked over their house, counted their cars, parking spaces, and commented on the décor. He announced that he was redecorating his house, but his own bookshelves and windows would be much higher and bigger than at her house.

And something about her infuriated him, as he kept looking from his own wife to her. His wife was a good cook, but he called her a chef, asserting there was a catering service interested in her. He also described his wife as a financial wiz that dabbled in the share market in her spare time. As he said that, Tana had glanced over at his wife, and the woman had smiled at her warmly, disarmingly. For her part, the wife said she was planning on training to be a gym instructor. Had Tana been rude to the braggadocious duo? She could not remember now, she must have said something terribly sarcastic that evening.

She remembered the story of a famous married actor having an affair, outed by a woman colleague who told his wife. He seethed for years, using all his society-given macho ascendancy to demean his colleague in every possible way before he decided to have her raped, the only acceptable revenge against uppity womanhood that could satiate his vengeance. Or the auteurs, that had insidiously toyed with women in films, and in life for years, and had manipulated a powerful publicity machine to feather and tar the women that dared to speak up. That was the provocation: the words, the speaking up.

A famous woman called her powerful ex-boyfriend a silly ex once, and it was as if a barrage had opened wide, and calumny poured upon her. Last she heard, that woman was still fighting back the deluge, but as a crazy doppelganger who had found power in a different bubble world, diametrically opposed to the world that had destroyed her. Tana had such mundane thoughts and concerns as she wriggled on the ground, dying…is this what they meant by death throes? She would miss the morning gossip rag, and she would miss the latest salvo from the other side. There was nothing worse in this world than surreptitious rage: hell hath no fury like a man with a veiled grudge. A woman scorned, why! she was just a pet rabbit boiled in a pot, gaudy, and flailing for all to see.

The hard ground could not help ease the spreading bruises on her hands and feet. Her tongue was chafing against the rough cloth of her gag. She managed to turn onto her side propping herself on her hip, trying at the same time to disregard the excruciating pain. She wanted to call herself a victim, but if somehow, she survived this, that word would be stripped away from her. They had attached the word 'playing' to victim. Feminine angst, to many men, and women, was silly make-believe, unreal. If feminine pain was not anchored in the male perspective, that of a distressed damsel or femme fatale, then it could not be substantiated. When enough women came out of the woodwork, from between the cracks they had fallen through, to substantiate themselves, their rage was chalked up to victimhood, which had been nuanced away, reframed as a populist guillotine with the sole purpose of persecuting perpetrators.

Tana stopped mid-thought. Why was she sounding like Humira? She had always wondered about Mira's bitterness and unceasing indignation. Something had happened to her, which she was not able to put into words. There were all these other, superfluous words, but the words she needed to utter…Mira was not permitted to sound those out into the world, like tolling bells for everyone to hear. Whenever she tried to speak, hands were figuratively clapped to ears. She had witnessed an argument at a family get-together at Humira's, between Mira and her aunt, her mother's favourite sister, a lawyer.

The older woman first declared herself a feminist before taking down women who seduced men as a means of attaining power. Tana had never seen Mira so still, so pale and impotent.

She told her aunt softly, "What do you expect women to do when they are educated in wiles and body size, not in science, technology, engineering or mathematics?"

Her mother had stepped in between the aunt and niece. By a dining table decorated with plates of pretty food, Mira said words to Tana she would never forget.

"So many people are stuck in the past, and they spend the rest of their lives trying to cover up what they did…it will be their singular obsession. And they will accuse others of being stuck in the past…You see that aunt of mine," she was pointing to her mother's sister at the other end of the room, "she is the much younger second wife to an influential man who was once married to a very nice woman."

Silently the two stared at the overconfident woman across the room. Mira then obliquely hinted to her friend that she had often considered death. Tana had been so uncomfortable that night, she remembered changing the subject. It was Tana who had clapped her hands to her ears. She, along with Jas and Alki…they were the three monkeys: Blind, deaf, and mum. With rude clarity, Mira's sister's wedding day came back to her—that strangely awful scene at the entrance to the hall with all of them confronting Mira's cousin, and how he had aggressively growled at Mira telling her she was stuck in the past.

"Stuck in the Past".

"Oh my god…" thought Tana.

From within the reedy towers of dry grass, Tana's low moan rose to resonate in the air above her. She felt Mira's anguish for the first time in her life. Tana knew. Tears for her friend flowed down from the corners of her eyes, dripping down to the scarred earth beneath the side of her face. The ground received her tears as a gift of rain and released in return the smell that came after new rain touched parched earth. Tana breathed it in to salve her sorrow. How had Mira gone on? Death would have been a release, as well as a defeat. The fuel for life had turned out to be suppressed white hot rage. And it could not go anywhere except inside, Mira had ignited into a burning star. Never having been gifted the redemptive mercy of compassion, what walked around in the name of Mira was just a bitter, fiery remnant of a person that once was. Mira had not always been angry. Her childhood friend had been an exultant tomboy who had loved to break into dance at every school picnic. It was at her wedding, ten years ago that she first acknowledged the change in Mira. While everyone else had got on the floor to dance, even conceited, conservative Alki, Mira had lurked in the background.

Tana had gone up to her and said, "Mira, what happened to you? You've lost your verve."

Tana winced at the memory. There was a recurring dream pattern in all of this: women stuck in irreparable pasts and unrepentant men who sought to cover up the irredeemable. And how did they get away with preying on women? They had support in numbers. They had implicit sympathy for each other and were inevitably linked together in a network of sneaky power. The women who colluded with them were bamboozled into assisting them in these networks and rewarded with doles from the system. Tana remembered a story about a woman who was murdered by her husband in a far-away village. His family had the help of a local politician, and the police dropped the case against him, then he was married to a second woman, who, when questioned by the reporter about the murdered first wife, said number one had it coming.

Arrogant; Ambitious; Stuck in the Past; Had it Coming; Asked for It. Slut. They were piling up now, the excuses…the justifications…the cover-ups.

She blinked her eyes. Patches of dazzling white were effervescing once again in her view. She blinked. He had kicked her again and again in the abdomen after she had collapsed to the ground. And the pain was now spreading like a contagion to the rest of her body. At least she had not had her innards pulled out with a jagged rod. Tana laughed and moaned to herself. A boy and a group of men had done that to a girl once. He was sent to juvenile detention for three years. Now he's a tailor. And she's ashes. Her image was banned from the news, for the sake of justice they said, the public was never able to substantiate her, or make her real. If she became real or was beatified, there was danger of the rapists getting lynched. Even before she died, they had turned her into an apparition. The irony was that she had never really existed, and she didn't exist anymore. Her mother's tears on television were the only things keeping her impaled ghost alive in public memory. Another patch of rainbow-bordered white dazzled Tana from above the grasses. The pain had made her delirious, as there was a woman in white with an ashy face and white eyes looking down at her. Tana could barely move at all now, even if she tried, the pain was too much.

"So, this is what death looks like," Tana thought.

The white woman spoke. Her desiccated, flaking lips parted to reveal pointed teeth.

"Get up now," she said rasping.

Tana closed her eyes, and the world went white. She mumbled. Names and faces. Tinu, lil Deep, big Deep, Amma, Papa, Jas, ohh Jas, Alki, Mira, Mamma, Mamma… Then she was looking down at herself, writhing, moaning, and babbling.

"How can this be?" said the floating Tana.

The white woman was beside her boring right into her with her snow eyes, and then she lifted her forearm to point towards the neighbour's house just visible over the old brick wall.

Tana, or at least some part of her unconscious self, found herself in their kitchen. There was her digging neighbour in quiet conversation with his unquiet wife, whose cordial warmth had been replaced by a hard-edged paranoia away from prying eyes. She pumped her fists in the air. Her child had done well at the hustings that were the school exams. He was trying to calm her, but that only seemed to make her more peeved. This was the price they paid for being in the rat race, of constantly competing with everyone over everything. They would never be able to reach a truce with reality. To them there was no such thing, no, that piece of wisdom had not come from them, this was according to the great texts of the world. To be ambitious was also to be clever and self-deluded, so clever that delusion would become codified as reality.

The wife was very ambitious, confident that she was smarter than most, but then someone smarter always came along and she would be forced to contend with her frustrations each time. Shiftily, she would linger by the edge of her window every morning clutching her cup of tea while her husband dressed for work. She watched her underqualified, middling neighbour Tana going to work, feeling foiled by domesticity, and bitter that she had not been able to substantiate her own merit. Her fenestral loitering, however, did not go unnoticed by her husband or child. During visits, the child would pocket small objects from Tana's house, a habit that had lately escalated to include money from Tana's purse, which the boy had stumbled upon one evening undiscovered by the adults.

The husband was quick to pick up on the wife's cues, always acting faithfully on her behalf, but he was tired of working to provide the bigger car and foreign vacations she insisted upon, or the nicely designed bathroom that had to be better than what she declared was the neighbour's ugly one. She could get unobtrusively nasty, projecting and accusing him of gasconading. In the end, neither of them could tell anymore if each was accusing the other of things of which they were themselves guilty. He found escape in an internal world where only he had volition. A cold, distant realm his wife could not touch, with her constantly seeking after herself, carefully couched in the language of concern for others.

Some, like Tana suspected something was not quite right having intercepted her neighbour's furtive stares, on occasion having also borne the brunt of her delicately spiteful commentaries. During a tour of Mamma's brand-new kitchen, she had disparaged it, not even bothering to be discreet. Almost instantly, Tana had identified the presence of a Jas-like persona, but this one was different, more virulent, irredeemably insecure and grasping. This was no Jas. When the woman's husband had civilly made a couple of admiring noises, she glared at him, cutting him short, and adding quickly that he said that in everyone's houses, regardless of whether there was any merit in their designs. Mamma had glanced at Tana, who touched her shoulder in support.

Floating Tana watched them for a bit, husband and wife, entombing their anxieties in ever-increasing bluster, then she returned to her motionless body in the field, the private realm into which her neighbour had disappeared, a place with no time, somewhere he could silently dig a grave, and no one would ever know.

27

Unfashionably, Gliricidia

A few yards from the entrance to the strange cave, Alki paused to survey the scrub where only skinny pale grasses grew in the bare earth. Someone had planted a couple of rat-repellent Gliricidia trees. These were trees that no one really looked at, they did their jobs invisibly as living fences, fertilising the ground for free with their bounty of nitrogen, and providing fodder for other people's wandering cattle. They were useful trees but were not native to the area or even the country and that was a problem for their continued survival. Many people had begun to hate the sight of them planted by the local forest department a decade ago to green the hills. Now like the ubiquitous Eucalyptus accused of drinking too much water, they were no longer fashionable. Trees, plants and birds were travelling the earth, crossing long-lost supercontinents and seas, adapting to new places, long before humans had migrated. Some, like hibiscuses and roses were a bit more welcome than others. Others like wheat, corn, rice, and chickens had piggybacked on humans and no one had a problem with them. The kudzu vine and mynas were deemed rapacious for their propensity to quickly adapt to their new homes and crowd out the plants and animals that had spent millennia adapting exclusively to that landscape.

In the late 1980s, nativist movements began to take off around the world in environmentalist circles, but soon the movement would become a crusade in the minds of conservative thinkers, and what was once a call to open-mindedness and acceptance of local weedy plants over formal exotic species, would turn into a compulsive worldview calling for bans on invading marauding outsider plants, known as exotic species.

The Gliricidia and the lone Bauhinia were about the only trees that grew above the mound clinging to the thin crust and its rock below, surviving while all else flourished just below a contour line where the earth was green. Alki too had come a long way, weedy, unseen and as useful as she could be without completely surrendering herself like her mother, just hanging on, in a bare place where her kind was not permitted to flourish.

She used to worry that she had inherited a lack of agency from her mother. This new term had arrived in her world from electronic newspaper columns at breakfast time with grouchy parents. To her, it meant that she had been born to a woman who existed low down in the social hierarchy. Her mother lacked confidence and self-assurance and therefore Alki too found herself deficient in fierce demeanour or as people nowadays called it, a resting bitch face. Without one, she appeared meek, and people took advantage of her. Jas and Mira were expert 'rbf'ers, and even Tana had caught up to them. Almost everything had to do with demeanour. If she gave in too easily, and always felt defeated, it all went back to one parental source. She had not inherited the privilege of position, that is, none of a parent's powers to be noticed or acknowledged in the world, like Jas or even Mira. Jas's mother was not as dominant as her daughter would prove to be, but both her parents were confident, assertive people. Jas's mother was also abidingly polite, while her father was pushy as he went about the business of living, and Jas had built herself up in the world thanks to them, a base on which she had founded her confidence.

Out of bodying herself, Alki could look back at herself to see that she suffered from all the symptoms of missing agency. Unlike her uppity friends, Jas or Mira, if she ever spoke up in public, her observations were dismissed, even when she knew something was wrong. She lived in a constant state of stiflement. Like her mother, she too did not speak anymore when in company. Absent privilege meant that she was easily passed over. Education had helped somewhat as a remedy, but, although now she was heard a bit more than her mother, she faced hostility when she tried to assert herself. Those same people who had ignored her mother begrudged the daughter for trying to be more visible, and audible.

She was angry at evolution for making her voice squeaky. Whenever she said anything forcefully, she was either hysterical or a fishwife. But her friends, positioned higher up on the social ladder, were permitted some hearing, and also allowed to bully women on lower rungs, women like her, and she had taken it. But when she talked back, she was speaking out of turn.

One day at Jas's, when Alki was tutoring Jas's nine-year-old daughter, the little girl had tried aggressively to correct her. Having been to school abroad, she tended to have disdain for the learning environment in the mother country. Jas had been nearby, watching the exchange but had not intervened. Unlike Mira who had several run-ins with the girl, Alki had been unable to chastise a child that was not hers. Jas was smug in her silence, indicating that the child was simply acting on signals given out by her mother. Whatever Jas could not do for herself she would use her progeny as tools to act on her behalf.

Alki was damned if she did and damned if she didn't. A simple skill like driving a car, for instance, had proved to be a monstrous endeavour. One day Jas had let Alki pull her hatchback out from the driveway only for one of Jas's visiting male cousins to step forward and tell Alki in the guise of chivalry that he would back the car out for her. Bemused, Alki refused, which seemed to prompt him to issue intrusive instructions as she reversed, to show her up for obstructing his chivalry. For once, her father was right, she was a motoring man-goader.

At the building site, she had found some confidence. At first, no one had listened to her. She was merely thankful for them letting her be, unmolested. Gradually, she asserted herself, mining an authority she did not know she possessed. After years of not being heard in her own home or outside, despite her volume steadily rising to fishwife levels, it was a high when at last she was heard, a high that men before her had routinely experienced. Her architect listened to her ideas, and even appreciated them. The brick house on the hill had rehabilitated her. She was a person again, not a woman.

At her house, her cupboard door had fallen out one day. Not being handy, she was forced to depend on her father to call in a handyman. She was not permitted to call one in on her own. Maddeningly, her father had refused to hire someone to repair it. A week afterwards, he brought in a poor neighbour who owed him money. Alki's cupboard door had remained hanging lopsided from its hinges following the aimless repair. There was nothing she could do about it as long as she continued to live with her father. Having hard-won the ability to organise skilled persons, and even learn some of these skills, she was determined to not let a broken cupboard door ever cripple her again.

How Humira had laughed out loud when the three of them, Tana, Jas, and Alki had greeted each other on Women's Day, their social media feeds having filled up with gaudy gif cards. Mira wanted to know what they were all celebrating — the three stages of womanhood that had kept them down these centuries?

"Coquettish damsel, femme fatale and nurturing wife/mother."

"Which one are you?" Mira had asked, pointing a reedy finger at Jas. There was a pause during which Tana, Jas and Alki were sheepish.

Under her breath Jas muttered, "Is she drunk?"

Mira said, "Jas, you have enjoyed all the perks of being in the boy's club, but you are a feminist, right? You never outgrew the damsel or the femme fatale, Tana there wants to become you...and my mother, all your mothers...you Alki, you don't raise your voice enough, Alki…you don't say anything to your architect even when he is incompetent, you are afraid he will get offended."

To no one in particular, she said, "You are like the scarfed woman weightlifter, trying to prove to the world she is better than the average uncovered woman or the news report boasting that our country has more women pilots than any other."

Then she turned to Jas again, who was beginning to feel picked on, and unsettled that the other two seemed not to want to stand up for her.

Mira said to her, "Under the makeup, you are over-compensating for being stuck in a nurturing role, defensive and passive aggressive till the day you die."

Jas gulped and turned away, tearing up.

She muttered, "I help a lot of people…"

But no one was really listening to her. They were spellbound by Mira's directionless fury squirting everywhere.

Mira said, "We are all feminists now. Women in veils who say it is their choice, the women who seduce to get their way, and carefully nasty…women who are horrid to other women, pushing them down at the slightest sign of success…do you know how many times I have been told by privileged people…women…I have airs, I mean come on, who even says that anymore…having airs..."

Humira had cackled at Jas's hushed consternation.

She had said again, "Be proud, you are all feminists. I would like to know who is not one."

Alki had been silent, but she empathised with her friend that day. They had learned to live their lives by imitating models available in columns, in fiction, and in their homes. What was culture but fiction writ large over the zeitgeist? Culture and fiction too were riddled with implicit post-truth. And fiction was supposed to uncover layers of untold truth through make-believe, but even fiction was made up of men and women's biases, more untruths. Even the very idea of choice had been renegotiated making it okay for women to be veiled and still be feminists.

When these forms of womanhood presented themselves in myths, stories and legends, in culture, when all expectations from gender were trapped inside straitjackets like romance and passion, a nest, a hearth, always the comforter, de-muscled and rewarded for suppressing her own wishes, what was a woman to do but live out her life in tropes: virginal, alluring, bitchy, beautiful, slutty, delicate, soft, maternal, veiled literally and figuratively. To be punished or honoured according to deviation from, or adherence to trope.

Light was filtering in over the horizon, through the forest from a buried sun still rising from behind the hills. In the waning darkness, Alki, Jas, Mira and Yug had found the path to the cave behind Alki's new brick house. They walked in single file past the quiet mound where an ancient house once stood. Mira stopped at the mound to concede to Alki and tell her she liked the new brick house, declaring she's never seen one quite like it. Alki squeezed Mira's hand in gratitude, conscious that her friend had stepped out of caricature to make the admission. The setting aside of ego was extraordinary for Mira. Alki was always thankful, relieved when someone, anyone, even she herself, was able to sidestep ego and peel back to a self, devoid of envy or malice. With each of her friends, she bore the brunt of their criticism, all the time unsure whether it was genuine or resulting from an emulous ego.

Soon, they were near the collapsed mud walls of the well where they came to a stop as if at an invisible wall of dread. A wave of disquiet washed over them. The four paused and stared at each other's unverbalised fear-struck faces.

Yug was the first one to speak.

"You all felt that, right?"

"Yes," said Jas.

Mira said, "Anyone who ever came up here must have felt this…this feeling, it has lived here a long time. It's old."

Yug, Jas and Alki turned to Mira.

Yug smiled and said, "Mira can't help but speak true..."

He left his train of thought unfinished, as both Jas and Alki glanced at him vexed. He knew immediately to shut himself up.

Alki said, "Maybe we are supposed to feel this way. It's evolution, you see. If we don't feel afraid, we will be eaten. Why do you think we always feel especially frightened at night? The ghosts come out at night. We are asleep, we have our guards down then, that's when we are at greatest risk, and our waking from fear serves to save us."

Yug and the others stared at Alki. Her voice was incongruous to them, as if this was another person, not their old friend, sounding out in a tone they did not recognise. But Alki knew from their expressions that amongst them she had been unheard, invisible, serving out her purpose till this moment.

They pushed through the dreadful miasma and were at the Bauhinia tree beneath which a dark woman's facelessness beckoned them. They had arrived at the cave's mouth.

One by one they stooped below the tangle of densely growing Bauhinia roots and stepped in, heavy torches lit and flashing brightly. The ground was littered with gravel and broken rock. Alki stopped abruptly to tell her friends she knew this place though she had never been in here before this moment. Over her head was the twisting root system of the Bauhinia holding up the roof of the cave entrance. They plodded slowly over shards of fallen rock, slipping up ever so often, as the path led them downhill into the bowels of the hill.

After about five minutes, the path became smooth rock, and Yug ran out of string. He had been uncoiling a big ball of it and also marking the route with chalk. As if to milestone the spot, a giant ligneous pillar cropped up before them in the light of their torches. It was definitely not carved by human hand, as its lumps and bulges were evidence of botany. It was plainly a massive root growing vertically, inexplicably through the hill. The narrow passage opened wide and within a minute they were surrounded by a forest of knotted wooden columns so breath-taking, they were rendered speechless. In between the columns were motes of thick ghostly light coming from above. Alki looked up and wondered how sunlight could have got in here so deep underground. She imagined a system of rock mirrors polished smooth by monsoon flows, which managed to reflect and pass down the summer light deep into the earth.

But her reverie was interrupted when she noticed something odd about each pillar of light. She looked around at her friends, and they were staring too. The columns of light were oddly humanoid.

Yug said, "I can't believe that no one knew about this place. Especially in your family, Alki."

"If they knew, no one told me."

Jas turned to Alki to ask, "Which way do we go?"

Alki directed her friends to shine their torches around the hall of roots.

Humira said pointing to the west, "We should be able to find our way out of here. I don't want to die here like those people."

At one end of the hall without end, they found bones, human bones. They were unnerved, each one glancing from one to the other, hands reaching out reflexively, hoping to find other hands in the sub-terranean gloom.

Jas said, "I don't think they were lost."

Yug stared at Jas.

He was concerned, "Are you alright Jas?"

Jas said, "Everybody that comes here can find their way out if She wills it."

Jas's eyes were glazing over, as if she were in a trance. Her skin was grey.

Alki took her friend's hand gently in her own hand and spoke softly, "Come back, Jas."

Yug regarded the bones, then he touched his wife's right shoulder anxiously. He said, "Alki we should turn back now, this place is beginning to affect Jas."

Wanly Jas said, "No, no, Yug, there's something here and we haven't found it yet. She wants something."

Humira said, "Jas, you are scaring us."

Jas said, "Can you all hear that hum?"

In the hush that followed they all heard it. Alki had heard it before. At the time it had reminded her of the melancholy low song of a blue whale. The four of them turned around towards the columns of light in the hall of roots. The light pillars had curves and undulations as if some kind of information was beaming into the cave through them. At the centre of the hall, a column of undulating light seemed to pare away from its wooden buttress. The four were now able to distinguish a woman made of pure light. She seemed to be beckoning them though it had no eyes, no face, only form. The light itself possessed an unnameable quality that moved the four, and Alki was compelled to tell her friends to follow the woman made of light.

As the woman of light led them away from the hall of roots down into the belly of the hill, her radiance mellowed and diffused. At last, underground at the end of a path, they arrived at a massive hollow dominated by a giant banyan tree on the edge of a shining, still pond. The canopy of the tree mushroomed outwards, underneath a basalt sky. It was a living bridge between sky and ground. The woman that was light had flowed into the cave and dispersed into the natural walls making the rock glow, then dim. There was a stream flowing into and out of the pond. The surface of the pond was a steely mirror reflecting the shadow of the tree's canopy and the twinkling surface of the cavern roof around the tree. Atop, the cave was studded with glittering globs of crystal-edged minerals. The effect was like looking up at a clear starry night sky.

Yug spoke.

"How…how can there be a such a big tree growing here… underground…it's impossible."

Humira said truculently, "And yet here it is."

Mesmerised by the glittering roof of the cave, Jas wanted to know, "Why do they look so familiar?"

Alki said softly, "Those are stars...those are the constellations."

Then it was Humira's turn to say, "But how can this be? Here deep inside?"

Raising her hand and pointing to the east, Alki said, "Somebody carved them here...and that bright one there, that's a planet...look it's so much bigger than the others. It's probably Venus."

She sniffed. The smell of the cave was familiar. She sniffed again. The cave had a background odour like every house she had ever known, her house, Jas's house, Humira's and even Tana's. Each home had an identifiable odour that marked it off as unique. Her house smelled old, ancient, musty. Jas's smelled of mown-grass, garden smells that cheered her every time she went over, but Jas's mother had a habit of spraying air freshener everywhere, which added a chemical note to the ambient air quality.

Humira's place smelled of wood and varnish, as her father liked wood panelling, armchairs, and antique furniture. Tana's mother-in-law's place smelled of cooking. They were always cooking over there from morning till dusk, no one there ever went out to eat. The sweet aromas from their kitchen had got into everything, into cushions and curtains. Though Jas complained about it, declaring that Tana's house could use a dose of air freshener, Alki had defied her saying the smell in Tana's house was inviting and friendly.

The cave and its musty odour reminded her of her own house, her parents' house. For her own red brick house, now raising itself near the mound, she wanted it to smell of old books, a fragrance that would disappear from the world, after the decline of paper and the takeover of blue screens. Some clever marketing type would find a way to bottle it and sell it to people with book pretensions like Alki, the people who dreamed of building phallic libraries to house their priapic book collections to show off to other more pretentious book owners. They could spray it around the house as air freshener. There was already talk of bottling petrichor, refreshing aerosols that soared from the earth after first rain.

The tree looked as if it was imbibing from the pond. Ropes of air roots streamed down from the tree and on one side these roots trailed down into the pond, which emptied into a stream. The flowing water in the stream made a gentle swishing sound, which echoed all around the cave as it flowed into and out of the pond, and somewhere on the surface far above them now, it found its way out to flow down the hill. Alki looked into the pond, and saw right through to the bottom. Strange prehistoric creatures were swimming about the sandy pond floor, kicking up the sand from time to time. They had flattened armoured bodies, reminiscent of the tiny woodlice she had seen scurrying around in the mulch in her parents' garden.

The meditative quality of the reflecting pond prompted her to recall the quieter moments that would descend on the building site when the geologist had called on them. She wished he were here to witness this.

28

The Unseen Cluster Fig

Open mouthed, the geologist was in a plaid blue shirt. He maintained a crop of short hair atop an oblong face, which he kept stubbornly unbearded, despite the social pressure to grow one. He had affixed himself by the base of a Goolar or cluster fig, all the better to stare up at unripe figs sprouting all over the tree. He cut a strange figure standing by the side of the busy road, unmindful of other people's stares and the grinding road dust. Several curious passers-by, who saw him poised with a magnifying glass, imagined he possessed the disposition of a slightly demented doctor examining a patient with a bad rash. The patient just happened to be a tree. If Jas's father could have laid eyes on him, he would have seen the legendary Howard Carter, backed by his benefactors, on a cool, dry Sunday in November 1922, flickering candle in hand, poised before a sealed rubble door inside KV62, the tomb of the ancient Egyptian teenaged king Tutankhamun. The geologist came by almost every day, giving the tree as much time as he could spare. He was awaiting the arrival of very tiny wasps—fig wasps. Having studied these insects in college, the subject fascinated him even after he had changed his course as his academic career advanced. He still kept up with the latest information on the diminutive wasps.

The cluster fig in particular interested him as these grew wild all over the place and people didn't seem to mind their presence as forgotten roadside trees with invisible insect partners. They were neglected and allowed to grow to maturity most wherever they sprouted. It was not as celebrated as the fruiting fig tree, or the Banyan or the Pipal, and it grew amongst them unobtrusively wild and arresting if only someone had bothered to notice. Because there were so many of them fairly close to each other, he was able to determine how generations of wasps migrated from tree to tree, which in turn affected the fruiting times of the trees in question. He was hoping to contribute a paper on the subject one day if he could accumulate enough data.

Beside the Goolar, his exaggerated concentration had just started to pay off with the landing of a tiny insect, almost impossible to spot, when his pants pocket started to buzz. He fished the phone out of his pocket to mute the unknown number. But then after 15 minutes it buzzed again and then again. At last, he sighed and abandoned his inspection to attend to the insistent caller. It was a woman calling about surveying a site she where she planned to build a house.

His chance arrival at Alki's building site as the surveyor would lead him to a bonanza of old-growth figs. The hill around the mound had become an ecological hotspot since it had been abandoned generations ago. A place like this so close to the city was a once-in-a-lifetime discovery. He came to an arrangement with Alki and her architect, a man who seemed to be acting as her guardian, and was given entry to the site for purposes of research. At first, he had come in search of his tiny wasps, but as he started to explore the hill, its oddly bald mound for which he could find no geological explanation, where once a house and a family had lived, the mysterious stream, and a blanket of basalt engirding the entire landscape, he became a devotee. But most of all there was Alki.

In numerous conversations with her, he realised here was somebody else like him that wanted to conserve the hill as it was. One afternoon she told him pensively that the stories of *Yekshis* haunting the area had actually helped preserve the landscape by spooking potential developers. The vampires prowling the local forests were not *Yekshis*, but the "Rangerovered" and their cronies who came around looking to erect concrete blocks.

And then she had said something that endeared her to him.

"The upper-caste middle classes flaunt their symbols of status and clout, their cars, laser light shows, god men and rain dances. Who am I to say to the villagers, you should not be like them? Save the land, save the trees…I am a hypocrite. It's okay for me to be a social-media crusader that hates plastic and developers. I already have a clean house to live in and enough money to keep myself fed and clothed. My parents' house, all the neighbours' houses were built on land that used to be paddy fields, before that it was probably swamp and forest. No one stopped them…It's funny we like to forget and even deny that we are all apes, at the most the cleverest say we are descended from them, but no, it's not even that, humans are simply a type of ape among so many others."

She was rambling, but he would not interrupt.

"That's why our brains have been engineered to be so imitative. Look at the way we are on social media, everybody's everything these days. We see someone else's feed, they are doing this, they are campaigning for that, and we feel the need to also become tree planters or composters or environmentalists. The upper castes and classes in our country believe that they are the ones being emulated, but it has cut both ways, every which way. We picked up nuances, grunts, head nods, mannerisms, and words from each other, and over aeons a whole culture was born…dolphins and humpback whales have cultures…we just don't understand them yet."

She had gone on for a bit, and he was silent. She looked at him and found him listening intently. She stopped self-conscious and mortified, unused to having someone be attentive. It was an odd sensation. The last time someone had heard her out that way was ten years ago, and that was Yug. Mostly, she was afraid of giving offence. Had she come off as aggressive, loud, and looking to show off her cleverness? Her friends did not enjoy her musings or her efforts to be a tall poppy amongst them.

Diffidently, she said, "I have said too much."

"No, you haven't…we are…apes, indeed."

Then he looked into the distance smiling thoughtfully.

Is he mocking me? thought Alki, self-conscious and a bit crestfallen.

One evening, towards sunset at the building site, he came down from the crown of stone above the mound in search of Alki and her architect only to run into a whole group of Alki's friends. He was introduced to Humira, Jas and Yug, and an older man and woman, who turned out to be parents to Jas and in-laws to Yug. Alki removed herself to the shadowy sidelines behind them to quietly watch them interact. Jas and Mira struck up almost instantaneous conversations with the geologist. Yug noticed that he kept turning around, not entirely absorbed in what the two were asking him. He seemed to be searching for someone or something. Behind the geologist were his in-laws who had found Alki hiding and had brought her out of the shell, into which she had retreated, to pepper her with questions.

Humira strolled over to them leaving Jas with the geologist and whispered brashly to Alki, "Why have you never mentioned him before Alki?"

Yug overheard the aside and glinted hotly at Alki. She looked away from him.

Humira continued, "Why! You didn't even tell Jas."

At that, the three—Yug, Mira and Alki—turned their attention to Jas who was still in conversation with the geologist. Jas was back to her usual sparkling self. She could be earnest and ingratiating when she chose. Yug and Alki observed her with unease. The geologist spoke a little and smiled at the lovely Jas politely. He turned once again and found Alki standing just a few feet away with Yug beside her. His eyes lingered on the pair for a second, then he smiled at Alki, warmly disarming her. It was unmistakeable to both Alki and Yug, but most importantly even to Jas.

She stopped mid-sentence to peek at her husband and her friend.

"Oh," she said, "I didn't see you both there. It's really very interesting, talking to this one…"

Yug said drolly, "Come on Jas, you…want to hear about wasps?"

Jas was very irritated.

"Who said I don't? Don't be so condescending…"

Jas said to the geologist, "You must come to our house tomorrow, we are having a little get together. See my father over there, he would love to talk to you."

Alki was surprised and annoyed with Jas. If there was anyone intriguing in their lives, then Jas had to have first dibs on that person before anyone else in their group could get to them. No one was allowed to like anyone in their circle before first paying obeisance at the feet of Jas, who was always conveniently blind to the exasperation she caused, or even if she knew, it simply made her feel more powerful. Jas had convinced herself that she was being protective, sussing out the new person before they could hurt Alki. Jas didn't want to concede that the ones that cut Alki down were the ones closest to her.

The geologist paused to think, then he said, "That's very kind of you, but I won't be able to accept..."

When they were all leaving, he asked Alki, pointing to the crown of rock above the mound, "Were you up there earlier?"

Alki was startled.

"No…why, did you see someone up there?"

He said, "Well, the sun was setting, it was all glare and colour, and for a second, I saw a glimpse of a woman in white. I was sure it was you…you're wearing white today."

Then he said, "Look, I wanted to ask you earlier. I was thinking of bringing a ground penetrating radar cart to the hill…to chart out the subterranean system beneath. This whole hill must be riddled with portals and entryways to the caves underneath, and the villagers who live around here probably know where all the entrances are…"

Alki said, "It's not safe…I know."

Then after a pause, she said, "Did you feel something up there on the rock? Did you hear anything?"

He said, "Other than a general air of misgiving, nothing else…" then observing her closely, "there's something more here that you are not able to tell me, isn't there?"

She said nothing because she didn't want to scare him off just yet. She appreciated his company too much. Alki didn't see him for a week after that and began to miss his appearances, but then one day at the site, he came up to her with a laptop. She smiled broadly at his arrival, a bit too broadly, she thought and checked herself.

He said seriously, "Here, I want to show you something."

They found a spot in her living room, newly laid with cement tiles with blue and white fleur de lis motifs. They sat down on dust-covered stools, and he made sure to wipe the one that she chose for her seat.

The screen flipped up and he said, "It took me some time, I had to bring in a colleague to help.

"As you can see here…," he said pointing at obscure patches of wispy blue amongst some blotches of red.

She had no idea what she was looking at.

"I went looking for the tunnels and caves, which I did find, but I found something more intriguing. Can you see that…? These are patches of extreme electrical conductivity in the earth, and most are not of recent origin. From what we can tell they seem to be from decades ago, possibly even centuries."

Alki was not following, and she regarded him with bewilderment. He continued, ignoring her bafflement.

"I found a whole network. And all these appear to be connected. They seem to be following the underground network of lava tubes and certain locations under particular trees. And it's strange, I found six hubs, where the electrical activity was strongest. There could be more. First was a path at which there was a Shami tree, then a little uphill from there underneath a clump of banana plants, under the Jackfruit tree above the new garden, and below, at the end of the new garden, under the old planting hole of the Ashoka tree, and weirdly even at the new planting site where the Ashoka tree stands now. Finally, the mound where the old house used to be."

Alki said, "I don't understand...what do you mean by electrical...activity?"

The geologist tried his best to explain.

"Well, initially I did not go looking for electrical conductivity. Like I told you I wanted to map out the tunnels using the radar cart. When we were doing that, we found these anomalous patches of resistance. In those places, we had to arrange for forensic probes to be sent down into the ground. Now...I don't want to frighten you, and neither do I want to spread this around in the area, though I think people in the village already know from the stories going around...but this kind of electrical activity in the soil is usually associated with decay from burials of some kind."

Alki stood up and inhaled audibly.

She said, "I...I didn't want to say anything to you earlier. But we have been experiencing some strange phenomena here at the hill..."

She stopped, unsure about saying more.

Sensing her reluctance, he said, "You can tell me about it…"

How could she tell him about what had happened to her, the architect, and even her friends? Jas, Yug and Mira had known her for years, but she was not able to explain it to them either, till they began to share the experiences with her.

The geologist stood up too and said, "The thing is…you have to understand…this electrical discharge, it behaves more like static charge, it can stick to you…"

Alki said, "Do you think it can make us hallucinate?"

Puzzled, he said, "Now that you ask me this…I am beginning to wonder about it, after what I saw on the rock above the mound. I was sure I would find some kind of a tunnel entrance very close to the rock. But the nearest one is below the Bauhinia tree, a few metres below. Before I saw what I saw, I didn't hear any rustling, or twigs breaking, footsteps, nothing…you know the kinds of sounds you would expect to hear when someone approaches you."

Alki said, "I have been holding this fright…inside me for a long time, but it's strange, I also feel maybe I should not be afraid. You know…my parents are against me building this house. Sometimes I feel like I am being punished for defying them…"

The surface of her face creased as if she was about to sob, and he reached out for her instinctively. But Alki checked herself quickly, unwilling as always to give away too much of herself or let her self-pity out into the world. For the briefest second, he had brushed her face then withdrew. But it was enough, Alki felt comforted and grateful.

<><><>

Humira said, "Oh my god! No."

Yug, Alki and Jas turned to Mira, who was staring into the darkness at the back end of the huge cavern behind the all-conquering Banyan.

Mira said hesitantly with genuine fear, "I think there's a body there."

Suddenly Alki peeled off into the darkness wailing, "No, no, no please nooo…"

Yug tried to pull her back to no avail, then he started after her with Jas and Mira following. Their eyes adjusted as they ran into the darkness in the back, which morphed into the merest of shadows. There was a form on the ground slumped against the basalt wall below a tangle of small roots strewing down from the roof. It was the geologist, his clothes grimy and tattered. Alki got down on her knees and put her palm against the side of his pale, cold face. His eyes were closed.

She was still muttering, "No, no, no please no…"

Yug was now beside her kneeling, and he tried to pull away her hand, saying, "Alki wait…"

Pushing him aside with her other hand, Alki said fiercely, "No…Yug."

Jas and Mira came up to them.

Jas glanced pointedly at Yug, then she said to Alki, "How did he get down here?"

Tears rolled down Alki's face.

She said, "He told me there were caves down here."

Suddenly the geologist stirred. Just as Alki took in a deep breath in relief, he raised his arm to his face to rest his cold palm against her warm one.

To Alki he said, "You are not being punished…"

She smiled through tears, then she said, "How did you get down here?"

He said softly, "I am not really sure what happened. I came down the southern side of the hill and I walked onto this clearing, a patch of land with all these weird wooden knots on the ground, all evenly spaced out, spread out over a couple of kilometres, I think. In between were all these little frilled plants sticking out of the ground, they were turmeric plants. Those wooden knots, some of them had leaves that belonged to some kind of a tree, a fig tree, a banyan, I was sure of it, I had studied enough of them… but where was the tree? When I examined the ground, it was draped in some kind of overgrowth from a spreading plant. At first, I thought it was sweet potato, then I realised they were all Banyan leaves. Then I saw you a few yards away, it looked like you at least…but your clothes were different…there was a swing on the ground next to you, the kind of old-fashioned makeshift rope-plank swing you tie to tree branches for little children… But then you…it became a sad little girl in a faded white frock, it had this wretched expression…and then I heard this low hum…like whale song. Then the ground just caved in, and I was falling. It was so...strange. You know that dream in which you fall suddenly, then you are jolted awake. This was like that. But I didn't wake, I just kept falling and falling through all these roots grabbing at my clothes. I looked up as I fell and there was this face, a white face looking down at me…"

Alki said gently to him, "I am so sorry, I should have told you about all this earlier."

He said, "It's okay, I know it's difficult to talk about…"

Alki said, "You mentioned the swing. I have this memory of my grandmother, my mother and my uncles, and a swing in a tree they had set up for me, that was a happy day…it happened here, up there I mean, and I had forgotten about it…They performed a ceremony. My father wasn't there though. I was a little girl; I had no idea what they were doing. But it was the same ceremony my mother did at our house two months ago when I told her about the white face…it was in my room at home. At that time, I thought it had followed me home from here. That's why I asked you if we could be hallucinating all this."

From behind Yug said, "We should try to get back Alki."

Then Yug said to the geologist, who was still holding Alki's hand, "Unless you know another way out."

He released her hand and got up as Yug stepped in between them to steer them forward.

Pointing, Jas said to Alki, "I think we are supposed to go this way."

In the shadows, Jas and Mira had found a portal.

The geologist said to Jas and Alki, "This should go to your new garden, to that yellow wall, where they transplanted your Ashoka tree. There are many more like this leading to different parts of the hill. You will also find one stretching all the way to the Bael temples. You will have to seal some of these off for your safety."

Yug was about to interject when his wife grasped his left hand. She shook her head ever so slightly in the gloom, the twinkling brown light in her eyes beginning to match the mesmeric reflections from the underground pond. All of a sudden, she seemed ethereal, as if she was reaching into his very depths, and she knew what was there, a dormant yearning, which should have gone away after all these years. He held his tongue. Then he squeezed her hand.

29

The Buzzing of Banyan Wasps

Once upon a time, beneath a Banyan, a perfect wife brought back to life a dead husband. Stories from past times, which were always written by eminent men, would never feature the resurrection of a dead woman. These stories became canon and even wives would rally to preserve what was written in writ, that it was holy for a wife to be drawn back into the ground or into flames; but restored to life, no, that was just profane. In the parched grasses, a couple of metres from the digging man, Tana lay aching on her side, her heavy eyelids starting to close from sleep. She grew tired of watching the man and returned her focus to the ground where an unusual phenomenon was manifesting around her. Shiny green mounds were poking through the hard red earth. Her eyes opened.

At first, she thought they were green gems, and then they weren't, because the emerald jewels unfurled as if they were flowers, but they weren't. They were leaves, and they seemed familiar, though she could not place them. Thick, dark green ones bursting through the ground and like spirited Lilliputians, climbing, then crawling over her, covering her over quickly. Instead of panicking, Tana relaxed inside her tight green swaddling. She felt comforted and held. That was when she heard the soft buzzing. She peered through the leaves spidering over her eyes, and she couldn't see anything at first. But changing focus, she began to see them, a vibrating, grey cloud made of very small insects that looked like flying black ants. Some of them landed on her face and made their way to her mouth, then inside, creeping into her throat. Tana gagged, trying to sputter and cough. But she could not move or breathe anymore. It was all too much. Her eyes bulged and reddened, then closed.

The insects were swarming all over the field and the man stopped his digging to swat them away from his face. He turned, suddenly acutely aware of where he had left Tana, only to look astonished. Where she was supposed to be, lay a blanket of the thickest leaves fanning from side to side as if animated. He dropped the spade, ran through the insect cloud and stuck his hands into the leaves. There was no one there and he was furious. He started to pull at the leaves maniacally, jerking this way and that, mangling the new-born jade carpet and its round ruddy fruits, squishing them, getting their berry blood on his hands. On the ground beneath the leaves, there was an ashy, white powder, which in the violence was transferred to his face, fingers, and forearms. He stood upright perplexed and angry, spitting out the disturbed ash, trying to dust himself off as best as he could, but then falling back abruptly, startled. On the earth below the peculiar leaves was the spectral form and outline of a woman, in ash. It was unmistakable.

Then a grating voice said, "What did I do that you had to do this to me? I am meek, and you will take from me…and hide what you did so that no one will ever know."

He looked down at his hands because the ash that had deposited there seemed to be writhing, at which he started to panic, then shrieked and gasped for air. On the ground, the crumbling white form became more than two-dimensional, rising into the vibrating cloud of tiny wasps. It was vertical now and flaking, but somehow fleshed out. Surrounded by a grey fog of tiny insects, the thing faced him with snow-white eyes and a hollow beckoning mouth that was dizzying, appearing bigger, darker than it was.

<><><>

Yug said, "We have to conserve the phone batteries. Let's not all use them at the same time."

With torches on, they were hiking through a dark tunnel, no more apparitions to be seen.

Mira said, "I hope we can find our way back."

"You will…" said a voice in a snarling whisper.

The five of them stopped in their tracks and switched on their phone torches despite the warning from Yug.

Mira said, "Who was that? Did one of you say that?"

None of them spoke.

The whisper sounded again.

"You can never go back to where you came from..." it said.

In the darkness, Yug, Jas, Mira, Alki and the geologist drew closer to each other.

The geologist said, "This can't be an echo. Or one of you is playing a prank."

Mira, Jas and Alki squinted at Yug.

Yug said, "No, it wasn't me."

They believed him.

Alki said, "Switch off the torches. I think I see something at the end of the tunnel."

Sure enough, there was a point of light shining at them from the far end of the dark hollow.

Mira said, "I hope that's our way out," and started briskly toward the light with some rapidity, the rest following her.

The little glow at the end of the tunnel got brighter until adrenaline mixed with speed had caused the five to scrabble their way over fallen rubbly bits to reach a hollow, a room with a naturally arching wall that seemed to be alight.

Alki was the first to speak out loud. "What is this?"

Jas said, "We have to go through. She's there on the other side."

The four of them pivoted around to Jas, who was pale and grey, her eyes distant, as if she was speaking to them from somewhere else.

Yug put his hand around his wife's shoulders to steady her, and Alki felt frightened for her friend, recalling that horrible secret day at her house with Jas and the old hibiscus.

Yug said, "Who's there, Jas?"

Jas said, "I don't know, but she needs our help."

A whispering voice called out. "Kalika…Kalika… My name… you changed it."

Humira said, "Who's Kalika?"

Alki said quietly, "That's my name."

Her friends stared at her.

"When I was born, they argued over what to call me. My mother wanted to call me Kalika after her goddess and my father wanted to give me a virtuous girl's name, Savitri. They called me Savi for a while. But my mother used to quietly call me Kalika all the time. And I couldn't pronounce it, all I could say was Alki. On my first day at kindergarten, the principal asked my parents and me my name. My father said Savi, my mother said Kalika, and I said Alki. The principal was a sweet, fearless woman, you remember her don't you Mira…Jas. She chose Alki, and my mother says my father did not try to confront her. My mother thinks he was afraid of her. He doesn't like women like that."

Smiling, Mira said, "Yes, I remember her…so, you named yourself. That's an advantage."

"How?" asked Yug.

Mira said, "You give yourself a form that someone else did not give you, your name is not based on your parents' ego, or their concepts of the world, or their hopes for what you should become. C'mon, how much do our parents really know us? Since we can't be clones, we are simply things for them to mould in their image, bigger and better, wish-fulfilment forms of the original. If we are lucky, if our parents are nice, caring folk, that form or image is benign. But most of the time it's not. Just look at all the women and men squabbling, fighting wars. Do they know what they are on about? If you name yourself, you set your own frequency to life. So many people try to free themselves from their given names or are trying to give themselves their own names. Name yourself, and life's energy is yours for the taking."

Alki said, "Except, it was not like that for me. My father refused to accept my name. He still says to people, even to me, what kind of name is Alki? It has no meaning. Your name is Savi...I tell him no...my name is Alki. It goes on like this every other week."

Looking past her, Mira said, "Yes...your name means something to you...Am I imagining things? Or is that wall getting closer to us?"

"Oh my god," said Alki, as the spreading light engulfed a part of her hand. The geologist who was standing next to her took hold of her and tried to yank her out. As the light consumed her, she looked into his eyes and finally saw what everyone else saw, that she had refused to see.

They had not noticed that the glow from the wall had burgeoned in radiance, obscuring the wall and everything else inside the hollow. Yug tried to push his wife out of the room, but it was too late. They were both overtaken. Reflexively, Mira too had turned around to get out of the hollow, but was taken by the light after Alki and the geologist.

At first Alki was discombobulated and could not see at all. Then her eyes adjusted, and she looked around for her friends overcome by a tightening in her chest. They were gone. The glow dimmed somewhat, and she was able to make out the form of a woman, and it was bizarre and reassuring all at the same time. For a moment, she thought it was her friend Tana. Her skin was a shining gold, and her thick black hair was tied back in a plait that flowed down one shoulder. A sprig of leaves sprang from the top of her head.

The woman said, "You think you see me, but I am not really here."

Alki said, "Where are my friends, what is this place?"

The woman said, "Your friends are safe. You are nowhere. Here there is no past, present or future."

Alki asked, "Are we still at the hill?"

The woman said, "The universe is not all forward momentum of that thing you call time. It's when you prefer order over randomness that you feel the illusion of time. You are in a bubble of possibility where there is neither and both."

Alki said, "Who are you?"

The woman said, "I was you; I am you, a long time ago, and now. I have waited a long time to meet you. The people who lived here before you, my people, were afraid of me, and they left this place, because they did not want their daughters to become me."

Alki said, "What are you?"

The woman said, "Living matter is stuck to the illusion of time and solidity. When life left me, I detached. You might say I am nothing, maybe a wave, of energy. I have intent only in your head and your mother's. Maybe a part of me did not die, the one idea that defined me stayed on, it defines you. That's why you see me."

Alki said, "Others have died here too, haven't they?"

The woman said, "Yes, there were many. There were always girls and boys born in the village who were different, weren't obedient. It was just easier for 'them' to be rid of them. Eventually, the family on the hill, our family, moved away assuming the hill was cursed, as it kept happening again and again. They thought it was my doing. But you see, I can't help being connected to you. There is something in me that keeps passing on, and now it's in you...life starts, gets old, then dies, but these atoms, they don't follow those rules, they were at the beginning and at the end…they have always been together, making and unmaking. Everywhere in the universe, it is now, though when we try to look at it, it is the past, or if we try to get somewhere it is the future."

Alki was confused.

"The hill was cursed…why? What kept happening again and again?"

"I told you, girls who would not learn the ways of their family. There will always be different girls and different boys. But they wouldn't stand for it. They needed the rote of order, as they understand it, no deviations will be acceptable."

Alki said, "Why did I just see my friend Tana? Something is wrong. Jas felt it."

The woman said, "In the world outside, she is dead. There was a man behind a gate. He wanted to steal her essence."

Alki's facial muscles slackened and collapsed under the weight of sudden grief. Tears started to flow down her face in rivulets.

Crying, she said, "No…how can that be? Please…not Tana."

The woman raised her palm in the gesture of reassurance that Alki had seen so many times in colourful pictures of gods and goddesses.

The woman said, "You have to go through the light. She may be dead, but in this place, you have a chance, take it. Don't let the same things happen generation after generation. To the universe, none of this has meaning. People and events come and go, they are cruel, and the cosmos goes on. But you can change that…take a step, choose a path, everything else that follows will be slightly different. That's enough, the unknown can be known, even by the likes of you, the meek. Now go, go, run through the light. Go."

Alki ran. There was no ground beneath her, and no air around her, only a granular, diffuse light that went on for years, or at least it felt like years to Alki, a light without end. At last, the light dimmed, until all that was left was a halo as the rest of it condensed and she recognised the form of a tree. She was at the Ashoka, at the end of her new garden, and it was laden with bunches of saffron flowers. The tree endured only an instant before it too luminesced and then she was running again between murky, gangling silhouettes of what must have been coconut trees. Then, she was through the light. She was in another familiar garden at dawn surrounded by a tableau of juvenile tomato plants, in the backdrop a Shami tree. Her friends were all there beside her—Jas, Mira, Yug and the geologist. Each looked from one to the other in confusion. They were unsteady and disoriented, screening their eyes from the newborn world.

Jas said, "This is Tana's garden…we are in Tana's garden…I don't understand. How did we get here?"

They all heard it at the same time, the squeaking of the gate opening and the scraping of a person's footsteps. Then they saw Tana. He was beckoning her and though she looked alarmed by his sudden appearance she made a move towards him.

Jas and Alki screamed, but Tana did not hear them, as they were transfixed and not really able to move or communicate in the dimension they had just entered. Jas and Alki summoned all their strength to materialise, and were the first to lunge at Tana, to grab her from behind screaming, "Nooo…"

Tana started in shock and squealed gutturally at the sudden appearance of a howling fog behind her, and an ashen face in the mist that dissolved in an instant.

Then she flailed her arms yelling, "Oh my god, Jas…Alki… what…how?"

<><><>

The man stole out of his house at dawn to go for his morning walk. Not far away was the low brick wall that marked off Tana's in-law's property. Over the wall, he spied Tana working in the garden. Even at this distance, he was sentient of an indefinable quality in Tana's demeanour. He couldn't be sure what it was, perhaps it was the way she held herself politely, condescendingly aloof even when she was alone, her hair perfectly coiffed so early in the morning, or the memory of the pleasure she took in her prized Czech onion pattern crockery that triggered an impetuous rancour. It was not as if he or his wife didn't have their share of trophies from aspirational foreign trips. She was a threat to his wife's super self.

He said to himself, "There's that snobby woman my wife doesn't like. My god, she puts on airs."

He looked around; the tarred weedy lane was deserted. Residents were safely asleep, all except for Tana. He felt an impulse, a tribal urge to wipe away her figurative smirk, to prank her and cut her down to size. He approached the gate unwilling to stop himself. He had felt it many times before and had always given in, as there was no other pleasure or gratification that could compare. It was an itch that had to be scratched till it bled, and even then, there was no consummation. The guilt he felt afterwards had never been enough to deter him.

As the days and years passed, no one had found out, and each time, he had been a little more emboldened. He had gone about his life listening to people talk, observing them closely for any sign of weakness. The stories they told were very important. People always gave away too much of themselves. And nowadays it was easier than ever, thanks to their digital need to share. They liked to repeat their tales of woe to him, not knowing that to him this was information, data he could use to manipulate them. He needn't have done anything special; people liked to set their own traps. One of his neighbours told him the story of how she was robbed once in broad daylight, and it was weird, she had said, how she did not raise an alarm even when she knew something was wrong. That meek neighbour was Tana.

He pushed open the iron gate, which was rusty and peeling. He could report that to his wife, as she liked him to take note of such discrepancies. They had painted their entire house, but had failed to paint the gate. He remembered how Tana's mother-in-law had shown them about the newly decorated house, exclaiming proudly that they had not needed a decorator as they had Tana. His wife had taken umbrage and had browbeaten Tana by touring the house pointing out the many flaws in her design, also fiercely cross-examining Tana, because she had been suspicious of the mother-in-law's claims. The rusty gate squeaked noisily. He didn't like that; what if someone heard it, took note of the time. He couldn't afford that in his line of work, he thought to himself smiling.

Tana looked up at the sound and he was still smiling, motioning her to come to the gate. As she stepped towards him a white spot materialised in his peripheral vision. There was an aura around Tana, and it was accompanying her to the gate. As she approached, he got a better look at what was behind Tana—a woman, pale and white all over, its dark mouth wide open as if it was howling soundlessly. Tana was almost at the gate and time itself seemed to slow. He heard a low hum, followed by a piercing, mournful wail. He became pallid, unable to stop the uncontrollable trembling that took over his body. He crumpled to the ground crying, bellowing. He had seen the thing before. And he knew what the creature had come for; it was here for him. Its mouth opened to the shape of an 'O' that traced out its gutted yowling. The dawn dimmed; its white eyes turned charcoal black. He was swallowed whole into the centre of its awful resonance.

Tana, Jas and Alki surveyed the bellowing man at the gate. He was on the ground, knees touching face, rocking back and forth, he had locked himself in foetal position.

Tana said, "What's happening…where did you all come from? What is going on...?"

Jas was still fiercely clutching Tana's elbow.

"Don't go anywhere near him, close the gate now, and lock it, Tana. He did not come here for anything good."

Perplexed and frightened, Tana said, "Jas, I don't know what this is? What do you mean? How do you know this?"

Jas did not answer. She was sobbing and staring at Tana. When Jas looked at her old friend, she saw what the rest of her friends could not see, an apparition from a different life. Her old friend's eyes were bloodshot, she was bleeding profusely from her forehead and her skin was blue and black from severe bruising. Then Alki spoke.

"She's right Tana, she's right. You would not believe us if we told you right now. Don't ever let that man in again."

Tana shut the gate and locked it with the man still rocking back and forth just outside. She had never bothered to latch it before this moment. There was commotion inside the house. Mamma and Tana's husband arrived at the front door awakened by the man's howling.

Mamma stepped down into her garden saying, "What on earth is going on? What are you all doing here?"

From the back, Mira said urgently, "Aunty please call this man's house and ask them to come and get him. We found him at the gate like this."

Mamma gazed at the dishevelled group in her front garden. When that gaze shifted to her daughter-in-law, she was startled. The colour drained from Mamma's face and tears rolled down her cheeks. She was momentarily confused and did not ask the question that popped into her head. Her voice quivered, but she collected herself to issue instruction to her son.

"Deep…Deep…go ring their house, tell them something is not right with him."

Her bewildered son ran inside and dialled the neighbour's house. The wailing was loud enough to wake a couple of other neighbours, who unbolted their gates and peeped into the lane. One of them walked up to their garden wall curiously. He bent down and touched the shaking, squalling man on the ground. No one knew what to do in unusual circumstances.

Mamma said to him over the noise, "My children's friends were visiting overnight. They were in the garden setting up for the Saturday prayer meeting today. Then this happened. We don't know what to think. Something is wrong with him. I think he needs to go to a hospital right now."

The man's wife and mother arrived, frantic and upset. The two women were not able to get him off the ground without help from Yug and the geologist, who unlatched the gate when the women scowled at them.

As the man was hauled off the ground, Yug said, "What is that?" And thwacked his forehead.

The geologist employed makeshift forceps, his index finger and thumb, to pick a dead insect off Yug's brow.

He said, "My god!"

"What is it?" asked Yug.

The geologist said, "It's a…fig wasp."

The man's wife turned on Mamma angrily.

"You are stone hearted. How could you not take him inside when you found him like this?"

Mamma did not reply immediately.

She asked calmly, "Have you seen him like this before?"

The woman was disconcerted and unable to look any of them in the eye.

"I don't know what you mean."

The man was still babbling and crying as the women led him back to their house.

Mamma said, "The louder they cry…the more they seek your sympathy, the more they have to hide."

30

Randomness Under the Ashoka

At the Ashoka tree in Alki's new garden sat Mamma, on a new cheerfully painted basalt platform, eyes closed, in communion with the disorder that bridged all pockets of life. A woman's voice spoke to her.

It said, "In the beginning was disorder and then tiny fluctuations, of what you call order here and there, which led to everything you see now. From randomness sprang devices useful to you, like life. What is consciousness but a self-referential programme buried in our brains to explain our thoughts to our thoughts. It beats back the automation of our biological systems, which too were means to get around what you call the meaningless random. Though life was a perchance fluctuation, it found a way to hang on in the granular ether through repeating loops that resisted the disappearing and appearing quanta. You, a biological being, are like a star or a galaxy, symmetry in the randomness. Deep inside you, the quanta are still coming and going, but those repeating patterns will corral the comings and goings of quanta into molecules, then brain cells, which will contemplate. And here you are… Now, why are you conscious of this, me? Many years ago, in a time you cannot fathom, my husband dug up the hillside here to make a well, but it didn't work. They abandoned the digging, and I made a garden here. It took me years of planting and burying kitchen and fire pit wastes. But when the trees grew well, I don't know why but it made my family unhappy. I disappeared into the garden here, and after that no one wanted to come here anymore, and this place became a jungly scar in the hillside. Consciousness is like the form of the tree here, beneath which you sit, and I am too. Like this present moment, like this place, it is a bridge, an in-between phase, between here and there, between me and you, it is taking in light from above and water from below, then sending them out into the world as something else. Inside that box in your head is a bubble of possibility. There's light going in, sounds, and even water, reactions producing life, then thought. These thoughts come and go, they can easily deceive you, lead you astray to dead ends, if you are not careful. That's why these thoughts don't make it necessary that those who possess life are conscious. The living are quite un-conscious. You will say, anything can become conscious—a programme, a stone, some sludge, if left long enough to produce, the way a leaf turns the uncertainty of light into something certain, starch. First life, then thought. But what is consciousness without self-reference?"

A few feet away from Mamma, stood the archaeologist. He had stopped to gaze at the ethereal stillness of the woman under the tree, her salt and pepper hair having come loose from the bun at the nape of her neck. Then he strolled up to her, awakening her to his world.

He said, "Where were you? You looked like you were somewhere else, not here."

She smiled, glad to see him.

She said, "When did you arrive?"

He said, "I looked for you at the courthouse. The wedding was such a simple affair, the children decided to come here afterwards."

She said, "I know. I was here setting up their little get-together. Tana and Jas asked me if I could do the food for them. How did the happy couple look?"

The archaeologist laughed.

"She never looks happy if you ask me. As for the learned groom, he's happy enough for the both of them."

The sound of joyful chatter made its way around the beautiful herringbone brick wall to the two in the garden, which was now a year past its new planting stage, and was sending up vibrant colour. As Mamma and the archaeologist walked away from the Ashoka tree, she turned around for one last look to the sad little girl in a faded frock beneath the tree waving at her. She waved back. The archaeologist by her side said nothing, although he noticed the shaking of a forearm. When he glanced back at the tree just before turning the corner, all he could perceive was a slight, white mist in the shape of a child.

Left alone by her husband and her younger daughter, who were politely mingling, Humira's mother was fidgeting with her dark shoulder length hair in Alki's unplastered living room. She was unhappy at the way her daughter, Humira had conducted her wedding. The girl had wanted no fanfare and wailed against calling any of their relatives to witness the occasion. Perhaps the most important aspect of Humira's wedding was the attendance of relatives. She had lived this long, certain that her daughter was doomed to be an ugly spot on her good name. Carping relatives needed to be present to see for themselves. But she was torn. She could not summon up enough interest in the man Humira had found, because of the un-glamorousness of what he did for a living. She had somehow convinced herself that her daughter, being finally hitched was just more significant. Those meddling friends of hers had done everything, and she was even fairly sure that Jas's parents had persuaded her daughter to not intemperately disinvite her own mother. Nearby, someone joked that Alki's dining chairs were the reason for Mira's predicament today and everyone laughed except Mira's mother.

A year ago, Alki had been seeking turned chairs for a three-plank dining table. The geologist was in a university far from her small town completing his PhD. She had been sad to see him go, two weeks after the incident in Mamma's garden. He had promised to write to her, but at the time she had not believed in promises because of one fairy-tale day in the library more than ten years ago. The day Yug had promised to be with her, swearing that if he ever went away, he would come back for her. Of course, she thought, it had been too good to be true. She had never mentioned it to Jas, and especially not to Yug, who had only started talking to her properly again a couple of months before the incident with Tana. Maybe at last, he thought, she had forgiven him, or maybe he just didn't remember after all these years.

It was customary for people to forget the bad they did to other people. It was human nature for people to assume they were essentially good and whatever bad they did was only because they had no choice. Their egos would not permit them to use words like covetous, or jealous, or selfish for themselves, these were adjectives meant to describe others. Those at the other end of the deeds would hold on to their tribulations, unable to forget, being slowly poisoned from the inside. The function that genuine apologies played in human life could not be underestimated, when there was such a thing called closure in fiction, apologies played the role of closure in life. But Alki like many others would never find closure in apologies. In a self-validating ethos, to apologise was to be weak.

Most people, especially those who were used to getting away with active or passive spite, were in-the-shadows people, taking comfort in never being here or there, occasionally getting caught for misdemeanours, but mostly never. To them, nothing was ever black and white. Apologies—closure was an end, a tag for a certain kind of fixed event in space and time, and they preferred to live indefinably, shirking the adjudications of other people for any trouble they had caused. They sought to move on quickly, shunning the light of definition, and if they had to, even resorting to disingenuous apologies to excuse themselves. For their casualties, the world was a diametrically different place. They were focussed on an end to their pain. Flailing for reparation, the sufferer would often seek to punish those who would wound them, so that they too could experience the pain of inflexibility, as pain was a tenacious beast refusing all attempts at nebulousness; this was at the heart of most troubles in the world.

For years, Alki had silently cursed Yug and Jas, even experiencing secret schadenfreude in Jas's troubles with her in-laws. Jas sensed a want of sympathy in Alki when she complained about her in-laws. Alki possessed a defect in her psyche that did not permit her the panacea of forgetting. Building the house on the hill had been therapy in so many ways, even helping her come to terms with an old sorrow. She was not able to forgive Jas. A big part of forgiveness was forgetting, and so much of the past was still too vivid for Alki, especially since Jas was always so confidently unremorseful. But at least now like Jas she too could move on to other things, perhaps not letting go of the pain, instead letting it be a milestone on a road behind her.

The geologist surprised her with an email two days after he had found his rooms at the university. And the letters kept coming, three to four times a week. He liked to describe his day, and write about the people he met. He enjoyed writing; also, it was easier, he said in his first letter, to describe in prose the eerie affair of the month before. It was an unspoken kinship and she understood what he meant by the need to put it all down in printable words. It was possible to access a kind of fixity through the world of writing; there were explanations and delineations to be had, which were not forthcoming in the world outside. The act of writing was a hieroglyphic affixing of the hopelessly abstract. The two-dimensional flat world on screen or paper possessed unique properties. It could spark off third, fourth, perhaps other unknown dimensions in the minds of readers. In this written realm, an end was indeed possible, even if that end arrived on the last page and the story had not officially ended. Some people like Alki, Mira, and the geologist, the dreamers, needed those conclusions, those elucidations, unlike Jas and Yug, the realists, who had learned long ago to shoot and scoot, always taking more than they gave, relying on self-delusion to make ends meet somewhere in between.

Alki remembered that shell-shocked Saturday at Mamma's after the incident in her garden. They were all sitting around the dining table nursing cups of coffee and tea, when the geologist tried to tell her that he was leaving for a year to pursue his grant, which hushed the entire table. Alki was instantly crestfallen, but self-consciousness set in, and she had endeavoured to hide her expressions before anyone noticed. Yug and Tana's husband inadvertently came to her rescue to curiously ask the geologist about his grant. The geologist kept glancing in her direction absentmindedly during his conversation with the two, but she had pivoted away.

Alki turned to Jas to ask very quietly instead, "Jas, what happened to you inside the light?"

Weary, Jas replied sotto voce so that Tana at the other end of the table could not hear.

"It was awful. I saw…Tana…lying on the ground bruised, beaten…de…dead. And you know what was stranger? I knew we could save her."

Overhearing, Mira said, "Alki…it was bizarre, I thought I was dead…I was weightless, floating horizontal…I could not move. I saw that sparkling green woman. She was upright…and she stroked my foot. She did not say anything, but I could hear her. She was saying I am going to be alright."

<><><>

In one letter to the geologist almost a month after the first, Alki described her hunt for turned chairs to complement a new dining table. He wrote back saying it was a coincidence that she liked turned chairs because he knew someone who made them, and if she didn't mind, he would send him over to the new house. It was his brother. Since the incident, and much to Jas's relief, Mira had been spending more time at the brick house helping Alki. And that was how Mira met the carpenter, a profession that defied all of her mother's notions of what a gloried middle class Indian profession ought to be. With his business-like conservative haircut, he was not a hipster or musical hippie sporting cornrows. He wasn't in any of the sciences, he wasn't in the languages in a university department, he was no engineer, neither was he a banker, manager, cricketer, or involved in information technology in any way. It defied all comprehension for Mira's mother. How was she to introduce him to their relatives? A part of her was even glad that Mira had not invited anyone to her wedding, the part that knew what those relatives would say. Her daughter had informed her that he was a designer and that was what she imparted to her relatives, knowing all along they were laughing at her behind her back.

Alki's wedding present to the couple was allowing them to build a workshop cum studio cum office downhill from her new garden. It wasn't an unselfish gesture, as she cherished their company. She liked having the two of them over every day arguing and pottering about in her brick house. At first, the downstairs bedroom had been converted into a workshop for the carpenter. This was the time Mira decided to accost him with what she believed was his dearth of a business model in selling his pieces for profit, and was pleasantly taken aback by the sparkling grey-green glint in his eyes. He did not shun her offer of assistance.

At the brick house, Mira no longer felt like an interloper, unremittingly angry and hopeless, a wanderer stuck in limbo between her house and Jas's parents. She had found a home, even if it was on a haunted hill. The haunted status of the hill even suited her confrontationist tendencies. Mira had spent less and less time at Jas's, with Alki designating a room for her in the brick house. Eventually Mira shifted all her belongings there after a little wheedling from Alki. Ironically, it was Alki who was still living at home with her parents, spending only a few days at a time at the brick house. Her mother was not looking forward to the move. Alki had already transferred some clothes and all her books to striking new shelves made from recycled scaffolding wood, crafted by the carpenter. There was not much more she owned anyway. Her shrouded comings and goings, away from the eyes of gossiping neighbours, were anathema to her father, and Alki realised she had to put a stop to the vacillation. When she moved out two weeks before Mira's wedding, it was a scandal in her neighbourhood, which worked to her father's advantage. He basked in the sudden shower of commiserations from neighbours, some of whom advised him to demand back rent for the time she had lived at home for free.

Alki felt awful and guilt-ridden turning her back that last day on her forlorn mother, but she didn't know what else to do. Stifled tears had flowed unbidden in the car, and she had gazed out the window as Mira drove them home to the hill in silence.

At their get-together, Alki contemplated the happy couple feeling a little sad—the carpenter with his dark brown hair and plaid shirt reminded her of the missing geologist, and Mira, though unsmiling was not scowling as usual. Alki knew that her friend was afraid to be happy. She just did not believe in it. Tana too glanced at Mira, but had a thought she had had in another tragic, but now forgotten, life, that Mira had suffered long enough and deserved a measure of happiness, whatever that maybe. Tana thought the insight had come to her spontaneously, then grimaced suddenly experiencing a phantom soreness down her sides.

For months now she had been overcome by a strange sensation, waking up in the morning, and looking into the mirror to think, "Am I supposed to be here?"

Jas caught the vacancy crossing Tana's face, and she crossed over to ask semi-casually, "What's up?"

After some hesitation, Tana said, "Since that day, I feel…how do I put it…out of place."

Jas knew instantly what day she meant, but said comfortingly, "Don't worry, we all feel that way."

Normally contemptuous of self-awareness, Jas realised that Tana could not possibly understand what she meant. Her efforts to comfort Tana could sound facile and maybe even a little selfish.

Tana smiled at her, then said, "What is even more strange is this, you, being nice."

Jas tried to laugh, but she was affronted.

She said, "What?! I am always nice."

Stumbling for words, Tana said, "Oh Jas…I didn't mean it like that…I feel like you all have been keeping something from me."

Jas replied somewhat frantically.

"I told you; it was just such a strange morning…Alki had this dream about you…then she called me, and everyone just turned up altogether…it all happened so fast."

Tana said, "Even the geologist...?"

The beautiful bride walked up to the quietly chatting pair, just as Tana said, "In her dream that man was trying to kill me… Mamma agrees with you all, she says, it was more than odd that he was there at that time of the morning calling me out of the gate… maybe that's what it is, he was trying to kill me…am I lucky to be alive…or am I undead?"

Jas fell silent. Then she said, "Why are you starting to sound like Mira?"

Tana said, "I am sorry, I shouldn't have said that."

Mira gave Tana a quick side hug.

"It's alright, at some point in our lives, no matter how well adjusted we are, we will feel exactly the way you feel now. It can go either way. But I like to think that your glass is half full, and just thinking that makes it so."

Jas said diffidently, "Humira…that's what I was trying to tell her. And you…you need to take your own advice."

Tana smiled at the scowling pair, and said, "But do you know what Mamma doesn't find odd? That you all appeared in the garden all at once and I didn't even see you come in through the gate."

Mira and Jas exchanged glances, which did not escape Tana's notice. Alki left the living room to fetch a tray from the kitchen where Yug was alone by the window brooding at the sunset.

Alki said, "You okay?"

Yug turned around and said, "You never asked me what I saw in the light?"

With the tray in her hands, Alki said, "Why don't you tell me now?"

There was a pause following which Yug said, "I saw myself. But you were there and so was Jas. We were all in the library back in college. And I saw what I did. Now how many people can say that Alki? How many people have the guts to look back at themselves and admit that they did something wrong?"

Alki thought to herself that even when he had an insight, he had to be boastful.

But she said, "You know most people do get chances to look back at themselves without having to go to a special place, but they always choose blindness over sight, that's easier. They make up whatever past story that suits them."

Yug was stymied in the midst of his bluster, still unused to Alki's voice, the quiet din of it speaking up for itself.

He said, "Okay, fine…I need to explain myself better."

Alki did not say, though she wanted to, that his words explained everything about him even if he claimed that he had not phrased his thoughts perfectly.

Yug said, "Do you know sometimes your phone records you when you are talking to an unknown caller, and you hear it back later and wonder who that stranger was? That's how it feels. That stranger in the light was me. I was so determined to succeed Alki…it's embarrassing now."

Alki said softly, "I would have come in the way, right?"

Yug said, "What? No, stop…God! your self-pity is frustrating… No, I came in my own way. I wanted to look, sound, and smell like successful people. I wanted to golf, speak French, play piano… never for pleasure…and imitate their mockery of American tourists, though I am a rent-seeking middle-class Indian tourist, which is perhaps worse. I don't remember the last time we paid for hotel rooms. Jas and I always find reluctant relatives and friends to stay with abroad…Did I tell you I've shifted to artificial intelligence? Why? Because that is the trend now. I was looking up my online profile one day, and I noticed that whatever I had worked on matched whatever was in fashion that decade. As they say be careful what you wish for. I can excuse myself, of course. I was young and all I knew was what I saw. I wanted it all then and there. I didn't take the time to look underneath because that was for people like you, the unsuccessful ones."

For the second time Alki winced, the first was when he reproached her for self-pity. But Yug kept going undeterred with his breakneck confessional.

"Jas undercuts you all the time because you let her. She can get her father to do it for her by being all child-like when he's around. That's why Mira intimidates her…Jas I mean…because Mira stands up to her. But secretly she wants Dozy to be independent and insolent like the two of you."

"Insolent?"

Yug said brusquely, "No, not you…Mira."

Alki said, "Oh!"

He continued, "Why do you think she wants you to tutor Dozy? She needs to make sure her children learn everything from you and turn out smarter than you. Though she thinks you are pretentious. That's her version of playing golf and mastering the piano, because somewhere in there she's insecure, and she channels it into her children…Mira was right…working to transform them into super versions of her, moulding them into these cocky know-it-alls, threatened by the hopes and desires of other people."

He was trying to apologise to Alki without uttering the actual words. But Alki wasn't sure exactly what he was penitent about.

Alki said, "And Jas was part of the plan for you?"

Yug stared at her, undone by the stillness of the question cutting into his meanderings.

He said, "I see now that she was. Though…you know how much I love her…I always have."

At those words an old pain flooded Alki, plummeting her to a depth she thought had long disappeared, but this time she was able to soar through to reply gently, "I know."

The doorbell rang and Alki left Yug in the kitchen with her tray, running out to get the door. Outside there was no one about and Alki was perplexed. She stepped out to look this way and that, as she would do back at home when naughty children in their neighbourhood would run up to their gate, ring the gate bell and run away giggling. When she looked again to her right, at the corner was a faded little girl in a white frock smiling at her and pointing into the garden towards where the Ashoka tree stood at the laterite wall at the end of her garden. Alki was overcome. It was the little girl she had seen months ago, the daughter of the construction worker.

31

The Exhalation of the Pipal

Near the mound, silhouetted by the sunset, stood the geologist, a ceramic bonsai bowl in his palms. The bowl housed a Pipal tree, in miniature, perched on a shard of granite.

Alki walked up the slope to him and he turned hearing her approach. She was smiling broadly, glancing curiously at the little Pipal.

With half outstretched hands, he said to her, "There's this myth doing the rounds of the internet, that the Pipal respires oxygen at night, and our ancients had declared it sacred after they chanced upon the secrets of photosynthesis long before the rest of the world. Someone made a mistake while reading a dense research paper long ago, which compared a Ficus tree to a Clusia tree that too had strangling capabilities, but that Clusia, like succulents, could let out day-made oxygen at night. It didn't help that there was also a cactus named Ficus. The Pipal was a regular tree, respiring carbon dioxide at night even if it had this amazing true story of tiny wasps that lived inside its figs."

Alki had left her doorstep behind in pursuit of the little girl she had met in the clearing so many months ago. The child that didn't exist had vanished round the corner. She had pointed to the Ashoka tree, but Alki found no one there. She had stopped a moment to soak in the purple orange radiance and look around. Up at the mound, there was a dark figure looking down at her. She took in a deep breath, unexpectedly happy. It was the geologist.

Still holding on to the bonsai bowl, he said to her, "Now I have gone on."

Alki's face glowed with amber light.

"So then…let me take the bait."

<><><>

She said, "So, what is a fact?"

He laughed and replied, "It's the oldest known thing in the world. A fact is something that has to be proved."

She said, "Haven't we been overconfident? How can you prove something that happens only to you?"

He did not answer.

With Mira on her mind, Alki continued, "…If something is true, truly true, it is only the rare person that will admit it."

He said, "Do you mean the truth can never be known? People will believe whatever they want to believe."

Alki shrugged yes.

He said, "Then we are back to square one. That's life for you in brief."

Alki said, "Going back to square one?"

He said, "Always. In circles we live."

She said, "If you can't prove it, then it is just a story. And people prefer stories. Each side picks a story they like better. The truth can't be realised."

He said, "Even when you are telling one story, the person listening to you might hear a different story."

They were quiet as the twilight darkened around them and their waltz of words.

Then he said, "If people prefer stories, why do they need the truth?"

She said, "There must be some value in it."

He said, "Yes…value…but it's only for some not for all."

The geologist looked past her, at a shadowy granular figure materialising in the dusk, watching them from the path that led up to the Bauhinia and the crown of rock above.

Then he turned to her to say, "You never asked me what I saw in the light?"

For the second time that evening, someone had asked her the same question.

"Tell me now."

He gave her the bonsai, saying, "I started this for you a few months ago. It reminded me of the tree down there."

Before she could thank him or ask him how he had managed the difficulty of carting it through quarantines and customs, he said, "I saw you in the light. And somehow it wasn't you. And you looked exactly as you look today. We were here at the mound. And you said to me…"

"…you have come to help me build my pond," she said, her eyes suffused with purple dusk.

The geologist was startled. "How could you know that?"

Alki said, "I don't know…the words were in my head all this time. I was going to ask you to help me with a pond with fish for an aquaponics set up. I was also going to ask you about a small hydro-electric plant for the stream."

They were quiet together for a mere second, then the geologist said, "How do you think your ancestors forgot this place?"

Alki said, "Ghosts frighten us, we don't want to understand more than what we already know. When we do try, the answers don't describe existence only the ego."

"Don't they frighten you anymore?" he asked.

"Yes, they do. I can't lie. But I am trying hard to understand them now. If I can get past the trigger of fear, or anger, there's so much on the other side I couldn't imagine before. Maybe a beautiful forest garden that leads to silver sands, disappearing into a turquoise ocean."

He turned to gaze at her.

Then he said, "There are so many things going on here, so much to study."

There was a pause and then a shared laugh.

She said, "I am beginning to realise that some things, no matter how much we know or understand them, try as we might to explain, we will be shut down, because of the stories going on in other people's heads. Stories that are also facts."

He said, "Don't we all do that?"

She said, "That's what it makes it so difficult. Working out how to be certain and uncertain of what we…know."

He smiled and said, "Uncertainty in certainty…that's something I…enjoy doing."

She was so glad for his presence.

"You know you have to come down to the house, everyone's there waiting for you."

She handed back the ceramic planter, and took his elbow gently, while he cradled the Pipal in the crook of his other arm. They started to hike down over the uneven path to the clearing bearing the brick house below, which to the geologist seemed as though it had sprouted out of the laterite overnight, a sacred thalloid Ficus made of brick. Alki turned back to glance at the old woman and the little girl whispering into the twilight. She waved goodbye.

Acknowledgment

The publishing world is a-churn. A tug of war is on between old influence and new money. Perhaps this has always been the case. Authors like me find themselves falling through the cracks, since they are not close to the powers-that-be, they haven't the networks of writing schools, nor are they mass-market whisperers. In this interregnum of being, neither here nor there, I want to thank Nu Voice for giving this being a voice.

About the Author

Neha P Lal is a pseudonym for an author who was a journalist in another life. Lal's passion for writing ignited at a young age, beginning with a simple classroom assignment that sparked a lifelong love for storytelling. As this is intended as a bio, the poem below by Lal is for those who may be tired of reading lofty author bios:

I can't stand reading bios,
they make me plain mad,
little listicles capping a life.

I don't want to know that a great one
possessed a gift of movement, slipping
through the world when I stood so baffled,
so plain still.

I can't stand reading bios,
these stories about my absence,
my lack of bio in a world that would have
each of us create one through an act of self.

Now that each of us is an autobiography
unto us, outing the world through feedback,
Please do not read me your titles,
I only want to see your work,
and sometimes not even that.